# CHARITY Case

# MELODY TYDEN

# Contents

# Chapter One

~**Naomi**~

Swallowing past the tightness in my throat, I ordered a drink and resisted the urge to bolt out of the hotel bar and run back up to my room.

I promised my friends I would do this. I promised *myself* I would do it, but actually sitting at the bar in my highest heels and shortest dress, I felt completely out of my element.

It had nothing to do with being in another country, although I'd only flown to Rome that afternoon. Along with two colleagues from the charity we all worked for, I would spend the next few days at a conference for rare medical conditions, including meeting with a non-profit foundation we hoped would provide us with a sizable donation. Months of effort went into making our pitch and we desperately needed it to work out.

That was tomorrow's worry, though. Nothing to do with my current discomfort.

No, what brought me out of my comfort zone and to the bar on my own had been months of my friends begging me to cut loose and have some fun.

"You need an adventure," they cajoled.

Or, more bluntly: "You need to get laid, Naomi."

They weren't entirely wrong.

Since Liam died, I hadn't been with anyone else. I hadn't wanted to be. For over a year, I went to bed alone. But recently, something shifted. I caught myself watching men a little too long. Noticing their hands. Their voices.

My skin felt too tight and the nights on my own were too loud.

I didn't want a relationship; God, no. Not yet. But I needed *something*. And if a night with a stranger wouldn't fix me, maybe, just for a little while, it would at least remind me I was still alive.

The bartender with grey flecking his beard set my drink in front of me with a friendly smile, and the sharp sting of the alcohol helped to ground me, bringing me out of my wandering thoughts as the cool liquid slid down my throat.

Freshly fortified, I pivoted in my chair, crossed my legs, and scanned the room to check out my prospects for the evening.

With dark wooden tables, sleek leather seats, and dimmed light descending from the hanging metallic fixtures, the bar gave off a sophisticated vibe just like the one I imagined when I pictured the scene back home in London. Unfortunately, the dark, handsome Italian man who starred in those daydreams was nowhere to be seen. Instead, a table of German businessmen sat in the corner and a loud, giggly group of American women took up most of the other end of the bar. A few other men were scattered around, alone or in pairs, but they all seemed to be working or talking business.

As far as I could tell, no one was on the pull that night except for me. *Just my luck.*

As I internally debated heading back up to my room and forgetting the whole thing, a voice spoke up from behind me.

"Are you waiting for someone?"

The deep, masculine tone would have been reason to rejoice if it weren't for the Home Counties accent accompanying it. I'd been hoping for an exotic fling rather than hooking up with someone from England. Even so, I turned around to take a look.

The man who'd just spoken leaned against the bar behind me, eyes fixed on me with interest. Handsome, I had to admit: probably a little older than me with dark hair cut short and just the right amount of stubble on his chin. Piercing blue eyes met mine confidently, almost arrogantly, and he wore a suit with a thin, light-blue tie that matched the shade of his eyes. Only a small scar above one eyebrow disturbed the perfect symmetry of his face.

In short, he looked like almost every City banker I'd ever met.

Not my usual type at all.

However, before I could open my mouth to rebuff him, my friends' voices echoed in my head: *You're too picky, Naomi.*

Though it pained me to admit it, they were right, at least in this scenario. I didn't go to the bar looking for someone to spend my life with. A warm body would meet my needs, and from what I could see, his would fit the bill. He might look even better out of that suit if the way his button-down shirt stretched across the firm plane of his chest offered any preview.

As I let myself imagine his hands on me, as firm and sure and confident as the look he gave me, a warm feeling I'd almost forgotten spread from my head to my toes, setting my whole body alight.

Perhaps talking to him wouldn't hurt.

"A friend was supposed to join me, but she had to cancel," I lied. Telling him I came there on my own seemed unnecessary. The depths of my desperation could remain hidden.

He gave a half-smile, nodding at the bartender as the man brought over a drink I hadn't heard him order. "You're British too. What brings you to Rome?"

Talking about myself didn't appeal to me either. The less he knew about me, the better. "Just sightseeing."

A suggestive eyebrow raised in my direction. "See anything you like?"

*Seriously?* A laugh threatened to escape at the rather obvious line, but at least those few words made it clearer that he'd come there looking for the same thing I had.

I tried to give him my best 'come-hither' look while I settled on a reasonably witty response. Unfortunately, it had been so long since I tried that look out on anyone, it felt utterly awkward and wrong, and the laugh that I managed to suppress before pushed its way out anyway.

The man's brow furrowed in confusion as he watched me, unsure whether or not to be offended by my laughter. "What's so funny?"

"I'm sorry, it's not you," I tried to explain, wincing at my own ineptness. I hadn't realized my seduction skills were quite so rusty. "I'm out of practice at flirting."

His brow cleared as he flashed me another smile, confidence fully restored. "That was you trying to flirt with me?"

"What if it was?"

"Then I'd agree it could use some work." His dry words were accompanied by a rather charming twinkle in his eye. At least he found me amusing and not pitiful. I'd take it.

"You seem to know what you're doing," I acknowledged. At the very least, he looked more comfortable than I did. "Tell me what you think I should say."

His eyes narrowed curiously, as if trying to gauge the sincerity of my request. "How you should flirt in general, or what you should say to me?"

"To you. Tell me what you, specifically, would like to hear from a stranger in a bar in Rome on a Monday night."

As he leaned forward, bringing his face closer to mine, his masculine scent, cologne and something else indefinable but unmistakably male, filled my nose and another strong pang of longing shot through me. It had been so long since I'd had a man's scent on me that I could hardly think straight. Was this what being in heat felt like? My body had complete control.

A hint of a smile graced his lips even as his gaze took on a harder edge. "I prefer to get right to the point, so you could tell me that you'd like to come up to my room, spend the night with me, and never see me again. That would work for me."

*Well, fuck.* Couldn't be much more to the point than that, and his suggestion aligned perfectly with what I'd been looking for. Anticipation surged through my veins and a dull pulsing started between my legs, another sensation I hadn't felt in a very long time.

Taking another deep breath, I screwed up all my courage and forced out my next words.

"Pretend I said that, then."

I kept my gaze steady on him, hoping he wouldn't actually make me repeat the words. I didn't know if I could, at least not in any way that would be considered sexy.

Surprise flashed in the man's blue eyes. Despite his confidence, he didn't seem to have actually expected me to agree. "You don't want to know anything about me?"

"Not really," I admitted.

"Not even that I'm married?"

Instantly, my eyes flew to his hands, one holding his drink and the other resting on the bar. Neither had any sign of a ring. I hadn't thought to check, which only proved how out of practice I was. My mind racing, my gaze returned to his face, trying to decide if his words were true. They must be, I supposed. Why would he lie about that?

"I'm not careless enough to leave it on when I'm looking for some fun," he explained, obviously having noticed my unsubtle examination.

As my hand tightened around my drink, a flicker of light caught my eye.

A glint of gold.

*My* ring.

My stomach lurched as I stared at the piece of jewellery, as though seeing it for the first time. I hadn't even thought about it when I got ready for the bar that evening, but there it sat, resting on my finger like a ghost of a promise I could never keep.

I flexed my hand, as if that might somehow make it disappear, but his voice cut through the moment before I could fully react.

"You might want to keep that in mind next time."

The sarcastic words sliced at my pride, letting a wave of guilt in.

He thought I was a cheater.

He thought we were the same, but my fiancé was dead while his wife, I assumed, must be very much alive.

A sharp pulse throbbed at my temple as I weighed my options. I should walk away. I should put his wife's feelings above my own. I'd never been someone to look twice at a man in a relationship.

And yet...

If he came to the bar specifically to pick up someone, as it seemed he had, it made no difference to his wife if he ended up with me or some other woman in his bed. He was the one breaking his vow, not me. It didn't make it right, but it also didn't make it any worse.

I glanced around the bar one last time, searching for another option, but found none.

Just me, a man who would take what I was willing to give, and a body that ached for something I could barely admit to wanting.

The weight of my ring dug into my skin, but instead of pulling away, I curled my fingers into a fist, swallowed the last of my drink, and let my need win out.

"It doesn't bother me if it doesn't bother you."

He searched my eyes one more time before putting his drink down on the bar and giving me an aggravatingly charming smirk. "In that case, let's go."

**~Kane~**

The woman from the bar stood next to me as we waited for the lift, keeping a safe distance between us. We didn't touch or look at each other and neither of us spoke. Small talk wouldn't serve any purpose when everything of importance had already been said.

I went down to the bar looking for a woman to take upstairs, as I usually did when travelling, and when I entered the room, the group of Americans caught my eye. I could spot some potential among them, but as I grabbed a drink before approaching them, I noticed the blonde woman on her own.

She didn't look like a woman who usually hung out in bars alone, and definitely not the type of easy pick-up I had in mind. I'd learned to read the signs a long time ago. Still, something about her appealed to me anyway. Figuring I had nothing to lose, I started talking to her while I waited for my drink. When she turned those gorgeous brown eyes on me, the other women in the room disappeared.

That would have been unusual enough even if the conversation hadn't quickly taken a turn I didn't expect.

I honestly didn't know what to make of her. For a start, the way she laughed at nothing threw me off. Then her question about how she should flirt with me struck me as almost impossibly innocent, and I had no interest in innocence. For that reason, I decided to be brutally blunt with her about what I wanted.

*Tell me that you'd like to come up to my room, spend the night with me, and never see me again. That would work for me.*

That should have scared her off.

It didn't.

Even more surprisingly, she barely batted an eye when I told her I had a wife. The words were a lie, one I often used to discourage anyone with long-term ambitions, but she didn't know that.

On top of that, she hadn't even bothered to try to hide her own ring. Clearly, she only played at being innocent. More than likely, a manipulative bitch hid behind her mask of openness, but that was her husband's problem. At that moment, my interest extended only as far as getting her naked in my bed. After that, I couldn't care less what she did.

When the lift door opened in front of us, I let her enter first before swiping my key card for the penthouse. If she noticed that I didn't select a floor, she didn't say so. Luckily, no one else got in with us, and as soon as the door closed behind us, I made my move, boxing her in against the mirror.

My mouth captured hers hungrily and rather than shying away from it, she met my desire with equal ardour. When my tongue plunged into her mouth, she twisted hers around it. When my cock, hardening with anticipation, pressed against her, her hips pushed back, leaving no space between us as our bodies sought the friction we both so clearly wanted.

The urge to start ripping her clothes off right there nearly overwhelmed me, but I managed to content myself with sliding my hand under the back of her dress and grabbing her ass beneath the fabric. The lace trim of her panties brushed against my fingers, sending another rush of need through me. I couldn't wait to see them and, even better, to get them off her.

The lift door opened directly into the penthouse suite and we stumbled out into the large, open space. The woman paused for a moment, glancing around at the opulent surroundings in confusion, but I didn't give her a chance to ask any questions. In one quick motion, I grabbed the bottom of her figure-hugging wrap dress and lifted it over her head, throwing it to the side before taking a moment to appreciate the view.

Magnificent in her matching red lace bra and panties, her blonde hair loose over her shoulders, her lips swollen from our bruising kiss in the lift and her brown eyes swimming with lust, I couldn't spot a single flaw. Finding such a stunning partner for the night was a real stroke of luck.

She shivered as I took her in, perhaps from the loss of heat from her dress or maybe simply from the intensity of my gaze, until eventually, she got tired of me staring at her.

Without a word, she pressed herself against me again, her lips finding mine as she pulled my jacket roughly over my shoulders and started on my shirt buttons. As much as I enjoyed her undressing me, it would take too long. Pulling back to yank my shirt over my head, I groaned as her fingers slid greedily across my chest, the skin-to-skin contact providing exactly the right level of heat. Reaching down to her panties, I could feel her heat through the thin fabric. Dampness met my fingers as I pressed them against her, and she moaned into my mouth. Willing and eager, her responsiveness turned me on even more.

As if I needed more. I'd been ready to go since the moment she agreed to come to my room.

Pulling her towards the bedroom, I discarded the rest of my clothes along the way. Original artwork lined the walls with fresh flowers on the desk by the window, but she didn't seem to notice her surroundings. Instead, the woman's eyes lingered on my cock as I released it, and from the heat in her gaze when she glanced back up, I could tell she liked what she saw.

That made two of us.

Before I had a chance to, she reached behind her back and unhooked her bra. She wasn't wasting any time, but I made myself useful anyway. Sliding the straps off her shoulders, I pulled the fabric away from her, revealing firm, round breasts just as perfect as the rest of her

My anticipation growing by the second, I pushed her down onto the bed and slid her panties off before taking another few seconds to enjoy the view of her laid out naked in front of me. She really was flawless. Luck had definitely been on my side that night and I didn't intend to waste it. Joining her on the bed, I brought my mouth to one of her nipples, already peaked with anticipation.

It fit perfectly between my lips and she moaned as I sucked it hard before flicking my tongue across it.

Before I could do anything else, though, she pushed me off of her, onto my back, and climbed on top of me. An unexpected move, but if she wanted to play it that way, I would happily let her take the lead.

"Where are your condoms?"

Those were the first words she said since we left the bar, and her voice, husky with desire, made me even harder.

"Top drawer."

I never took any risks and it seemed she didn't want to either. She found the strip I'd stashed in the nightstand earlier, pulled one out, deftly rolled it onto me, and gave my hard cock a couple of firm strokes before climbing back onto the bed and lowering herself onto me. As her warm wetness surrounded me, I let out a groan of pure pleasure. *Fuck.* We were skipping foreplay, apparently, but I couldn't bring myself to complain about it when she felt so fucking perfect.

For a long moment, she simply sat there, her eyes closed, enjoying the feel of me inside her as much as I enjoyed her engulfing me. When her eyes opened again, such intense lust filled her gorgeous brown eyes that my cock twitched in her pussy, my hips bucking up into her. Spurred back into action, she leaned forward over me and began to move herself slowly up and down the length of my cock, rocking her hips every time she reached my base so that her clit ground against me.

Her breasts hung over me, irresistibly tempting, and I craned my neck to take one of them into my mouth again. She grabbed my hand and guided it down to her clit while I hummed in appreciation. I loved a woman who knew what she wanted. My mouth continued to suck her nipple as my fingers circled her clit, her hips still rising and falling on my stiff cock. Her moans and whimpers grew louder until I could tell her orgasm wasn't too far off. To be fair, mine would be close behind, even though we'd only been at it for a few minutes. She felt too damn good to fight it.

"That's fucking good," I whispered, encouraging her. "You look amazing riding my cock. Just the dirty little fuck I needed tonight."

That did it. In a matter of seconds, she shuddered on top of me, her pussy clenching my cock tightly as she came. As soon as I felt her pulsing around me, I let myself go, drowning in the pleasure she gave me. My cock pumped hard and my body flooded with satisfaction.

*Damn.*

The world blackened and I floated there for a moment or two, savouring the total surrender. I hadn't had an orgasm that good in a while, and in my post-orgasmic haze, I found myself wishing she'd called out my name in that sexy voice of hers while she fucked me.

That would have been impossible, though.

I hadn't even told her my name.

We both remained silent, catching our breath while we came down from our mutual high, until she slid off me. Without a word, she removed my condom and tossed it in the rubbish bin. I lay there, watching her and appreciating the view, but instead of coming back to the bed as I expected her to, she picked up her underwear and walked back out to the living room.

Propping myself up on my elbows, I called after her. "Where are you going?"

She reappeared at the bedroom door, already slipping her dress back over her head. "I have a busy day tomorrow." Her tone remained friendly enough but not overly warm. "I need to get some sleep, but thanks for this. I had fun."

With that, she turned around and disappeared from my view, leaving me staring after her in consternation. Was she seriously leaving just like that?

By the time I got off the bed and walked to the bedroom door, she already stood in front of the lift, the call button pressed as she stepped back into her panties and pulled them up underneath her dress. The last glimpse I got of that red lace covering her rounded ass made my mouth water all over again.

"I wouldn't have kicked you out until the morning." I tried to keep my tone light and hide my disappointment at her departure. Why the hell did I feel disappointed? She gave me exactly what I asked for and did a damn good job of it too.

"I know." She pressed the button again, not looking at me. "But we're done here, right? There's no need for things to get awkward."

The lift opened and she stepped inside, giving her full attention to the buttons rather than me. She didn't even say goodbye. Only at the last second before the door closed did her eyes briefly meet mine again, and she was gone.

# Chapter Two

~**Naomi**~

The memory of my orgasm, the first in more than a year that hadn't been self-procured, brought a smile to my face as soon as I woke up the next morning.

The previous night's encounter had been just what I needed. I found a handsome stranger, went to bed with him, and left immediately afterwards, exactly as I planned. To be honest, I hadn't been sure I had it in me, but not only did I pull it off, the sex was actually *really* good. The feel of his hands on me and the dirty words he whispered would fuel my fantasies for a long time to come.

And the very best part? I never had to see him again. No awkward goodbyes. No complicated feelings. Just the memory of his touch, lingering in my skin like a secret. I didn't even know his name and he didn't know mine. The experience could remain pure and undiluted and perfect, with no pesky real-world details contaminating it.

It couldn't have gone any better.

Still, as I stared at the ceiling, warmth from the night before still humming through my body, a strange hollowness crept in at the edges. For so long, I hadn't wanted anyone's touch but Liam's. Now, a stranger's hands had erased some of that grief, however briefly. Did that mean I was actually moving on? Or just distracting myself?

Before I could dwell on it too much, Pauline stirred in the bed next to me, stretching before rolling out of bed with an energy I envied, especially considering she had a good thirty years on me. "I'll shower first," she offered, already moving toward the bathroom.

We were sharing the room to save the charity money, but thankfully, she was a deep sleeper. She had no idea I hadn't spent the whole night in bed, and I wanted to keep it that way.

As we got ready, we chatted about the day ahead of us. The conference centred on drugs and treatments for rare disorders, and since our charity supported children with a rare genetic condition, we had a lot to accomplish. Between the three of us - me, Pauline, and our colleague, Simon - we would split up to cover as many of the sessions as possible. We each had a personal reason for getting involved with the charity's work which made it more than just a job to all of us.

I dressed carefully, opting for my navy suit and a lighter blue blouse that made me look, I hoped, professional and confident. Pulling my blonde hair into a neat twist, I tried to push aside any lingering thoughts of last night. The day wasn't about me but the children who needed our help.

Simon was already waiting for us in the lobby, dressed in a suit of his own, and together, we walked the few blocks to the conference center in the crisp Italian morning. The city bustled with life: smartly dressed professionals weaving between tourists, the smell of espresso curling through the air, ancient churches casting long shadows across the cobblestones. Maybe on another visit, I would actually have time to explore some of them.

Pauline's phone rang as we entered the main room to take our seats for the keynote speaker, and she turned to us with a smile after a brief conversation with the person on the other end. "That was our contact from the foundation."

Nobody needed to ask which foundation she meant, not when we'd been working on our pitch for the Abel Foundation for months. The small, private foundation put out a call for grant applications at the start of the year, setting off a buzz in the rare disease community. All the information for our proposal had been submitted and they'd agreed to meet with us over lunch that day. Hopefully, the informality of the lunch meeting meant they had good news for us, but we really didn't know for sure. They were keeping their cards close to their chest.

"What did she say?" Simon asked before I got a chance to.

"The foundation's main donor is also in town." Pauline nearly squealed in excitement, reminding me more of a teenager than someone nearing retirement. I hoped I had half as much energy at her age. "He's agreed to meet with us."

Although I'd made a point to learn about all the staff at the Abel Foundation, I didn't know anything about their donors. "Is that a big deal?"

"It's a *huge* deal," she assured me. "Apparently, he makes the final decision on all major donations. If he's meeting with us, it must be a good sign."

The three of us shared smiles of nervous anticipation; excited but trying not to get our hopes up too much. "What do we know about him?" Simon asked.

"Not a lot. They wouldn't tell me his name in advance. He must be very wealthy and apparently, there's some family connection to the foundation, but beyond that, I don't know. They were pretty secretive about it."

In that case, we couldn't do much to prepare, and to be honest, I didn't feel too worried about it. As a major donor to a foundation that did so much good, it stood to reason that he must be a good person. We all believed in our cause deeply and that would come across when we met him.

We *would* make a good impression.

We had to.

The morning sped by in a flurry of presentations and networking, and almost before I knew it, we broke for lunch. A private room had been reserved for us to meet with the foundation representatives, and the woman we'd been dealing with, a beautiful brunette woman in her 30s named Catherine, already waited for us when we arrived.

"Please, have a seat," she greeted us, gesturing to the circular table and the plates of food laid out on it. "Mr Davis will be with us any minute. He told us not to wait."

"Mr Davis is your donor?" Simon asked as he slid into the seat next to Catherine.

"That's right. Mr Kane Davis."

A sharp intake of breath came from Pauline and recognition flickered in Simon's eyes while I blinked at them both. They clearly knew the name but I had never heard it before.

I shot Pauline a questioning look, but she just shook her head slightly, as if to say, *I'll explain later.*

Curiosity flared but I didn't press. Instead, I took my seat across from Simon, leaving an open space beside Pauline for our mysterious benefactor.

Over small talk, the others began to eat. I also picked up my fork and took a careful bite of my pasta, but a subtle, restless energy crackled in the room. I adjusted the cuff of my sleeve, trying to shake the feeling, as the door opened behind me.

Swallowing my bite, I quickly wiped my napkin across my lips, forcing a pleasant, welcoming smile onto my face as I turned to greet our potential donor.

**~Kane~**
The woman invaded my thoughts as soon as I woke up.

She'd been there as I tossed and turned the night before - blonde hair wild against my sheets, warm brown eyes flashing with heat, her soft moans still imprinted in my memory - and she picked up right where she left off the moment my alarm went off.

It didn't help that I could still smell her on my skin.

It only took a few seconds of remembering the way she looked on top of me, her body moving in perfect rhythm with mine, for my cock to stir to life again. With a groan, I pushed myself out of bed and strode into the bathroom, turning the shower to ice-cold in an attempt to erase her from my system.

Fixating on a hookup had never been my style. If I wanted more, I would find someone else. One woman was the same as the next.

And yet, this one lingered.

Maybe because not only had she been fantastic in bed, but she'd left before I had the chance to.

By the time I dressed in a fresh suit and stepped into the penthouse sitting room, my assistant, Natalie, already sat there waiting for me. She greeted me with a bright, white smile.

"Good morning, Kane. Breakfast is on the way, and we can review your emails once it arrives."

I adjusted my cufflinks, that restless feeling still simmering under my skin. "I'd rather eat in the hotel's breakfast room."

Natalie blinked, caught off guard by the deviation from routine, but recovered quickly. "Of course."

She gathered her things and followed me to the lift, quietly canceling the room service order. I ignored the questioning glance she shot me as the lift carried us down to the ground floor.

Inside the dining room, with its pale-yellow tablecloths and neatly set tables, my gaze swept the room. I told myself I was just surveying the space. That I wasn't looking for anyone in particular.

But when I didn't see her, irritation flickered.

*Fuck.*

I should have stayed upstairs.

The meal passed in a blur of business updates and calendar reminders but my thoughts kept drifting. My mind replayed the previous night on an endless loop, and the more I tried to shake it, the more firmly the memory lodged itself in place.

I didn't like it. I didn't like that this woman had gotten under my skin and I didn't like that I had no idea who she was or how to find her, even if I wanted to.

By the time lunch rolled around, I had fallen a few minutes behind schedule. I slid into the car when my meeting ended, barely glancing at Natalie as she handed me a file.

"The charity you're meeting over lunch supports children with a rare genetic condition," she summarized. "The foundation has reviewed their grant proposal and Catherine is ready to approve it if you give the go-ahead."

I flipped through the documents. "How much are they asking for?"

"A hundred thousand pounds."

I nearly handed the file right back to her. That kind of pocket change was barely worth my time. However, Catherine was simply following my orders. I'd told her I wanted to be involved in the foundation's major decisions. Maybe I needed to redefine 'major'.

"Keep the car ready," I told the driver when we arrived. "I won't be long."

Natalie led me through the busy conference centre to the room Catherine had arranged. "I'll wait out here," she offered, and I pushed the door open, stepping inside with the intention of saying a quick hello, giving my blessing to the project, and making an equally hasty escape.

In the small meeting room, four sets of eyes turned towards me.

Catherine, I recognized immediately. The other three, I assumed, were from the charity. My gaze skimmed past the middle-aged man and the larger woman with a warm smile until I locked eyes with... *her.*

*Well, well.*

The blonde woman's warm smile vanished as her eyes met mine. Her shoulders tensed and I bit back a smirk as I clocked her obvious unease.

Every strained muscle made it clear she hadn't expected to see me there.

When she walked out of my room the night before, she held all the cards. Now, the tables had turned, and nothing suited me better than having the upper hand.

What I would do with it, I still had to decide.

Catherine rose, oblivious to the tension crackling between us. "Mr. Davis, let me introduce you to our guests."

She rattled off the name of the condition the charity represented, a string of genetic letters and numbers, while I walked around the room to shake hands with everyone. I left the blonde woman until last.

When I reached her, she stood, but there was no polite warmth in her posture. Her fingers clenched into fists at her sides.

"And you are?" I asked, my voice smooth and controlled. A small, knowing smirk pulled at my lips.

Her jaw tightened. "Naomi Law. It's a pleasure to meet you."

The look in her eyes said otherwise.

I dragged my chair slightly to the left as we sat, ensuring I had a perfect view of Naomi. She kept her gaze firmly on her plate while Pauline, the older woman, launched into her pitch. I half-listened, but the bulk of my attention remained fixed on the woman across the table.

Naomi was trying her damnedest to ignore me, which only made me more interested.

Catherine thanked the older woman as she wrapped up the presentation, then turned to me. "Naturally, it's up to you whether the foundation approves the grant."

I leaned back, still studying Naomi, and the path forward suddenly seemed clear. "It sounds very interesting. I wonder if Miss Law would be willing to tell me more about it over dinner tonight?"

Naomie's head snapped up, her eyes wide in alarm as all the attention in the room shifted to her.

"Or is it *Mrs* Law?" I added.

Pauline, eager to help, chimed in. "It's Miss. And we have no plans tonight, do we, Naomi?"

So, the ring wasn't a wedding ring. Engagement, then? I almost felt bad for her fiancé, whoever he might be, but not bad enough to stop me from manipulating my way into more time with Naomi.

Naomi found her voice at last. "Pauline and Simon have both been with the charity longer than I have. I'm sure they would be better able to answer your questions."

"Pauline mentioned you all have a personal connection to the charity." At least I'd been paying enough attention to pick up on that. "I'd like to hear about yours."

Her colleagues turned pleading eyes on her, all of them knowing what was at stake, and as I hoped she would, she gave in to the peer pressure. "If that's what you'd like."

Triumph swelled in my chest, but before I could celebrate my victory, Naomi struck back.

"Will your wife be joining us?"

The sharpness in her tone and the way she tilted her chin told me that she thought she'd landed a winning blow, but Catherine and Pauline simply exchanged nervous, tittered laughter.

"Mr Davis isn't married," Catherine informed her, shooting me an apologetic glance that I dismissed with a wave of my hand.

Naomi's eyes narrowed on me before she offered a stiff apology. "My mistake."

The words held no sincerity. She knew as well as I did that her only mistake had been believing me, and rather than being annoyed at her attempt to expose me, a slow, deep satisfaction settled in my chest.

She wouldn't give in easily, but I had her exactly where I wanted her.

I stood, not needing to prolong the encounter any longer. "I'll have my assistant send you the details. Lovely to meet you all."

A new anticipation energized my steps as I walked back to the car with Natalie, all my frustration from the morning evaporated with the prospect of seeing Naomi again. "I need you to change my dinner plans for tonight. Something has just come up."

**~Naomi~**

The second Catherine left the room, Pauline whirled on me. "How do you not know who Kane Davis is?"

I barely heard her, my mind still spinning from the last twenty minutes. Of all the men in Rome, why did it have to be him? The one man who had the power to make or break everything we'd been working toward for months? I just wanted one night of escape, one night to forget about my grief and my loneliness. One night with no complications.

Instead, I'd walked straight into the biggest complication of all.

"Who is he?" I mumbled, still dazed.

Pauline gaped at me, as if I'd committed a crime by being unaware of his existence. "Self-made multi-millionaire? Tatler's most eligible bachelor? More money than he knows what to do with? None of this is ringing a bell?"

"Even I've heard of him," Simon piped up.

I shrugged, trying to act indifferent even as my pulse pounded in my ears. Wealth and status never interested me, so I hadn't given his expensive hotel room a second thought. I didn't care about his background because he wasn't supposed to matter, not supposed to play any role in my life besides our fleeting encounter.

Clearly, I had miscalculated.

"Why did you think he was married?" Pauline asked next, still breathless in her disbelief.

*Because he told me he was?* The words sat heavy on my tongue, but I swallowed them down. If I admitted I'd met him before, I'd have to explain how and why, and I wasn't about to do that. My face burned at the thought.

I repeated my attempt at a casual shrug. "He just seemed like someone who would be."

Pauline's brow knit in suspicion at my weak excuse, but mercifully, she let it go and we prepared to return to the conference for the afternoon sessions.

That left me alone with my unanswered questions, none of which I could figure out.

Why did he lie about being married? Why did he look pleased to see me when, at the bar, he'd been the one to state he never wanted to see me again?

Most importantly, why the hell did he want to have dinner with me?

All I could come up with was that he enjoyed making me squirm. He might not have been a cheater, but that still made him an asshole.

Dinner with him sounded like pure torture, but how could I refuse? The grant meant everything. If I walked away now, I'd be throwing months of work down the drain. Pauline and Simon were counting on me. The children and families who needed this funding were counting on me.

Kane knew it.

And so, I had no choice but to play whatever game he had in mind.

*Bastard.*

The rest of the conference passed in a blur. I nodded through pre-sentations, answered questions, even smiled when appropriate. But in the back of my mind, the same thought played on a loop.

*I cannot screw this up.*

Back at the hotel, Pauline took it upon herself to prepare me for my "date," as she insisted on calling it.

"It's not a date," I corrected for the twentieth time. "We're discussing the grant. That's it."

"Right, because men always insist on dinner meetings with women they have no interest in." Pauline shot me a knowing look as she rifled through my suitcase. When she pulled out the dress I wore to the bar the night before, she gasped. "Oh, this is cute! Maybe you could wear this one."

I grabbed the dress from her and tossed it onto the other side of the bed like it was contaminated. "Absolutely not."

I could still feel Kane's hands on me, still see the heat in his eyes when he pulled it off me. I didn't need him thinking about that too.

"I need to look professional."

Pauline sighed dramatically. "Fine. Be boring."

We finally settled on a short-sleeved white blouse, a black skirt, and dressy sandals. Businesslike, but not too cold. The perfect balance.

As I dressed, my phone buzzed with a message.

> Good evening, this is Mr Davis' assistant, Natalie. He'll meet you in the lobby at seven.

"Pauline?" I called through the bathroom door. "Did you give Catherine my number?"

"No. Why?"

"No reason."

I stared at the message a moment longer before shaking my head and setting my phone down. How the hell did he get my contact info? If he hadn't gone through the Abel Foundation, how *would* he have found it? I wasn't sure I wanted to know.

When I stepped out of the bathroom, Pauline clutched her heart dramatically. "You look gorgeous."

"It is *not* a date," I muttered one last time, grabbing my purse.

Her eyes sparkled. "Call it whatever you want, but a sexy billionaire just rearranged his entire evening for you. Even if you're technically using him for money, it's still exciting."

*Using him for money.*

Those words lingered in my mind as I pressed the button for the lift, doing my best to ignore the way my fingers trembled with nerves. I supposed that was one way of looking at it. And just because he was the one with the money didn't mean he held *all* the power.

I'd gotten what I wanted from him once. I could do it again. All I had to do was keep things professional and appeal to his sense of decency. How hard could it be?

# Chapter Three



**~Kane~**

While I attended my afternoon meetings, I set Natalie the task of finding out everything she could about Naomi before our dinner. It didn't take long. Used to pulling together files on my clients or competitors, anyone I needed leverage over, my assistant had the information waiting for me by the time I finished my final meeting for the day.

"Do you want the full report or just the highlights?" she asked as I slid into the car beside her.

"Highlights." I didn't need Naomi's life story, just enough to understand the lay of the land so I could figure out exactly what I might be able to get out of the evening. Having her in my bed again that night went without saying, but based on how she'd dominated my thoughts since then, I had a feeling just one more night wouldn't be enough. I'd rather overshoot than under.

Natalie skimmed the pages in front of her. "Unmarried. Twenty-six years old. Has worked at the charity for two years; before that, she was a teaching assistant at a special school No criminal record, decent credit rating..."

That level of minutiae didn't interest me, and she hadn't gotten to the most important detail yet, so I cut her off to ask the question foremost in my mind: "Who's she engaged to?"

A frown tugged at the corners of Natalie's mouth. "Nothing in the file about a fiancé. What makes you think she's engaged?"

"She wears a ring."

"Give me two seconds." She tapped on her phone, apparently sending a message to someone since her phone dinged with a reply a few seconds later. "She was engaged to a Liam Howard, but he passed away last year. No current partner listed."

*Passed away.* The words hit heavier than I expected, a dull weight pressing against my ribs as I exhaled slowly, thinking back to our conversation the night before. When I mentioned the ring, she neither confirmed nor denied its meaning. I assumed she was hiding a relationship, but this information reframed everything.

The awkward tension at lunch. The way she flinched when I brought up her ring but didn't correct me. I thought she was nervous about being caught, but she was holding onto something no longer there.

In that case, why hadn't she cared when I lied about being married? She obviously believed me since she brought it up again at lunch. But if she owed no loyalty to anyone, why had my lie not mattered to her?

I leaned back against the seat, considering this new development from all angles. Natalie's findings had given me answers, but not clarity. If anything, Naomi Law was more of a mystery now than she had been before. At least I'd have the chance to ask her those questions myself.

I played games of strategy against clients and competitors every day. This was no different. She wanted something from me and I wanted something from her. All we had to do was come to a mutually satisfying compromise.

Back at the hotel, I changed into something more casual: a light blue button-down shirt with cream trousers. When I stepped into the lobby, heads turned, as they always did. Normally, I welcomed the attention, the subtle invitations in lingering gazes, but that night, I barely noticed.

At three minutes to seven, Naomi hadn't arrived. I pulled out my phone, scanning through emails as a pretense of patience, but doubt crept in. People didn't keep me waiting. Would she? I had no idea what to expect, making her an intriguing opponent.

Just as I considered tracking her down, the elevator doors slid open.

Even if I hadn't been waiting for her, I would have noticed her the moment she stepped into the room. There was something about the way she carried herself, an unspoken challenge in the set of her shoulders and a deliberate lift of her chin.

She wasn't as done up as last night. Her skirt hung lower on her thighs, her blouse more modest, but it didn't matter. The soft fabric clung to her in just the right places, teasing rather than revealing. As she walked toward me, I could already picture the way she had looked spread across my sheets, flushed and breathless beneath me.

The memory stirred my blood, and the anticipation of getting her back in that position later that evening set it simmering.

When our gazes met, Naomi squared her shoulders, preparing for battle, and a slow smile spread across my lips. I still hadn't figured out *why* I wanted her again when once was usually enough, but her determination to fight me on it only made me want her more.

"Mr Davis." Her tight smile when she greeted me didn't reach her eyes.

"Kane," I corrected, letting my gaze linger on her mouth. I couldn't wait to hear my name on her lips, gasping it, moaning it, but that would come later. For now, I simply offered her my arm. "The restaurant is just a couple of blocks away so I thought we could walk."

She refused to take my arm, unwilling to give me an inch. "I can walk on my own. Which way?"

My amusement deepened with every attempt she made to resist me, and as we stepped onto the street, the autumn air cooler now that the heat of the day had faded, I kept a leisurely pace, forcing her to slow her steps to match mine.

"Have you been to Rome before?"

She kept her eyes ahead, not glancing at me. "No."

"When did you arrive?"

"Yesterday."

"Will you have time to do any sightseeing while you're here?"

"No."

A one-word answer met every query, each syllable carefully measured. She didn't ask me anything in return. Still, I kept going, volleying questions like moves in a game of chess until we reached the restaurant I'd chosen for the evening.

Housed in an old mansion, 17-century frescos decorated the intimate rooms above a mosaic of thousands of pieces of coloured glass on the floor. At my request, Natalie had booked us a private room with only one table for two overlooking the courtyard garden with its gurgling fountain and the sweet scent of late-blooming flowers.

Anyone would have been impressed.

Naomi barely spared it a glance.

"Would you like to choose a wine?" I asked, offering her the wine menu when we were both seated.

"I'm not drinking. Sparkling water, please."

I motioned to the waiter who stood unobtrusively in the doorway, waiting to be called. "A bottle of the Chianti with two glasses, and a sparkling water."

I suspected Naomi might change her mind about having a drink when she heard what I had to say.

She studied the menu, eyes fixed downward in deliberate avoidance, but once our orders were placed, she had no choice but to meet my gaze.

"Tell me about your grant application," I invited, easing us into what I hoped would lead to an actual conversation.

Wariness lingered in her eyes, but she finally gave me a proper answer. "My colleague, Pauline, already told you the main details over lunch: we have an arrangement with a biotech company to work on developing a new pharmaceutical treatment for our patients. It's a two-year project.

No one has ever developed a treatment specifically for this condition and we haven't been able to find a drug to repurpose either. At the moment, there isn't any kind of treatment available for these kids."

"And this two-year project costs £100,000?"

I already knew the answer since Natalie provided me with the full proposal that afternoon, but I wanted her to state it out loud. I wanted us to be on the same page when it came to the financial situation.

"No," Naomi admitted, her lips twisting in an unhappy grimace around the word. "Our grant application is to cover the cost of some of the supplies. The full project will be closer to half a million pounds, so we're working on fundraising the rest."

"That's a daunting amount to raise for a charity of your size."

"It is, but we have a dedicated group of volunteers. The patients with this condition are so special. Everyone who meets them loves them. If the Abel Foundation agrees to give us this grant, it will help take some of the pressure off and allow us to focus on the rest of what we need to do. We really appreciate the work that the foundation does and we believe that this proposal fits your mission extremely well."

She grew more earnest as she spoke, warming to the subject, showing a conviction and passion I hadn't seen from her before, so I decided to set her mind at ease on this one point at least.

"The foundation will be making the grant, Naomi. It's already approved."

She blinked, and a second passed before her surprise melted into something softer.

"That's wonderful, Mr Davis. Thank you. It will mean so much to us."

Her smile reached her eyes this time and something warm unfurled inside my chest. Though it shouldn't have mattered, I liked it when she looked at me that way.

"It's Kane," I reminded her, taking a sip from my wine glass to prolong the warm feeling still blooming inside me.

It didn't take long for her expression to shift, though, her brows knitting in confusion.

"What's wrong?" I asked when she didn't say anything.

Her mouth opened and closed again, as if she were debating whether to speak what was on her mind, before she spoke. "If you've already decided to make the grant, what am I doing here?"

I held her gaze as I set my drink down, focusing all of my attention on the beautiful woman across from me. "I wanted to see you."

With the grant out of the way, the real negotiation could begin.

**~Naomi~**

Kane smiled at me over the flickering candlelight, as if his statement was all the answer I needed. As if I should be *grateful* that he wanted to see me. As if he were doing me some kind of favor.

What was he playing at?

Some women might have been naive enough to believe that dinner at a high-end restaurant meant he was actually interested in them, but I knew better. I had pegged him the moment I saw him and Pauline's stories that afternoon only confirmed my instincts.

Kane Davis: playboy billionaire. A different model on his arm at every event. Never attached, never serious, never with the same woman for more than a few weeks. The textbook definition of a fuckboy.

But if all of that were true, why was he going to such trouble to impress me when we'd already slept together?

I could spend the rest of the evening trying to untangle his motives or I could just ask him.

I settled on the latter.

Leaning forward, I lowered my voice even though we were alone in the room. "You said last night that you wanted to spend the night with me and never see me again."

His smile didn't waver, looking so smug I wanted to reach across the table and wipe it off his face. "I'd started to think you didn't recognize me."

I narrowed my eyes, giving him my best withering glare. "I'm more than happy to stick to what we agreed, and since you just told me the grant is approved, I don't see the point in continuing this charade."

I pushed my chair back and stood, fully intending to walk away.

Kane leaned back, utterly unbothered, and swirled the wine in his glass before murmuring, "Unless you want to talk about the rest of the money."

My body stilled mid-motion. "The rest of what money?"

"The other £400,000 your project needs."

His response stunned me into silence.

Was he serious? He probably *had* that kind of money, but would he actually consider donating it? Or was this just another way to amuse himself at my expense?

"What about it?" I finally managed.

"Why don't you sit back down and we can discuss it?" He gestured to my empty chair. "Besides, you haven't eaten yet."

My pride screamed at me to walk away, but if there was even the smallest chance of securing that donation, I had to at least *try*.

Hating myself for giving him the upper hand yet again, I sank back into my seat. The satisfied smile that tugged at his lips did nothing to improve my mood.

Fine. If we were going to drop the pretense, I might as well ask what had been bothering me since lunch. "Why did you tell me you were married when you aren't?"

Kane shrugged as if the effort of lifting his shoulders bored him as much as the question did. "It's a standard line I use. Helps me weed out anyone looking for a commitment."

The sheer *audacity*. Were there really women in the world who found this self-congratulatory tone attractive?

"I clearly *wasn't* looking for a commitment. And yet, you're still bothering me."

He laughed, as if I were joking. "You didn't seem too bothered by me yesterday. Except in a hot-and-bothered kind of way."

I refused to dignify that with a response.

"Besides, you let me believe you had a partner too," he added smoothly. "I assume your reasoning is the same?"

My fingers twitched against my napkin. How did he know I *didn't* have a partner? I never told him that, and I didn't intend to talk about it now.

Liam's name didn't belong in this room. Not in this conversation, and not anywhere near this man.

Instead of answering, I shifted the subject back to what *actually* mattered. "You mentioned the rest of the money. Are you considering making an additional donation?"

Before he could answer, the waiter arrived with our food, pausing the conversation. I barely took notice of my meal, my mind still spinning. Kane, on the other hand, picked up his fork, twirling his pasta with an easy confidence that made me want to reach across the table and stab him with it.

"I could be persuaded to provide the additional funding," he finally said, glancing at my untouched plate. "Eat before it gets cold."

I picked up my fork reluctantly, my stomach too twisted in knots to eat. My energy was better spent figuring out what game we were playing.

"What kind of persuasion would you require?"

His lips curled. "I'm so glad you phrased it that way."

My grip tightened on my fork. "Just get to the point, Mr Davis."

"Kane," he reminded me again. "And the point is: I have a problem. One that you might be able to help with."

I already knew I didn't *want* to hear the answer, but I asked anyway. "What problem is that?"

"Every time I take a woman home, she ends up thinking I'm going to marry her."

I waited a beat. Then two.

No punchline.

He was actually *serious*.

I called on all my self-control not to roll my eyes. "How awful for you."

His lips twitched as he picked up his wine glass. "It is, actually. It leads to endless awkward conversations. Scenes from hysterical women who think they're in love with me after an hour in my bed. It's a nuisance."

"You could try not sleeping with so many women in the first place," I suggested sweetly, feigning innocence.

His smirk grew as he lifted the glass to his lips. "I've never been particularly good at denying myself pleasure. Especially when I don't have to."

God, he was insufferable.

How would he react if I picked up my plate and flung my pasta in his smug face? The mental image nearly made me smile, until he kept talking.

"I didn't have that problem with you, though." He set his glass down, studying me. "We had fun - and I know you did, don't bother denying it. But afterwards, you were happy to leave."

"That's what I *tried* to do," I muttered.

His low chuckle sent an uncontrollable shiver down my spine, my body reacting to him in spite of everything else.

"Exactly. And that's what I need right now: someone to have fun with, who'll be there when I want them, but not when I don't. Someone who isn't going to imagine they've fallen in love with me or, God forbid, think that *I* love *them*."

"You want a fuck buddy," I clarified.

"If you want to be crass about it."

I arched a brow. "You do know there are women who do that for a living, right? I'm sure you could afford as many as you want."

Kane nearly choked on his laughter before replying. "Even the most discreet professionals have leaks sometimes and I have a reputation to protect. It would be much easier for me if you and I could come to an arrangement."

I still wasn't sure exactly where I fit into this, but at least we were finally getting to the point.

"What kind of arrangement are you suggesting?"

His slow, deliberate smile brought to mind a hunter closing in on his prey. "A very simple one: you make yourself available to me whenever I want you and in return, I'll donate the rest of the money for your project."

**~Kane~**

I kept my eyes trained on Naomi as I got to the heart of my proposal, watching her body language carefully for all the clues that her words might try to hide. Every flicker of emotion that crossed her face. She was rare among the women I usually surrounded myself with: sharp, perceptive, and completely unimpressed by me.

That made her a challenge, and there was little that I loved more than a challenge.

It didn't even occur to me to stop and wonder why exactly I cared so much about winning.

"You want me to be 'available' to you?" Her voice squeaked in indignance as she glared at me. "Forever?"

I almost laughed. "No. Let's not get dramatic. Three months should do it."

I made it sound like an arbitrary number, but I'd actually given it careful thought. Never had I spent that long with one woman, and it should be more than enough time to get Naomi Law out of my system. Originally, I thought just one month would be enough, but for the amount of money involved, three seemed more reasonable. If I got bored, I'd simply stop calling. The donation would be paid at the end.

As plans went, it was clean. Simple.

Foolproof.

She blinked at me a couple of times before scoffing. "Let me get this straight: you want to pay me four hundred thousand pounds to sleep with you for three months?"

She made it sound insane. Maybe it was, but I'd always gone after what I wanted, and right now, I wanted her.

"I wouldn't be paying you," I corrected. "I'd be supporting a worthy cause."

Naomi shook her head, still in disbelief. "That doesn't make it any less..."

She stopped herself, inhaling sharply.

"This is ridiculous."

I shrugged. "It's my money. I can spend it how I like." I let the words settle before adding, "Besides sex, there would be a few other expectations."

Her posture stiffened. "Like what?"

"You don't tell anyone about our arrangement and you don't see anyone else while we're together."

"I'd expect the same from you," she bit back, and I couldn't hide my smirk. That was the first sign she was considering it, even if she didn't realize it yet.

"Of course," I said smoothly. "What else?"

She exhaled sharply, clearly trying to suppress whatever internal argument she was having with herself.

"I won't go out in public with you," she said at last. "I don't want people thinking I'm your girlfriend."

"Obviously."

Her lips pressed together before she continued, more hesitantly this time. "I can refuse to do anything I'm uncomfortable with."

What exactly did she think I had in mind? "Based on last night, I have no doubt we'd find plenty we both enjoy."

She shifted in her seat, clearly suppressing whatever images flashed through her mind with the reminder of our night together.

I leaned forward, lowering my voice. It was almost time to move in for the kill. "Anything else?"

She swallowed, her jaw tightening. "I can change my mind at any time and walk away."

I pretended to consider that. "Fair. But the donation is made at the end of the three months. Are we agreed, then?"

Her gaze met mine, steady but uncertain. "Can I have some time to think about it?"

"I leave for London tomorrow. I want an answer before then."

Technically, I could have waited longer, but I knew that giving her time would only give her the chance to talk herself out of it. Nerves and her imagination would take over. If I got her back in my bed that night, though... the deal would be made.

She hesitated, exhaling through her nose before asking one final question.

"What guarantee do I have that you'll actually follow through?"

I smiled a slow, calculated, utterly insincere smile.

"You'll just have to trust me."

# Chapter Four

~**Naomi**~

*Trust him?* Not a chance.

But if he was so determined to keep this secret, that would be my insurance policy. If he tried to back out of our agreement, I could always go to the press. Sure, it would be humiliating for me, but for him? The gossip rags would have a field day exposing a man like Kane, someone who had everything, resorting to paying for sex.

And why would he even need to? I doubted he had trouble finding women willing to warm his bed, and even if they got more attached than he liked, was that really such a big deal? No, this wasn't about convenience or whatever excuse he tried to give me.

It was about control.

He got off on power, and this arrangement gave him the ability to have me at his beck and call, for no reason other than because it amused him.

But did his reasons really matter when I could use it to my own advantage?

*Four hundred thousand pounds.* That kind of money could change lives. It could jump start the charity's research and provide hope to people who desperately needed it.

*That* was the reason I was even considering it.

The primary reason, at least.

Maybe not the only one.

I ended up in Kane's bed because I missed sex but had no interest in a relationship. He had a great body, and he knew how to use it; he'd already proven that much. His proposal, crude as it may be, gave me the perfect cover to have more of that, no strings attached. I didn't have to admit I wanted him. I didn't have to tell anyone in my life about it. In fact, I couldn't. I could claim the money as my motivation while secretly getting exactly what I wanted, too.

Sure, the guy was an asshole, but just the thought of riding him again had me squirming in my seat in a way I really hoped wasn't too obvious.

*Fuck.* I was actually going to agree to this.

Dreading the inevitable smugness that would follow my assent, I grabbed the bottle of wine, poured a full glass, and downed it in one go. Kane chuckled, clearly enjoying my turmoil.

"Is that a yes?"

Would it be too late to add a clause that I'd only sleep with him in the dark so I wouldn't have to see that insufferable smirk?

"Fine," I muttered.

I caught the gleam in his eyes as I set the empty glass down. Sure enough, that arrogant, knowing smirk spread across his face like he'd just won a bet.

"Excellent. Let's go."

He stood, and I frowned, glancing down at my barely-touched plate. "Right now?"

"Whenever I want," he reminded me. "That's what you agreed to."

My glare did nothing to shake his confidence. Arguing would be pointless. With a resigned sigh, I shoveled one last forkful of pasta into my mouth before standing and following him out of the beautiful restaurant.

Back on the street, he extended his arm toward me.

"I thought we agreed we wouldn't be seen together in public," I said, raising an eyebrow. If he wanted to stick to the rules he set, so would I.

"At home," he clarified. "Here, nobody knows who we are."

"Nobody knows who I am in London either."

He laughed as I rolled my eyes, but I took his arm anyway, trying to ignore the way his warmth seeped into me and the way my pulse picked up the moment we touched. My body recognized it for what it was, though.

Anticipation.

As soon as we reached the hotel, I dropped his arm, putting space between us. There were people there who knew me. I had no idea if he had colleagues with him or what he was even doing in Rome beyond our brief meeting. Not that I was about to ask. The more impersonal we kept things, the better.

We waited in silence for the lift, but my mind was anything but still. It wandered back to the night before and the way he kissed me the moment we got inside, how his hands roamed over my body with a confidence that made my knees weak. A flush crept up my skin at the memory, warmth settling low in my stomach.

I should *not* be so turned on by him.

It didn't change the fact that I was.

When the lift doors opened, we stepped inside, joined by two other guests. I kept my eyes fixed on the screen as the numbers ticked upward, doing my best to ignore Kane's presence beside me. But when his hand brushed lightly against my ass, the contact sent a jolt up my spine.

I wanted his hands on me again. I couldn't deny it.

The two people got off at the next floor, leaving us alone, and the doors barely closed before his mouth was on mine.

He wanted me as much as I wanted him, and *fuck*, I wanted him.

The eagerness in my kiss spurred him on even more. My back hit the wall as his body pressed into me, his erection pushing against my stomach. When the lift finally reached his floor, he reached down and scooped me up, his hands under my ass, and with my legs wrapped around him, he walked us both into the living room. His stiff cock rubbed against my pussy through the layers of clothing and I rocked my hips against it.

I needed friction. I needed *more*.

Kane didn't pause in the living space, heading straight to the bedroom where we had sex the night before. With my legs still around his waist, we fell onto the bed, him on top. Releasing his grip on my ass, he brought his hands up to my blouse instead, undoing the buttons while I worked on the ones on his shirt. It felt like a race, and I won, pulling his shirt down over his shoulders before he reached my final buttons. My fingers traced the lines of his chest, the defined muscles tight and warm beneath my fingers, and it was all I could do not to moan as he reached down to roughly yank the rest of his shirt off before he finished opening mine.

This frenzied need wasn't typical for me, especially when aimed towards a man who had done nothing but frustrate me all day long. I didn't like him but I wanted him anyway, and somehow, that dichotomy made the desire even more intense.

My hands dragged down his back as his mouth moved downwards, kissing the rise of my breasts over my bra. A hiss whistled through my teeth as he pulled one side of my bra down and sucked the nipple in his mouth. Nothing in his movements was soft or gentle. Everything he did felt as urgent as the pulsing inside my body. Almost against my will, my back arched in pleasure, my hips pushing into him as my hands grabbed hold of his hair.

My body had a mind of its own.

Without warning, he pushed himself off me and I almost cried out from the loss of contact. "Where are you going?"

He smirked at the breathiness of my voice, and though his expression should have annoyed me, it only made me hotter, especially when he grabbed my skirt and panties and pulled them both down, leaving me naked other than my bra and the sandals still on my feet. While he got rid of his trousers, I unhooked my bra, wanting nothing between us. My body ached with relief when he returned to the bed, and as his naked body covered mine, he slid one finger inside me without any further preamble.

That time, I couldn't hold back my moan as he felt his way around inside me.

"You're so ready for me, aren't you Naomi?"

Part of me wanted to deny him the satisfaction of admitting it, but what would that achieve? He could feel it for himself, and I didn't want to wait any more. I needed to come and I knew he could take care of me.

"Yes," I breathed out as he sucked on my neck, his finger still exploring.

"Say my name," he commanded, lifting his head to look in my eyes while he added a second finger to his probing.

Gritting my teeth, I forced myself to meet his gaze. The desire lurking there made me breathless all over again, and I gave up the fight. We *both* needed this.

"Yes, Kane. I'm ready for you. I want you, now. Fuck me."

My pussy clenched as he hummed in appreciation, the sound rumbling deep in his chest. His lips captured mine, his tongue pushing deep into his mouth, and I felt his fingers withdraw and the tip of his cock press against my entrance instead.

Pushing back on his shoulders, I broke our kiss. "Wait. You need a condom."

His handsome nose wrinkled in confusion. "Why?"

Was that a joke? "Because you're a literal stranger to me and I don't know anything about the hundreds of other women you've slept with."

He had the nerve to look slightly offended but he didn't bother correcting me on the number. Instead, he got up once more to open the same drawer where I found the condom the night before. I stared up at the ceiling as I waited for him to roll it on, my body still on fire, aching for him.

After what felt like an eternity but must have only been a matter of seconds, he crawled back onto the bed one more time, spreading my

legs wide around him. This time, there were no more kisses. Position-
ing himself between my thighs, he thrust into me without any further
warning.

"Fuck!" I cried out as he filled me and that smirk spread across his face
once more. We both knew exactly how good it felt. My ankles crossed
over his back and I lifted my hips to meet each thrust as he pistoned
into me, hard and fast. Any tenderness in our fucking had disappeared,
leaving only primal need and desperation behind.

My body loved every second of it.

His breath grew ragged as the tension inside me built until it felt like
I literally couldn't take anymore. "Oh, God," I whimpered. "Don't stop.
There... fuck, Kane, yes."

With one more cry, I crossed over the edge of my orgasm, my legs
trembling as the wave of pleasure crashed over me.

"Yes... fuck..." he muttered in response, his body tensing and his cock
pulsing as he emptied himself into the condom.

Panting and sated, we stayed locked together for a long moment
before he pulled out of me and moved away. Emptiness replaced the
wonderful fullness, leaving my body craving more even if I didn't *want*
to want it. After discarding the condom, he lay down on the bed beside
me on his back, exhaling deeply in satisfaction.

Gradually, the lustful haze cleared and reality settled back in.

What the hell were we supposed to do now?

**~Kane~**

Lying on my back, staring at the ceiling, it took me a second to
recognize the feeling drenching me in warmth.

*Contentment.*

My body was sated, my mind at ease for the first time all day. Things
went even better than I'd hoped. Naomi hadn't just given in to my

proposition; she had matched my impatience the second we were alone, her fiery passion stoking me to orgasm even faster than usual.

Hearing her moan my name as she came was just as satisfying as I'd imagined.

I wanted to hear it again.

When she didn't say anything, I rolled over to face her, only to find her already sitting up, reaching for her clothes. A frown tugged at my lips.

"What are you doing?"

"I have to get back to my room."

She stood, bending to pick up her shirt, and my gaze trailed down her body. Just like that, my blood heated again.

"You can stay here tonight," I said, my voice deliberately casual. "I might want you again."

Naomi glanced over her shoulder, her expression dripping with disdain, and my frown morphed into a slow grin. Apparently, she planned to resume her pretense of indifference whenever we weren't actively fucking.

I was more than up for the challenge.

"I'm sharing a room with my colleague," she explained, slipping her arms into her blouse. "She knows I went to dinner with you. If I don't turn up until morning, she'll have her theories, and she's never been one to keep things to herself."

*Fuck.* I hadn't considered that.

"Fine," I conceded. "But back in London, I'll expect you to stay the night."

The way she rushed to dress and put distance between us left a sour taste in my mouth. It was one thing for her to resist me in public; it made the game more fun. But scrambling to leave my bed like it was some kind of crime scene? That made me feel... dirty. And not in the way I usually enjoyed.

"Where do you live?" she asked, buttoning her blouse. "I'll need to get home in the mornings before work."

"Canary Wharf." I watched her expression carefully as I answered. "You?"

"Ealing."

A grimace pulled at my mouth. Opposite ends of the city. While she might believe me to be a self-serving bastard, and quite rightly, I had no desire to actually make her life more difficult merely for the sake of it.

"I'll set you up with a car service. You can get where you need to go whenever you want. And if it's easier, you can keep a few things at my place, so you can go straight to work from there."

That seemed to catch her off guard, so before she could refuse, I pushed ahead.

"There's one other thing." I let my voice drop into something firmer. "I don't want to bother with condoms every time we have sex. I already agreed I wouldn't be with anyone else for the duration of our arrangement. What would you need to be comfortable with that?"

Normally, I always wore a condom, but when she asked me to put one on that night, it didn't sit right. And if we were doing this for three months, it seemed unnecessary.

Naomi stilled for a second, and I half-expected an argument, but she relented instead as she straightened the sleeves of her blouse.

"I guess I'd be okay with it as long as you get tested. I will too, naturally."

"I can do that. Do you need any kind of birth control, or are you covered?"

She hesitated before turning her back to me as she pulled her skirt up. I thought I saw the slightest flinch.

"That's under control."

Her answer was clipped, final. I didn't press.

By the time she finished tucking in her blouse, she looked fully composed. Too composed. As if she wasn't naked in my bed just minutes ago, panting my name. I missed the sight of her bare skin already.

"When do you get back to London?" I asked.

"Friday."

Three days.

My sharp prickle of frustration surprised me. Or was it something else?

Disappointment?

I already had plans for Friday and Saturday, which meant I wouldn't see her until Sunday. The realization irritated me more than it should have.

"You can come to my flat Sunday evening," I said. "I'll send you the details of the car service so you can use it that night. Anything else you need to know for now?"

"I don't think so."

She glanced around the room, checking that she hadn't left anything behind. My gaze locked on her lips as she pulled the lower one between her teeth, and my cock twitched in response.

*Fuck.* If she didn't have someone tracking her whereabouts tonight, I'd already have her beneath me again.

Before I could do something as desperate as ask her to stay, I forced myself to dismiss her instead.

"I'll see you Sunday, then."

For a moment, Naomi held my gaze, as if she had something else to say, but in the end, she simply turned and walked out without another word.

# Chapter Five



~**Naomi**~

The lift door closed in front of me, sealing me off from the surreal penthouse hotel room and the frustratingly attractive man inside it. In an attempt to bring myself back to reality, I inhaled deeply, but that only made things worse. Kane's cologne still clung to my skin, a lingering ghost of our time together. The rich woodsy scent, edged with something citrusy, curled around me in a whisper of temptation, and my thighs clenched involuntarily, heat pooling low in my belly.

I'd need a long, cold shower before bed or I'd spend the night tangled in dreams I didn't want to admit to craving.

Why did being with him feel so good? No emotional connection existed between us, and I'd always believed that really good sex required at least *liking* the other person.

Apparently, I had that wrong.

When he told me we wouldn't see each other until Sunday, I should have felt relieved. Three days to breathe, to regain control. Instead, I felt... what? A little disappointed? A flicker of doubt? Honestly, I didn't know. The agreement we made was nothing but a transaction, and yet, the idea of putting space between us, of letting this strange thing between us cool before it had fully ignited, left an ache I didn't want to examine too closely.

How in the world did I get myself into this?

"There you are!"

Pauline's squeal when I let myself into our room nearly made me jump out of my skin. I thought she'd be asleep already, but it seemed she'd waited up for me, sitting in the chair by the window with a book that she closed on her lap as she looked eagerly over at me.

"How did it go?"

I stuck to the important part: "We got the grant."

Her eyes widened in surprise before her whole face lit up in delight. "For certain?"

"That's what he said."

"Oh my days! Naomi, that's amazing!"

Hauling herself out of the chair, she beelined for me and wrapped me in a strong hug before I could protest.

It only took her a few seconds to smell Kane on me.

"Is that Mr Davis' cologne? Did something happen?"

An uncomfortable laugh was the best I could manage. "All that happened is that he confirmed the grant. I'm going to shower and get ready for bed; it's been a long day. Why don't you go and share the news with Simon?"

Unable to resist the opportunity to be the bearer of such good news, she left me alone, and I made sure to be tucked in bed and pretending to be asleep by the time she got back to avoid any further questions about exactly how my evening went.

With the grant secured, we could all relax and enjoy the rest of the conference. I assumed that Kane left the next day as planned since I didn't see him at the hotel again, nor did I hear anything from him. Too often, I found myself checking my phone for messages only to find none there, and eventually, I forced myself to stop looking.

When we touched down on the tarmac in London on Friday morning, I switched my phone back on and found a text message waiting for me from a number I didn't recognize.

> Welcome home.

Instantly, my heart beat a little faster. Could that be him? How would he know my arrival time? I told him I'd be back that day, but to receive it immediately on landing seemed a little too coincidental.

After staring slightly too long at the two words, I decided that since I couldn't be sure of the sender and it didn't seem to require any sort of reply anyway, I would ignore the message.

By the time I got out of the airport, it had just passed noon, and with the rest of the day off, I headed directly for my local sexual health clinic, still hauling my little suitcase. I'd made an appointment for a screening after my conversation with Kane even though I knew for certain the tests would be negative. Liam was the only man I ever slept with without using protection and our last time together had been over a year ago.

However, since I insisted on Kane getting tested, I would go through the motions too.

For me, having sex without a condom was a sign of intimacy and trust, but I knew that for him, it had nothing to do with emotions. He only cared about how good it felt, about the physical pleasure of it. Kane Davis had already proven himself to be a very pleasure-focused man, and given his wealth and good looks, I couldn't begin to imagine how many women he had been with.

No matter how good it felt, I wouldn't be risking my health.

On the other hand, getting pregnant didn't concern me. A couple of years earlier, I discovered that I couldn't have children thanks to an infection that got out of control and caused an autoimmune reaction that attacked my ovaries. When Kane asked about needing birth control, I brushed it off, barely feeling the sting of loss anymore after years of coming to terms with it. Besides, it paled in significance compared to the other things I'd lost.

Long story short: no chance existed of an accidental pregnancy and he didn't need to know the details why.

My phone buzzed as I sat on the cool metal chairs in the clinic waiting room, revealing another message from the same number as before.

> Are you home safely?

Since this one asked a question, I replied.

> Kane?

> Yes. Where are you?

So, I hadn't imagined him after all. There were times over the past few days when I really did wonder.

I went into my contacts and added his name to the number before replying.

> London, but not home yet. I'll be there soon.

He didn't respond immediately so I flipped to my news app, catching up on current events while I waited for my name to be called.

A few minutes later, another message came through.

> What are you wearing?

I could nearly picture the smirk on his face as he typed the words, and a smile spread across my lips as I tapped out my reply.

> An unimpressed expression.

> I can picture it. It's like you're right here.

I couldn't help it; I laughed out loud just as the nurse called my name. With my cheeks heating, I put the phone away and followed her into the office.

Once the tests were complete, I took the bus home to my flat. No seats were available, so I needed to keep one hand on the pole and the other holding my suitcase, trying to avoid jostling into my fellow passengers and giving me no opportunity to check my phone again until I got home.

At last, after four full days away, the familiar Victorian facade of my house came into view, one of a long line of row houses built in the late 1800s, all made of brick with bay windows and tiny front gardens. Travelling always took a lot out of me and this trip had been more eventful than most. By the time I carried my case up to my first floor flat and walked into the stuffy front room, I was knackered.

The flat had been my home since a month after Liam died, when I needed a fresh start and found this one-bedroom unit advertised on a local bulletin board. Nobody could call it spacious or special in any way, but for me, it had been a haven. I spent more time on my own within these walls in the last year than I cared to admit to anyone.

After opening the front windows to get some fresh air in, I flipped through the post that had accumulated during the week until my phone buzzed again. I'd almost forgotten about my messages with Kane, but when I pulled it from my pocket, I found *twelve* messages waiting from him.

*What the fuck?*

Didn't he have anything better to do with his time? I thought Pauline said he was some important businessman, so why would be texting me like a bored teenager in the middle of the day?

What did he do, anyway? How did he get so rich? I had no idea, and should probably try to find out a little more about him the next time I saw him.

Scrolling through his messages did nothing to increase my desire to see him, though.

> What are your plans for tonight?

> Are you home yet?

> Why aren't you answering?

The flirty teasing vanished after I stopped responding and each message got progressively more impatient with my silence.

Rolling my eyes at his entitlement, I sent off a quick note.

> I was in the middle of something. At home now.

His reply came quickly, as if he'd been waiting for me.

> I told you I wanted you to be available.

He had to be kidding. He expected me to drop everything to respond to his texts?

> I'm seeing you on Sunday, as you requested.

> That doesn't mean you can ignore me until then.

Could this actually be the same guy who told me he didn't like when women got clingy with him?

> My humblest apologies, my liege.

Hopefully, the heavy sarcasm in my response would translate over text.

> I prefer 'my lord'.

I felt 99% sure that was a joke. It had better be, so I responded with an eye roll emoji.

Ignoring that, he sent another message.

> I'll be out of touch for a while now. My assistant will send you the details for the car service. They have my address. You can arrive between eight and nine on Sunday, no later.

My eyes rolled again at his micromanaging, but I kept my response simple.

> Okay.

My fingers hovered over the keys as I debated wishing him a nice weekend, but ultimately, I decided against it. Honestly, after the hissy fit he just threw, I didn't really care whether he had a nice weekend or not. The best plan of action would be to not think about him again until I absolutely had to.

**~Kane~**

The screen of my phone cast a pale glow over my hands in the shaded back seat of the car.

Okay.

Just one word, curt and final. I exhaled sharply, forcing my grip to loosen around the device before I crushed it in frustration. The leather seat creaked as I shifted, running a hand down my face. I needed to stop acting like a desperate idiot.

What the fuck was wrong with me? Scrolling back through the messages made me cringe. God, I sounded needy. I didn't text her during the rest of her stay in Rome, though she crossed my mind often, and I only intended to send one message to remind her I still expected her at my flat on Sunday.

Instead, I sent a string of increasingly unhinged messages and managed to come across as an entitled and demanding prat. At least she seemed to understand I was joking about the 'my lord' thing but that didn't excuse the rest of it.

The whole exchange left me with one big, unanswered question: why did this woman throw me so far off my game?

She wouldn't even tell me where she'd been that afternoon. No woman had ever been this evasive with me before and it frustrated me. Hell, it infuriated me. Did she think I was someone who'd be satisfied with waiting on the periphery of her life, accepting whatever crumbs of attention she decided to throw my way? The thought made my jaw tighten. I wanted to be at the front of her thoughts the same way I'd been unable to shake her from mine.

After our second night in Rome together, I had Natalie do a bit more digging and she assured me there was no other man in the picture. As far as my investigator could tell, there hadn't been anyone since Naomi's fiancé died. That probably explained her delightful artlessness in the hotel bar. She needed to find her feet again and I could definitely help her with that.

At least I *should* be able to, if I could stop acting like a whiny little bitch.

Telling her I would be out of touch until Sunday was the only way I could think of to stop making an ass of myself any more than I had already.

"Here we are, Mr Davis," my driver announced over the intercom from the front of the car. I'd been so distracted I didn't even notice we'd arrived.

"Thank you. You can pick me up here on Sunday afternoon, I'll send the exact time when I know it."

"Yes, sir. Enjoy your weekend."

I would, as long as I could put Naomi out of my thoughts as easily as I slipped the now-silent phone back into my pocket.

"There he is!" Mum's voice rang out from the front door, warm and familiar, cutting through the restless thoughts still lingering in my mind. The moment her arms wrapped around me, a tension I hadn't even realized I'd been holding melted away. Dad clapped a firm hand on my shoulder, steady and reassuring as always

Then there was the other person I'd gone there to see.

He tilted his head up at me, eyes searching mine, as if gauging how long he could make me wait before I caved first. I huffed a laugh and leaned down, pulling him into a tight hug.

"Hi, Abel. I missed you."

**~Naomi~**

As promised, Kane's assistant, Natalie, sent me an email with all the details about using the car service, leaving me to wonder exactly what Kane told her about me. Did she know where I would be going in the car and why? Did he usually have her arranging his booty calls?

She better be paid damn well for putting up with him.

I managed to put all thoughts of the infuriating man out of my mind until Sunday afternoon, when I reluctantly began to pack a small bag to take with me to Kane's flat. He offered to let me keep a few things there and it made sense if I would be spending the night. Into the small overnight bag, I neatly folded a few work outfits, some pyjamas, a toothbrush and my other toiletries. That seemed like all I'd need but I couldn't get rid of the niggling feeling I'd forgotten something.

At last, it came to me: *underwear.*

*Fuck.*

The red set I wore that night in the bar in Rome was in a league of its own; nothing else I owned even came close. Half-heartedly, I flipped through the contents of my drawer, hoping something had fallen to the bottom that I'd forgotten I had.

No such luck. I would have to go buy some.

Not that I cared about impressing him, I quickly reminded myself, but there was a middle lane between going over the top and showing up in faded knickers with holes in them. With that sweet spot lacking in my current belongings, I gave in and went shopping.

"Do you need any help in there?" the cheery shop assistant's voice called out as I stood in front of a full-length mirror an hour later in the changing room of a lingerie shop I hadn't visited in years. It had been a long time since I could guarantee someone would actually see what

I wore beneath my clothes, and my cheeks flushed red as I imagined Kane's reaction to the set I currently wore.

"I'm okay, thanks," I called back, doing my best to ignore the tremor in my voice that betrayed my nervousness.

By the time I got home, I barely had time to swap into one of my new purchases, throw on a striped t-shirt and jeans, and head out the door. Leaving my hair down, I spritzed a small amount of my favourite perfume on, trying not to think about how the bottle had been one of the last gifts Liam ever bought me.

The car arrived promptly at seven and I ran down to meet it, knowing that even with no traffic, it would take an hour to get to Kane's place. It had just passed 8:14 when we pulled up outside a massive high-rise building that couldn't be more of a contrast to my cozy Victorian terrace back in Ealing. It looked brand-new, and a doorman came out to open the car door for me, taking my bag from my hand before I could say anything.

After thanking the driver, I followed the doorman into the lobby where he led me straight to the lift and pressed the button. The man hadn't asked for my name or where I was going, so I thought I better say something. "I'm here to see Mr Davis."

The man turned to me with a smile. "Of course, Ms Law. He left instructions that you can head right up." As the lift doors opened, he entered with me, placing my bag on the floor and swiping a card over the keypad. While I watched, he pressed the button for the 24th floor: the *top* floor. Once the button lit up, he stepped back out of the lift. "Have a nice evening, ma'am."

The door closed behind him, leaving me slightly flummoxed. What exactly had Kane told him? Did all his fuck-buddies get this kind of special treatment? Everything about this was so far out of my comfort zone that I felt off-balance leaning back against the rear wall of the lift as it sped upwards.

When the door opened on the 24th floor, it opened directly into the living space, just as it had at the hotel in Rome.

*He owned the whole fucking floor.*

Why was I even surprised?

Clutching my bag, I took one hesitant step out of the lift, then another. The space in front of me looked like something out of a designer magazine, all sleek lines and minimalist decoration. Floor-to-ceiling windows offered a picture-perfect view over Canary Wharf and the City, but inside, the room felt cold and impersonal, nothing like my little flat or the one I previously shared with Liam and Michelle.

It belonged to a completely different world than the one where I lived.

"What do you think?"

Kane's voice came from my left, and with a start, I turned to find him standing in a doorway, leaning casually against the frame like some kind of model. Frustratingly, he looked just as good as he had in Italy. His clothes were a little more casual than they'd been in Rome but the obvious quality of them remained the same. Everything about him oozed wealth.

Privilege.

Control.

I couldn't tell if he'd been waiting there for me, but he'd obviously noticed me checking out the room. Denying it would be pointless but I didn't need to feed his ego either so I did my best to keep my reply cool and not too interested.

"It's nice. Who decorated it?"

A smile played at the corner of his lips. "What makes you think I didn't?"

I took another quick look around at the stale, lifeless elegance. "It doesn't feel like you."

"Is that so?" His words were barely more than a murmur as he took a handful of steps towards me. "What do I feel like?"

My lips pursed as I reached for a sarcastic reply, but he took another step closer and the look in his eyes stopped the words in the back of my throat. Naked desire lurked just beneath the surface and my body temperature instantly rose in response.

We both knew why I was there, and it had nothing to do with commenting on his interior design choices.

In a desperate attempt to keep some distance between us before I gave in to the urge to start tearing his clothes off, I held up my bag in front of my body. "Where should I put my things?"

Kane blinked in surprise, almost as if waking from a trance, and offered me a small nod. "I'll show you around."

Before I could protest, he took the bag from my hands and turned back to the doorway he'd just entered through.

"Bedrooms are this way."

He moved quickly down the hall and I followed behind him, peering through the open doorways we passed. Two guest rooms each seemed to have their own ensuites, along with a separate bathroom that sat between them. He didn't stop in any of those rooms, heading for the last door at the end of the hall instead, flipping on the light as he entered.

My feet skidded to a halt as I stepped into what had to be the master bedroom. My entire flat would fit into it twice over, but I managed to stop myself from saying that out loud.

Fitted wardrobes covered two of the walls, interrupted only by a door which I assumed led to another bathroom. Abstract art hung on the walls; originals, I would bet. Dominating the space, a massive bed sat centered along the back wall, facing another row of floor-to-ceiling windows.

The space was immaculately clean but utterly impersonal, no different from the hotel room where we'd slept together in Rome. The room told me nothing about Kane Davis except that he had more money than I could begin to imagine.

Oblivious to my thoughts, Kane tossed my bag onto the bed and slid open one of the wardrobe doors on the left wall. It was completely empty.

"You can use this one."

Had he emptied it for me, or did he just have more space than he knew what to do with? The second option seemed more likely to me.

Giving him a nod of thanks, I moved towards the bed, ready to open my bag and unpack, but Kane came up behind me, placing his hand on top of mine and pressing his body against my back.

"That can wait."

The gruff desire in his voice sent an answering wave of need shooting through me. He obviously had only one thing on his mind, and even though his breath on the back of my neck made my knees weak, I forced myself to stick to my game plan.

Unzipping the top of my bag, I pulled out the paper sitting on top of it and passed it over my shoulder to him without turning around. "These are some of my results. I won't get the rest until next week, so if you want to wait until then to stop using condoms, that's fine."

Taking the paper from my hand, he took a step back, giving me space to turn around to face him. The corners of his lips quirked into an amused smile as he skimmed the paper's contents. "I didn't expect you to do this."

Did that mean he hadn't done the same? "I thought we agreed we would."

"I agreed *I* would. You didn't need to."

With effortless calm, he set the letter on the bedside table, pulled out his phone, and tapped the screen a few times before handing it to me. It showed an email from a private clinic with the negative results of his screenings. Apparently, they worked a little faster than the public clinic I'd visited.

After quickly reviewing everything, I handed the phone back to him. "Thank you for doing that."

"Trust me," he said, voice thick with promise. "It will be worth it."

Setting the phone down on top of the paper, he reached out and pulled me towards him. My resistance evaporated as I melted into him, his mouth finding mine in no time at all. His tongue pushed against my lips, forcing them open as he dove deeper into my mouth, and my whole body reacted, my nipples hardening and my stomach flipping as my thighs clenched against the gathering wetness. *Fuck.* Why did I want him even more now than I had before?

*How* could I want him more? I hadn't even known this level of desire existed.

With his usual forwardness, Kane grabbed the bottom of my shirt and lifted it over my head. Appreciation shone in his eyes as he took in the sight of my breasts in my new silky black bra, making me glad I had gone shopping after all. However, when he reached behind me to undo it, his fingers hesitated for a moment. Pulling the bra free, he held it out in front of him, his blue eyes dancing gleefully.

"Did you buy this just for me?"

"N-no." I stammered out the lie, not sure how he could possibly know that.

With a smirk, Kane twisted the bra around in front of me to reveal the tag I'd neglected to remove.

"Shit," I muttered, making Kane laugh as he tossed the bra over his shoulder.

"I'm flattered. Should we see if it's a matching set?"

Firmly, he pushed me back onto the bed, my back hitting the mattress as his fingers undid my jeans and pulled them down, not wasting a second.

"Just as I thought."

Still smiling, he bent down and tugged the top of my black panties down just enough to drag his lips across my hips. A moan rumbled deep in my throat as his touch sent a bolt of electricity straight through my core.

"You like me down here, huh?"

My eyes gave him all the answer he needed when our gazes connected, and with a devilish grin, he removed the remainder of my clothes, sinking to his knees on the floor and spreading my legs with his hands. Anticipation thrummed through my veins as he kissed the inside of my thigh, his breath teasing my centre, and I gasped as his tongue found my clit.

It had definitely been too long since I felt *that*.

My gasp only served to encourage him, and with a hum of satisfaction, he licked downwards until his tongue plunged inside me. The sounds I made were indecent but by that point, I didn't care. My hips rocked towards him as his tongue explored every inch it could reach, and when he added his fingers while his tongue moved back to my clit, I nearly saw stars.

He was fucking *amazing* at this.

Circling my clit, licking it, sucking it, he drove my need higher and higher while his fingers continued to stroke me from the inside. Every other thought left my head, every reason why I found myself there with him, everything I disliked about him, all of it vanished in the pleasure he provided.

"Don't stop, please." My voice seemed to be coming from someone else, some desperate, feral woman I barely recognized. "I'm so close. Yes... fuck!"

I cried out as I came, my body pulsing under his touch and squeezing him tightly. He reduced the pressure but didn't stop, his tongue still lapping at me as I came back down from my high, the gentle touch sending shivering aftershocks through me.

No one... *no one*... had ever made me feel that way before.

The thought made me feel disloyal and a little out of control, but it didn't change the fact of the matter: I wanted *more*.

**~Kane~**

My tongue continued its lazy swipes until Naomi's legs stopped twitching, and I licked my lips as I pulled back, savouring her taste a little longer. Although I enjoyed giving oral, it had been a while since I went down on a woman. To me, it felt more intimate than sex, and true intimacy hadn't factored into my relationships in quite a while.

I hadn't planned on doing it with Naomi that night either, but her reaction when I kissed her hip intrigued me enough to keep going. That and the fact that she went out and bought new underwear for me. The idea of her in a shop, picking things out with me in mind, pleased me more than it should.

At the moment, though, I had other things on my mind, primarily things involving my cock. With a grunt, I pulled down my trousers, relieving the strain that had built up stronger with every sigh and moan Naomi made. Fresh from her orgasm, she was ready for me, and I couldn't wait to feel her wrapped around my bare skin. I'd been looking forward to it for days.

"Back up," I instructed gruffly and she immediately obeyed, pulling herself further back so her whole body rested on the bed. Kneeling between her legs, I lifted them up, placing an ankle on each of my shoulders. Her slick entrance welcomed the tip of my cock eagerly and I grabbed hold of her arms, pulling her towards me as I pushed into her.

"Fuck," Naomi groaned and I grunted in agreement. Her tightness in this position, her legs squeezing together around my cock, increased the friction to an almost painfully pleasurably level, especially without the rubber between us. She felt every bit as good as I imagined she would.

Naomi's hands gripped my arms, tugging me towards her even as I pulled in the opposite direction. My hips rolled slowly, withdrawing from her almost completely before slowly pushing into her again. Her mouth hung open, eyes closed as she moaned softly, and as much as I appreciated the view, I wanted to see those gorgeous brown eyes of hers more.

"Look at me."

Instantly, her eyes flew open, her gaze locking onto mine as I kept up a slow rhythm. Her fingers clawed at my forearms, urging me to go faster, but I was too close to the edge already just from the feel of her. I had to get her closer before I really let go.

Her hips raised to meet me each time I buried myself in her, our bodies moving together in perfect harmony, and as I dragged myself back out, her body shuddered, a gasp slipping through her lips. *There* was the spot I wanted. I thrust again, more shallowly, aiming for it, and Naomi groaned, still clinging to me, her eyes fixed on mine.

Electricity sizzled between us as I finally increased my pace, my body tensing in both pleasure and the anticipation of even more. Her name whispered its way over my tongue. "Naomi."

"Yes," came her gasp of an answer, and her eyes closed once more as another orgasm took her. Her pussy clenched around my cock and I couldn't hold on any longer, my breath coming in short spurts as I emptied myself deep inside her.

For five days, I'd thought about this moment, remembering how it had been to be with her and imagining how it would feel to be there again.

Somehow, reality exceeded my expectations.

Still breathing heavily, I pulled out and lay down beside her to savour the lingering bliss of release. Naomi rolled onto her side and pressed herself against me, her hand resting lightly on my chest. She fit there perfectly, her breath warm against my skin, blonde hair spilling over my shoulder.

In some ways, holding her that way felt more intimate than anything we'd done up to that point. The rest was just sex, but this... this felt...

Something tightened in my chest, sharp and unwelcome, and I sat up quickly, forcing Naomi onto her back. When I glanced down at her, the confusion and vulnerability in her brown eyes only heightened my discomfort. We were supposed to be having fun, nothing more, so why did this feel different from the other women I brought back to my flat?

Not willing to share the thought, I cleared my throat and reached for a safer topic. "Are you hungry? We can finish that tour of the flat now."

Naomi studied me for a beat but didn't press. Instead, she sat up, letting the moment slip between us. "I've already eaten, but I'd like to take a look around."

As I watched, she stood up and picked up her bag from where it had tumbled off the bed, a casualty of our earlier urgency. From it, she retrieved a simple navy-blue slip nightie and pulled it over her head, covering herself with practiced ease before disappearing into the bathroom.

I exhaled, running a hand through my hair before grabbing a pair of loose cotton trousers from the wardrobe. By the time she emerged, fresh-faced and composed, I had my mask of indifference firmly back in place.

The flat was silent except for the whisper of our bare feet against the hardwood as I led her down the hall. Past the living room, I pointed out the kitchen, dining room, and my home office. She took it all in, her expression more observant than impressed, as though she were gathering details about me rather than the space itself.

Back in the kitchen, I pulled out a few ingredients for a sandwich while Naomi wandered to the floor-to-ceiling windows, gazing out over the City.

"Don't you feel exposed in here with all these windows?"

"They're tinted at night," I explained, setting a plate on the counter. "And we're high enough that no one could see in without some really high-powered binoculars anyway. I like the openness. The whole city is my backyard."

She hummed in understanding, if not necessarily agreement. "How long have you lived here?"

"A couple of years. Are you sure you don't want anything to eat? I've got some leftover chocolate cake."

Her head whipped around, eyes bright with excitement. "You didn't mention cake."

I laughed before I could check the urge. "Help yourself."

I retrieved the cake my mum had insisted I take home, still wrapped in tinfoil. I never ate the leftovers she sent, knowing they'd only end up in the bin after my housekeeper cleared them out. But refusing them outright would hurt her feelings, so I took them anyway.

Naomi cut herself a generous slice while I grabbed a plate and cutlery. The second she placed the first bite in her mouth, she let out a quiet moan of pleasure.

My body reacted instantly.

"I thought you only made those kinds of noises for me."

A tinge of pink tinted her cheeks but she ignored the comment, taking another bite. "This is amazing. Where did you get it?"

"Someone I know made it."

Her lips pressed into a pout. "Damn. I was hoping it came from a shop so I could get my own."

A response leapt to the tip of my tongue - *Mum would make another if you asked* - but I managed to swallow it back down. Where the hell did that thought come from? Mum would go mad if I ever brought a woman home, no matter how I framed it. She would never meet Naomi. She would never even know about her.

"How was your weekend?" I asked, shifting gears as I sat down on a stool and took a bite of my sandwich. It tasted good, but nowhere near as good as she had.

Naomi shrugged, her attention still mostly focused on the cake. "Fine. Nothing too exciting. A few friends met me at the pub last night but we behaved ourselves. What about you?"

I regretted the question immediately since I couldn't share much about my weekend without getting more personal than I wanted. "Saw some family. Nothing too exciting."

Naomi perked up. "Does your family live in London?"

Desperate to change the subject, I gave a vague answer. "Not too far away." Then, before she could ask anything else, I countered, "You never told me where your office is. Where do you need to go in the morning?"

"It's in Acton. I can walk there from home."

"So, this is really out of the way for you."

She waved off the concern. "I'll take the tube in the morning. It's probably faster than driving."

It probably was, and I pushed down the twinge of guilt at the thought of her crammed into a crowded train during rush hour because of me.

"Where do *you* work?" she asked.

Rather than answer outright, I motioned for her to follow me. She shoveled the last piece of cake into her mouth before trailing after me, making me smile again.

At the far end of the dining room, I pressed a button on the wall, and the window in front of us slid open.

"Fuck," Naomi breathed, stepping onto the wrap-around balcony that stretched across two sides of the flat. The city sprawled beneath us, a sea of golden lights. "This is amazing."

For the first time since arriving, she looked genuinely impressed. Most women were in awe the moment they walked through the door, but Naomi had been harder to win over.

At the balcony's corner, I pointed to my office building, a few blocks away. The red neon sign at the top that read *Kane* was just visible from this height. "I work there."

"That's convenient." Her tone teased, so I teased her back.

"You said you can walk to work too."

"True, but my office doesn't have my name on it." She smiled at me, hair catching in the breeze. "What does your company do?"

She really didn't know. That was rare. Most women I brought home knew exactly who I was and how much money I had.

I hesitated a beat too long, and Naomi's expression flickered into embarrassment. "I'm sure Google could tell me. I should have looked it up."

"No, it's fine." Actually, I liked that she hadn't. Her impression of me was based on our interactions, not my reputation, and that made a refreshing change. "We're involved in artificial intelligence. AI."

Her eyes sought mine, her lips twisting in a sheepish smile. "I don't really know what that means. Computer stuff?"

"Mostly," I agreed with a chuckle. "Using computers to simplify or automate processes. Helping machines learn to do things better."

"Can you give me an example?"

I searched for an easy entry point among the various projects I'd worked on. "Well, the first company I sold created 3D maps."

"Company you sold?" she repeated. "What does that mean?"

If I'd had any doubt that she genuinely had no idea about my work, this line of questioning would have erased it. "I created the company and the product, then sold it to a bigger tech firm."

She blinked. "That's how you make money?"

"More or less."

"What are you working on now?"

Her gaze drifted to the cityscape before us but I knew she continued to listen carefully to my response.

"A lot of complicated, probably boring things, but there's one side project that I'm pretty excited about."

She must have heard something in my voice because she turned to face me again, her eyes bright with curiosity. "What is it?"

"It has to do with turning brainwaves into sound. Essentially, the computer could detect thoughts and turn them into text."

Naomi's breath hitched. "That's *possible*?"

"We'll see. It's still really early days, but we've seen some positive signs."

Excitement bubbled inside those expressive brown eyes. "So, if someone isn't able to speak, the computer could read their thoughts and speak for them?"

"Yes. At least, I hope so."

If it worked, the program would have multiple applications, but somehow, she picked up on the precise reason I decided to pursue it. That had to be a coincidence; if she didn't know about my work, she certainly wouldn't know anything about my personal life. I kept those details very closely guarded.

To my surprise, tears appeared to gather in the corners of her eyes. "That would be incredible. It would mean so much to those people and their loved ones."

"It would." My head cocked to the side as I took her in, trying to understand the strength of her reaction to something most people would see as interesting but not tear-worthy. "Do you know someone who has trouble speaking?"

"A lot of them. The patients that my charity supports are almost all non-verbal."

*Of course.* Understanding hit me and I felt like an idiot for not putting it together sooner. If I'd paid more attention during my meeting with her team in Rome, they'd probably mentioned communication difficulties then, but I'd been too focused on Naomi herself.

It seemed we had something in common.

"I'll let you know when we make any progress," I offered, and her smile widened, warming something in my chest that usually stayed cold. "Come on, let's go back inside. I haven't finished my snack yet.

Almost reluctantly, Naomi followed me back in and sat down again at the island, her empty plate in front of her.

"Do you want more cake?" Based on how she devoured the last piece, she might as well enjoy it. At least someone would.

However, she shook her head with a laugh. "I would love some but I better not. I could easily eat the whole thing. It's that good."

Again, the thought crossed my mind that Mum would be thrilled with the compliment before remembering I couldn't tell her about it. Not without telling her who it came from, and that was out of the question. My private life stayed private for a very good reason and it would continue to stay that way, no matter what.

# Chapter Six

~**Naomi**~

When Kane finished eating, we returned to his room where he headed into the bathroom while I began to unpack my bag. The few items I brought didn't take up much space in the large, empty wardrobe he'd assigned to me. Did Kane ever get lonely in this cavernous space, night after night on his own? At first impression, he didn't seem to be missing anything in his life, but the longer I stood there, the more the luxury and excess hinted at overcompensation.

Was that part of the reason he wanted me to spend the night? Did it explain why he offered me this deal in the first place? Maybe it went deeper than the superficial, fuckboy explanation he'd given me.

Or maybe he liked being alone and was exactly as much of a selfish asshole as he appeared. Who was I to say?

The sound of the shower turning on in the bathroom drew me out of my thoughts and back to the present moment. Kane didn't mention taking a shower, but it shouldn't surprise me that he didn't share his plans. I doubted I took up much space in his mind whenever I wasn't directly in front of him.

With my unpacking finished except for the items to go in the bathroom, I took a seat on the bed, trying to decide what to do with myself until he came back. There must have been a TV somewhere in the enormous room, or I could scroll on my phone, no different from what I'd do at home.

At home, though, I didn't have a naked man showering a few feet away from me, and as my mind drifted to thoughts of water running down the hard lines of his body, that rediscovered ache deep inside me started up again.

What were our boundaries? He said I needed to be available whenever he wanted me, but what about when *I* wanted *him?*

No time like the present to find out.

Creeping quietly to the bathroom door, I tried the handle, and finding it unlocked, I took a steadying breath and let myself in.

The bathroom was bigger than any room in my flat, and when I'd been in there earlier, I noted the jacuzzi-style hot tub in one corner and the large walk-in shower opposite it. As I expected, Kane stood silhouetted behind the shower's tinted glass doors, facing away from me. With water from the rainfall shower head cascading around him and splatting onto the floor in a steady rhythm, he hadn't heard me come in.

Before I could lose my nerve and change my mind, I lifted my night-gown over my head, tossed it on the floor next to his discarded trousers, and strode over to the shower door. It opened silently, giving me a spectacular view of his backside as he washed his hair. Muscles danced across the broad plane of his back with each scrubbing motion, and with his eyes closed to keep the shampoo out, he still didn't see me.

He jumped as I wrapped my arms around his waist from behind.

"Fuck, Naomi." My name came out in a throaty gulp as he swallowed his surprise. It sounded sexy as hell.

I lay my cheek against his back, my hands roaming over his slippery chest and stomach. "You didn't ask if I needed a shower too."

"Are you dirty?" he teased, and the throbbing inside me deepened. By the time he rinsed his hair and turned to face me, his striking blue eyes heavy with lust, his cock was already half-rigid.

"You tell me."

Emboldened by his obvious desire, I slid my hand around the back of his neck to pull his mouth down to mine. My other hand reached down to stroke his cock, the water helping to smooth my path as I stroked him firmly. He pulsed beneath my touch, blood rushing to the spot as quickly as it raced through my body.

Kane groaned as he spun us both and pushed me back against the wall, the tiles cool in contrast to the warm water still falling. His hips ground against mine as our tongues tangled, and with a grunt, he grabbed the back of my thighs and hauled me up so I was at the right height for him. Wrapping my legs around him, I reached between us to guide his cock to my aching entrance, my hips rolling forward in invitation. He didn't hesitate, pushing into me as he bent down to kiss my neck, and a desperate whimper, which might have come from me, filled the space between us.

He rocked me hard against the wall, pulling out and thrusting back in again with growing intensity. His need seemed just as strong as mine, and mine was off the charts.

"I think you're *very* dirty," he panted as he drove into me again and again.

"For you, I am," I agreed, letting my guard down in the heat of the moment. "You make me feel... oh, God, Kane!"

I didn't get a chance to finish the thought before I hit my peak, my body tensing in pleasure before I fell apart. Only the strength of his grip kept me upright as he continued to fuck me, thrusting a few more times before he followed me over the top.

Gradually, my self-awareness returned along with the shape of the room, the tiles against my back and the sound of us both breathing heavily over the backdrop of the shower's spray.

Kane slid out of me as he lowered me back to the ground, but before he let me go completely, he lowered his head and kissed me one more time.

Gently.

Deeply.

Not quite like any other kiss we'd shared to that point.

Before I could wonder exactly what it meant, he tugged me beneath the water with him and ran his hands over my head. "Did you bring shampoo?"

"It's still in the other room."

I shifted towards the door, intending to go and grab it, but he moved quicker. "I'll get it. Stay in the warmth."

A minute later, he returned with my products, bringing a wave of cooler air with him. Although I held out my hand for the shampoo, he ignored me, pouring a small amount into his own hand instead and beginning to massage it slowly into my hair.

My eyes closed in bliss. "That feels so good."

Not having someone to wash my hair anymore was one of those little things I hadn't realized I would miss so much when I lost Liam. Doing it myself wasn't the same, and the firm, steady pressure of Kane's fingers felt amazing.

After rinsing the shampoo out, he moved onto the body wash without me asking. With his bare hands, he rubbed my whole body down, his fingers finding every inch of skin. Despite the jolt of pleasure I got when his hands slid over my nipples or between my legs, it didn't feel overly sexual. Erotic, certainly, but not as if he were doing it purely as a lead-in to more sex.

Indeed, when he finished and I offered to return the favour, he switched the water off instead.

"It's getting late. We should get some sleep."

Stepping from the shower, he grabbed an extra towel from the warming rack and handed it to me before towelling himself dry. I snuck glimpses of his naked body as he worked, still trying to work out how I felt about what just happened.

The way he washed me was tender and sensual, careful and deliberate. If this was just about sex, why did it feel like something more?

Unless I was overthinking it? Did I *want* there to be more?

That would be dangerous, especially with a man like Kane. I had to remember to keep our agreement in perspective at all times.

Kane finished before I did, leaving me alone to complete my bedtime routine, but the absence of his presence lingered, the warmth of his hands still ghosting over my skin.

By the time I stepped back into the bedroom, he stood near the window, phone in hand, bathed in the soft glow of the city lights. His broad shoulders, still bare and a little damp from the shower, looked tense despite the ease with which he always carried himself.

I glanced at the bed, still undisturbed on both sides. "Which side do you sleep on?"

A smile tugged at his lips but he didn't look up. "I have no preference. Take your pick."

Who didn't have a preferred side? Someone who never shared their bed, maybe. Or someone who didn't care who occupied it.

Shrugging, I climbed onto the left side, sinking into the plush mattress with a quiet sigh. The sheets were cool against my skin, and as I set my alarm, I wondered how long it had been since I felt this comfortable. *This* kind of luxury, I could definitely get used to.

A minute later, Kane switched his phone off and slid in beside me. There was enough space between us for another person, maybe two, but after a moment, I felt the mattress shift. He moved closer, the heat of his body pressing against mine, his arm wrapping loosely around my waist.

For a beat, I froze. The last time I fell asleep like this, it was with Liam. I never imagined I'd share my bed with someone else, never thought I'd let another man hold me this way.

But I had to move on, and whatever else I thought about him, Kane was making sure I did.

"Goodnight, Naomi," he whispered near my ear.

"Goodnight."

I let out a slow breath, placed my hand lightly over his, and let myself drift off to sleep.

**~Kane~**

A pleasant tingling sensation in my groin woke me up. It had been a while since I got turned on by a dream, but my mind must have come up with something good. Pity I couldn't remember it.

A second later, something warm pressed against my cock and my eyes flew open. I definitely didn't dream *that.*

Propping myself up on my elbows, I took in the rumpled sheets streaked in early morning sunlight and the large shape moving beneath them on Naomi's side of the bed.

*Naomi's side.* Strange that I already thought of it that way, but rather than dwell on that, I flipped the covers off of us both, revealing a mess of blonde hair between my legs.

Naomi giggled at being discovered, the sound light and airy in my usually quiet bedroom. "Good morning."

Without waiting for a response, she continued with her task. Without waking me, she'd somehow got my cock out of my thin cotton trousers and was swirling her tongue up and down my shaft, flicking the tip of it back and forth as my cock twitched to life beneath her. Now fully awake and enjoying the visual almost as much as the feel of her tongue on me, I propped an arm behind my head and relaxed as I took in the show.

My cock rapidly hardened under her attention, and once its stiffness satisfied her, she grabbed hold of the base with one hand, brought it to her lips and sucked the tip into her mouth.

*Fuck.* Having her spend the night had definitely been the right call.

As I watched, she alternated between licking long strokes down my shaft and sucking lightly on my head, one hand still holding me tight at the base and the other drifting down to tease my balls. Just when I started to get used to her rhythm, she took me deeper into her mouth, drawing out my sharp inhale as I hit the back of her throat.

Her mouth looked fucking amazing wrapped around my cock, and at this rate, I wouldn't be lasting too much longer.

Rising onto her knees, Naomi began to work my cock in earnest, the hand circling my shaft stroking up and down while her head bobbed in the same rhythm. Each time, she took me in a little deeper, or at least it felt that way as the tightness of her throat made me groan.

"That feels too good. I'm going to come," I warned her as my balls began to tighten, just in case she didn't want me to let go in her mouth.

Naomi didn't stop, though. She kept pumping me until I shot straight down her throat, my head pressing back into the pillow as pleasure surged through me.

Almost immediately, her grip loosened but she kept me in her mouth, gently milking every last drop from me and swallowing it all.

I could fucking get used to waking up like that.

While I regained my composure, her face appeared above me. "Good morning," she repeated, her lips quirking in a wicked grin before she hopped out of bed.

I huffed out a laugh, shaking my head. Waking up to a woman between my legs wasn't exactly new, but seeing Naomi so playful and pleased with herself, made it feel different. "What time is it?"

Despite the light through the window suggesting we needed to get up, I would have much rather pulled her back into bed with me.

"Just after seven. I need to leave soon."

Still dressed in her nightie, she stepped over to the wardrobe and opened it, revealing just a few items inside. Something about the sight unsettled me. It looked... temporary. Like she didn't want to get too settled. Which was good, right? That was the whole point.

So why did it feel like a problem?

I checked my phone for my schedule, groaning internally when I saw my first meeting was at eight. At least it only took me five minutes to get to my office.

"I need to get ready too," I said, swinging my legs over the side of the bed. "If you need a bathroom, you can use one of the others. There's food in the kitchen, so help yourself. Your keycard is on the table by the lift."

Naomi froze mid-motion, her hand pausing over a hanger in the wardrobe. "My keycard?"

I barely glanced up as I continued to scroll through my schedule. "For the building, so Tom doesn't have to let you in every time."

"Oh." Her tone was neutral, but something flickered across her face. Uncertainty, maybe?

"I trust you're not going to break in when I'm not here and steal from me," I added drily. "And you can't just knock on my door when you get here. It's more convenient for you to have a card."

As I expected, her eyes rolled at my explanation and she stopped looking for a deeper reason behind the gesture. "Alright. Do you want me to come back tonight?"

I stood, stretching out the stiffness in my muscles, and noted the way her eyes slid down my body, as if she couldn't help it. It made me wish I *could* see her again that night, but unfortunately, I had a business event I couldn't get out of.

"No, not tonight," I said, keeping my voice even. "I'll text you when I know my plans for the week."

She nodded, her expression as unreadable as my tone. "Okay. Well, have a good day, I guess."

*I guess.* She still had to put up a bit of a fight somewhere, and I smirked at her as I walked past her. "You too."

With that, I stepped into the bathroom, closing the door behind me. Another quick shower would clean me up after the unexpected orgasm that started my day, but as I got ready, my mind lingered elsewhere.

The keycard really *wasn't* a big deal. It was practical.

Just because I'd never given any other woman one before didn't mean anything.

By the time I emerged from my room, Naomi had already gone. The clock read 7:55 when I walked into the office, and the nervous tapping of Natalie's pencil against her desk made it clear she had been worried I would be late.

"Get the head of the charity Naomi Law works for on the phone for me, as soon as he or she is in the office," I instructed on my way past her desk and into my office.

"Of course," she agreed, hurrying after me with my coffee and the notes for that morning's meeting. "I'll connect you as soon as possible after your meeting."

I leaned back in my chair, my fingers drumming against the desk as I waited for my first appointment of the day. I'd make one call to Naomi's work, and then I could put her out of my mind for the rest of the day.

**~Naomi~**

No one would ever call the tube at 7:30 on a Monday morning a good time. As I squeezed onto the crowded train at Canary Wharf, it didn't take long to remember why I made the decision to move closer to my office. The air inside the train was thick and unrelenting as a bead of sweat trickled down my spine, my blouse already sticking to my skin. When the train jerked to a sudden halt in the tunnel before my station, the collective groan of the passengers mirrored my own frustration.

"Sorry I'm late," I apologized when I finally made it to my desk. With only five full-time employees, everyone knew everyone else's business in our tiny office. Our CEO, Jane, had her own office but the rest of us worked at one big table, our computers all facing each other.

"Did you sleep through your alarm?" Simon asked, his head tilting in sympathy as he gave me a smile. He'd done that more than once.

I kept my reply honest and brief. "No, I was delayed on the tube."

"Since when do you take the tube in?" Michael wondered. He lived just a few blocks away from me and we often walked most of the way home together.

I really didn't want to go into detail, but I had to offer some further explanation for my uncharacteristic tardiness. "I stayed at a friend's place in the east end last night."

Jane appeared at her office door, cutting off any further discussion. "Ah, Naomi, there you are. Can I borrow you for a second?"

*Damn it.* I'd hoped she might be on a call and not notice me coming in late, but no such luck. I set down my bag in front of my computer and headed to her door. "Yes?"

She had already moved back towards her desk, taking a seat behind it. "Come in and shut the door."

With some trepidation, I did as she asked. Normally, we kept things very informal in the office. Jane's door stayed open unless she was on a call or working on something confidential, so the privacy seemed like a bad sign.

However, she smiled as I took a seat across from her, lessening my worry a little.

"I had a conversation this morning with Mr Davis, the donor from the Abel Foundation," she began and it was a good thing I had already sat down or my knees might have buckled.

My palms suddenly clammy, I forced my expression to remain neutral as my pulse thrummed in my ears. Kane had no reason to speak to my boss, so why had he?

"Oh?" I managed to squeak out.

She beamed at me, completely unaware of my inner panic. "He told me how much you impressed him during your conversation in Rome and said he's considering making an additional donation."

Discomfort twisted my stomach. Why would he tell Jane that? I hadn't planned to mention it until things were confirmed. Now, if for any reason I didn't complete our arrangement, I would have to explain why the donation fell through.

Was this another way to control me, or did he just want to make things awkward for me at work? Either way, it felt like a dick move after what I thought was a pretty enjoyable night together.

"He seemed very interested," I mumbled since she seemed to be expecting a reply.

Jane nodded, still oblivious to my unease. "He said he might need to speak with you again from time to time to keep up to date on what we're doing. So, I just wanted to let you know that whatever time you need to do that, you have my blessing. This takes top priority. The rest of the team can pitch in to take over anything else you need help with."

That made things a little clearer, and my blood began to boil as I realized what it meant. Basically, he called my boss and lied to her so I could be more 'available' to him, free to run to his side whenever he deigned to call on me.

And to think I had actually been a little disappointed that morning when he said he didn't need me tonight.

Who the fuck did he think he was?

I did my best to thank Jane sincerely for her support but I couldn't pretend to match her level of enthusiasm. As I made my way back to my desk, my anger grew stronger with every step. Apparently, I misread every sign he gave me the night before. There I was, thinking the connection between us might be evolving, that he might actually be a little fond of me and we might actually become friends, and all the while, he still viewed me as nothing more than a sex doll to be brought out and played with when it suited him.

How could I be such an idiot?

I stabbed at my keyboard, the keys clacking louder than necessary, each stroke an outlet for the anger bubbling under my skin, but Kane refused to leave my thoughts. Finally, I grabbed my phone, tapped out an angry text and hit send. Releasing a little of my fury reduced the pressure enough that I could concentrate, and I shoved my phone back into my bag and exhaled, slow and controlled, determined not to look at my phone again all day.

Let him stew over my message. He thought he could pull my strings, but I wouldn't be manipulated quite so easily.

**~Kane~**

With ten minutes between meetings later that morning, I pulled out my phone. The sight of Naomi's name in my inbox nearly made me smile, but that impulse quickly faded when I opened the message.

> What. The. FUCK.

My forehead creased as I stared at the three words. What the hell was that supposed to mean? A message like that usually followed a disaster. Had something happened? Was she hurt? Did she send it to me by mistake?

I typed out a quick response before overthinking it.

> What's wrong?

Leaving the phone on my desk in case she replied straight away, I turned my attention to the emails on my computer, but when Natalie knocked on my door with the clients for my next meeting, I had to put the phone away, my response still unread.

An hour later, after the clients left, I checked the phone again but it still only showed as delivered, not read.

I tried again.

> Naomi? What's going on?

A lunch meeting was followed by a pitch of one of our new systems to a company we were trying to interest in buying it, so I didn't get a chance to check my phone again until nearly three o'clock. By then, the message was showing read, but she hadn't replied.

My jaw tightened. If she had time to open it, she had time to reply. I had no interest in playing games or whatever passive-aggressive bullshit this might be. Didn't I make it clear last week that I expected her to respond to me promptly? Things went so well between us the night before, I thought we'd moved past her pretending she didn't want me.

Jamming my finger down on the call button, I listened to the phone ring out before going to voicemail.

"Answer my text," I instructed in a terse message before putting my phone away again and heading into my last round of meetings for the day.

After work, I stopped at home to change for the party that evening. I waited until I was ready to check my phone, figuring Naomi would have to be finished work by then, but still, no new message had appeared. What the fuck was she playing at?

I sent one more message.

> I have an engagement tonight. If you haven't responded by the time I get back, I'll expect a damn good explanation.

Although anger had taken over as my dominant emotion regarding all of this nonsense, I was still confused as well. What changed since the wonderful wake-up call she gave that morning? She initiated that blow job *and* she took the lead in the shower the night before, so what on earth was she pissed off at me about?

I excused myself from the party just after ten, and it didn't really surprise me to see no reply waiting on my phone.

Enough of this bullshit.

She wanted to ignore me? Fine. But I was getting my answers, one way or another.

My driver tipped his head in greeting as he held the door open for me. "Home, sir?"

I slid into the seat, gripping my phone tightly.

"No. There's someone I need to see first."

**~Naomi~**

The longer the day went on, the more upset I got, and Kane's texts did nothing to improve my mood. I didn't appreciate him playing dumb about what had upset me, and I *really* didn't appreciate his snippy tone when I didn't respond. Maybe leaving him on read was a tiny bit childish, but he needed to get it through his head that, despite our arrangement, he did *not* own me.

Making him wait until the next day before confronting him over his conversation with Jane wouldn't do him any harm. He must be so used to getting his way all the time that letting him sweat it out a bit might actually be good for him.

Set in my plan, I went to bed just after ten, but an hour later, loud, insistent pounding on my front door jolted me awake. Disoriented and groggy, I stumbled toward the door, rubbing my eyes. My first thought was that one of my neighbors had gotten too drunk and confused their flat for mine. It had happened before.

I barely cracked the door open before Kane shoved his way inside.

His expensive cologne hit me first, even in the dark. The next thing I knew, his solid frame moved past me, only to immediately slam into the back of the chair I kept near the entrance.

"For fuck's sake," he muttered, barely more than a silhouette in the darkness. "Where's the light?"

Heart still racing from the rude awakening, I shut the door and flicked on the switch. Harsh yellow light filled the tiny space, and I finally got a proper look at him. His suit jacket was undone, his tie missing, and his crisp white shirt unbuttoned at the collar. He looked expensive and irritated as hell.

My voice came out hoarse from sleep. "What are you doing here?"

A better question might have been, 'How do you know where I live?', but my brain hadn't caught up yet.

Kane spun to face me, his scowl darkening his already sharp features. "What is your problem?"

Something about the way his brows pulled together made me think he truly didn't get it, but the sharpness in his tone immediately brought out my fight-or-flight response, and in this case, I chose 'fight'.

"You're the one with a problem. How dare you speak to my boss behind my back?"

His confusion morphed into something closer to disbelief. "*That's* what you're mad about? That's why you've been ignoring me all day?"

My arms crossed over my chest, braced against the pounding of my heart. "Yes, Kane. Believe it or not, I have an issue with you *lying* to my boss and interfering in my job. It's not something that can be pushed aside to make things more convenient for you."

"I was trying to make things more convenient for *you*," he countered, his tone still sharp. "In case the commute became an issue, I didn't want you to have to stress about it. Your boss didn't seem to have any problem with it."

"Because you told her I was working on getting us a donation."

"Aren't you?"

The smirk he gave me landed like a lead balloon and my glare brought his scowl back out.

"You need to grow up, Naomi. If you have a problem with something I've done, tell me so instead of throwing a tantrum or giving me the silent treatment."

"*I'm* throwing a tantrum? You're the one who gets in a huff if I don't respond to you within seconds, and you're the one storming into my flat in the middle of the night."

As if to illustrate my point, my upstairs neighbour banged on the floor of their flat, letting me know the noise had definitely filtered up through the ceiling.

"Sorry," I called before lowering my voice and addressing Kane again. "Why are you here anyway? I thought you were busy tonight."

"I was." He turned down his volume too but the tension remained. "I came here because you weren't responding to my texts or calls. You didn't leave me much choice."

That might have been true, I had to admit, as my eyes flicked over him again. The way he looked, he'd clearly gone straight from whatever event he was at without stopping at home first.

He'd travelled across the city to come here. To sort things out.

Even if I didn't like his methods, he made an effort.

And maybe he had a point. I had the right to be angry, but the silent treatment wasn't solving anything. Something about Kane brought out my most defensive instincts, but if we were going to make it through the next three months without killing each other, I needed to learn how to handle this better.

We would *both* have to try a little harder to see each other's perspective.

With a deep breath, I softened my tone and offered an olive branch. "I'm sorry. I could have reacted better but I wish you had talked to me before going to Jane. I'm used to handling my own problems."

The apology helped to diffuse Kane's anger and he exhaled too, making a conscious effort to release the tension in his shoulders. "I didn't realize it would upset you so much. Honestly, I only wanted to help."

I supposed I could see how he might have thought speaking to Jane would be helpful. He'd gone about it the completely wrong way, but maybe, in his own alpha-male, take-charge style, he'd actually *meant* to do something good.

Uncrossing my arms, I offered him a small smile. "I guess we still have a lot to learn about each other."

"I guess so."

The energy between us shifted, no longer crackling with anger, and Kane took a step back, eyes scanning my flat for the first time.

It didn't take long. The whole thing was visible from where we stood. To our right, the lounge area opened onto a bay window. Straight ahead, the small, open-plan kitchen and dining space blended into the living space. To the left, two doors led to the bathroom and my bedroom.

It couldn't have been more different from his world.

But if he had any thoughts about it, he didn't share them. Instead, he looked back at me and asked, "Is there room in your bed for two?"

I blinked. "What?"

His expression didn't change. "Your bed," he repeated, slow and deliberate, as if speaking to a child. "I'm tired. I don't feel like going all the way home."

*Oh.* He actually wanted to sleep. In *my* flat.

Not sex. Just sleep.

"It's not huge but it is a double," I stammered.

"I'm sure we can make it work."

His smirk returned in full force as he turned and strode towards my bedroom, leaving me standing there, completely off-balance and staring after him, still trying to process the last five minutes.

Kane Davis never did exactly what I expected him to.

And, maybe, just *maybe*, I didn't entirely hate it.

# Chapter Seven

**~Kane~**

I woke to find Naomi snuggled up against me, her body soft and warm as she slept, and strangely, I didn't mind her closeness.

Not that either of us had much choice in the matter. She hadn't been kidding about the size of her bed, and while I could have suggested she get a bigger one, the room wouldn't accommodate anything larger. Her flat could hardly be more of a contrast to mine, but in some ways, it reminded me of the house I grew up in: warm and comfortable despite being small and cluttered.

Disentangling myself as gently as I could, I slipped out of bed and used the tiny bathroom before venturing into the living space. Morning sunlight filtered in through the bay window, casting a golden glow over the room. I wandered toward it, taking in the view of her Victorian-terraced street, a world away from the sleek glass towers of Canary Wharf. Leafy trees lined the pavement, their branches swaying slightly in the morning breeze. Cars parked on either side of the street left a narrow one-way lane for traffic and most of the small front gardens had been paved over with bricks or stone.

As an older woman strolled past with a small dog on a lead, she glanced up and did a double take, startling us both. *Right.* The window worked both ways, and given that I was standing there in nothing but boxer-briefs, I probably should have thought that through.

Turning my back to the outside world, I let my gaze drift around Naomi's flat, curious about the life she led when she wasn't with me. Luckily for me, the room offered up its secrets in plain sight. Books stacked on shelves flanking the fireplace ranged from classics to Booker Prize winners to romances with half-naked men on the covers. A small basket on the hearth held some kind of sewing or needlework, the delicate threads tangled in a way that suggested frequent use.

But it was the framed photo on the mantle that caught my attention, and I stepped closer to examine it more carefully.

Trees framed the shot, flowers blooming in the background. In the centre, a young girl sat in a wheelchair, beaming at the camera. Beside her, Naomi smiled, looking fresh and beautiful as the wind played with her hair. On the girl's other side, a man with shoulder-length hair and a slightly unkempt beard stood. He looked away from the camera, his attention focused on the two people beside him, his smile lit with quiet affection.

Taking another step, I picked up the frame to look even closer. On Naomi's hand, the one resting on the girl's shoulder, the same ring she still wore sparkled in the light. Did that make the man in the photo her fiancé? He didn't really seem like her type to me, but what I was basing that on, I couldn't really say. Maybe just because he didn't look anything like me?

Taking another step forward, I picked up the frame and the details came into sharper focus, including Naomi's hand resting on the girl's shoulder, the same ring she still wore sparkling in the light. That must make the man in the photo her fiancé.

He didn't look like her type, though why I thought that, I couldn't fully explain.

Maybe because he didn't look anything like me?

"Are you hungry?"

Naomi's voice startled me so much, I nearly dropped the photo. I'd been so lost in the image that I hadn't heard her approach. When I turned, she stood just outside the bedroom doorway, watching me. Her neutral expression gave me no hints about her mood that morning or which version of her I'd be dealing with: the one who flirted and teased, or the one who took offense at everything I said.

Playing it safe, I matched her casual tone. "I'll eat at the office, but coffee would be nice."

With a nod, she walked the few steps to the kitchen and put the kettle on. From the cupboard, she pulled out two mismatched mugs, a tea bag and a jar of instant coffee, her movements efficient and controlled.

She didn't ask what I'd been doing, but since I still held the photo in my hands, pretending that I hadn't been looking at it seemed pretty pointless.

"Who are they?" I asked, setting the frame back on the mantle.

A nearly imperceptible shift in her shoulders suggested I'd hit something raw, but when she spoke, her voice was measured. "That's Liam and his daughter, Michelle."

I recognized the name of her dead fiancé from the sleuthing Natalie had done on my behalf but my assistant hadn't mentioned a daughter. Not wanting to admit that I'd already looked into her background, I feigned ignorance. "Are they family?"

The kettle whistled and Naomi switched it off, filling both mugs. She stirred them slowly, her gaze never straying in my direction.

"Liam and I were engaged."

Rather than waiting for her to bring the mug to me, I walked over and picked it up from the counter myself. I sipped the hot, strong liquid while Naomi blew on her tea.

When she didn't elaborate, I asked a simple follow-up: "What happened?"

At last, her eyes met mine, and my chest tightened at the unshed tears pooling in them. Normally, an emotional display like that would have me running for the door, but with Naomi, I found myself reaching for her instead. Gently, I took her arm and steered her toward the sofa.

"Come sit down."

She let me guide her into the lounge, settling beside me on the sofa. Our legs brushed, the skin-on-skin contact warm, and Naomi stared down into her tea, turning the mug slowly between her hands. "I don't talk about this very often."

We sat together on the sofa, close enough that our legs touched, and Naomi took a sip of her drink before saying anything. Her eyes followed her mug as she lowered it into her lap. "I'm sorry, I didn't expect to get so emotional. I guess it's because I don't talk about this very often."

I understood that better than she realized. "You don't have to tell me if you don't want to."

"I know." A small, tired smile stretched her lips. "But if we're going to be spending time together, it's bound to come up."

Silence stretched between us, strangely comfortable in its weight. Her blonde hair, still unbrushed that morning, flew in chaotic strands around her face, and I had to resist the impulse to smooth it down. To run my fingers through it and wrap my arm around her shoulders.

Where the hell did those instincts come from?

Finally, she spoke, tracing the rim of her mug with a fingertip, as if grounding herself. "We were together for three years. Michelle was in my class at the special school where I worked. That's a school for kids with additional needs."

That she thought she needed to explain that to me would have made me smile, if it weren't for the sadness in her tone.

"She was the sweetest, most wonderful little girl. I fell in love with her first, and then I met her dad. Before long, I fell in love with him too."

Her fingers skimmed over her engagement ring as she said the word 'love', but I couldn't tell if she even noticed she did it.

"His wife left them after Michelle was born. The reality of raising a child with disabilities was too much for her, so Liam raised her alone. He was completely devoted to her and she adored him."

Glancing back towards the photo, the meaning of Liam's gaze shifted in my mind. Not just affection, as I'd originally thought, but pride, love, and unwavering commitment. *Devotion*, she said.

That seemed like the right word.

"As I got more involved in their lives, I became more interested in Michelle's condition. That's how I ended up at the charity. That's why the research is so important to me."

*Of course.* She told me she had a personal connection to the charity, but somehow, our discussions had never delved into exactly what that connection was. Now that she said it, I could see the full picture.

"And that's why you needed the grant from my foundation."

Naomi nodded, her gaze still on her tea as she swallowed. "It would have been incredible for her to get any kind of treatment to make things easier for her. Especially if we could have heard her speak, that would…"

She trailed off, her voice wavering, and my chest tightened in response as I noted her use of the past tense. "*Would* have been?"

At last, Naomi glanced over at me, and though the tears had dried, pain filled her brown eyes. "She died last year. They both did."

"I'm sorry," I said, knowing it wasn't enough. The words were useless but I didn't have any other ones. Although I knew Liam died, I had no idea about his daughter. If they both died, there must have been some kind of accident, but asking for details seemed crass. How didn't matter as much as the effect their loss clearly still had on Naomi.

A heavy silence filled the small space, the clock above her mantle ticking quietly as I processed everything she said and gave her time to add any further details if she wanted to. She seemed to be finished, though.

As she took a drink from her tea, the ring on her finger caught the light from the window as she lowered the mug back to her lap, and I couldn't help asking about it.

"Is that why you still wear your ring?"

Her gaze dropped to her hand as she flexed her fingers, studying the delicate diamond. "It probably sounds silly, but I feel like if I take it off, it'll be like it never happened. Like they were never here at all."

It didn't sound silly to me, but neither did I know what to say next. As I took a drink of my coffee, Naomi glanced back over at me.

"Does it bother you that I wear it?"

I nearly choked on the liquid halfway down my throat, coughing as I forced myself to swallow it down. "It has nothing to do with me."

Why would she ask me that?

The words felt too sharp. Too revealing.

Too close. Too personal.

The walls of the flat seemed to press in on us, making the small space even smaller. None of this had anything to do with our arrangement. What the hell was I even doing there?

I stood abruptly, striding back to the kitchen and setting my half-full mug on the counter. "I should go before traffic gets bad."

Naomi didn't try to stop me, staying where she was while I returned to the bedroom to collect my things. A simple tap of the screen in my car service app alerted my driver to come and pick me up as I pulled on my clothes from the night before. When I was ready, I walked briskly to the door. Naomi still sat on the sofa, her gaze on the window and the world outside, but she spoke up as I put my shoes back on.

"When do you need me again?"

Every cell in my body rebelled against the idea that I *needed* her at all, but I forced myself to remain calm and not overreact. We didn't need to begin another fight when she hadn't done anything wrong. This was 100% my issue. "This week is busy for me but my weekend is open. I might go out of town. You can come with me."

The words 'if you want to' were on the tip of my tongue but I swallowed them back down. It didn't matter if she wanted to. That was the whole point of our contract and the absurd amount of money I intended to donate in exchange for her keeping to the terms.

Her head turned, her eyes meeting mine over her shoulder, curious and open. "Where do you want to go?"

Relieved that she didn't intend to argue, I offered her a tight smile. "I have a house in Norfolk that I sometimes visit on weekends."

If that surprised her, she didn't show it. "That sounds nice," she said instead, returning my smile. "Will I need to bring my wellies?"

"That's up to you. There are some nice walks and you'll have to entertain yourself some of the time while I do some work, so bring whatever you like."

Naomi nodded in acceptance. "Should I meet you at your place?"

"That's probably easiest. Let me check with my assistant and see what time I finish on Friday. I'll get back to you." The phone in my hand buzzed, indicating my car had arrived. "That's my ride. I'll see you in a few days."

I let myself out without waiting for her to say goodbye, but for the first time in a long time, walking away didn't make me feel any lighter.

**~Naomi~**

Having a conversation with Kane reminded me of being on a roller coaster, full of ups and downs and twists and turns. One second, he'd be completely invested, asking questions and showing sympathy. The next, he bolted out of my flat like someone had set his ass on fire.

I hadn't expected him to ask about the photo, and I certainly hadn't expected to tell him as much as I did about the people in it. My words barely scratched the surface, but they were more than I'd told anyone in a long time. If he'd asked for more details, would I have told him how Michelle and Liam died? Or how I stopped working at the school when I found out I'd never have children of my own?

Maybe. Maybe not. Since he didn't ask, I couldn't be entirely sure how I would have responded, but it still surprised me that I'd opened up as much as I did, and it surprised me even more that he had invited the conversation in the first place.

I sat on the sofa for several more minutes after he left, finishing my tea and thinking it all over. Despite his abrupt departure, he still asked me to spend the weekend with him, so he couldn't have been *too* put off by my confessions.

Why Norfolk, I wondered? If he had work to do, why not stay at his flat, close to his office? A change of scenery would be nice, though, so perhaps I shouldn't dig too deep and accept the mini-break as the escape it seemed to be.

Swallowing down the last of my tea, I pushed all thoughts of Kane aside and got ready for work.

The week fell into its usual rhythm: work during the day and the pub with friends afterwards when I got invited. When they asked if I met anyone in Rome, I told them that I struck out. Too many questions might lead to me letting something slip, and I had no intention of anyone in my life ever finding out about Kane.

When they asked what I was doing that weekend, I told them I had a work event. When the people at work asked the same question, I said I'd be with my friends. It was easier that way. With everyone satisfied I wouldn't be sitting around my flat alone, no one would call me up with last-minute invitations.

The text from Natalie, Kane's assistant, arrived on Thursday afternoon, short and to the point.

> Mr Davis will expect you as soon as possible after six o'clock tomorrow.

Once again, I had to wonder exactly what Kane told her about why we were meeting.

Since London traffic on a Friday afternoon would be a nightmare, I decided to skip the car service and took my overnight bag to work with me. That way, I could get on the tube straight from the office. Luckily, since the start of my journey headed into the city centre instead of out of it, I managed to snag a seat, tucking my bag between my feet. I read the book I'd brought, snacked on the granola bars I packed since Kane hadn't said anything about dinner, and tried to ignore the slightly sour odour coming from the man sitting next to me.

It had just passed 6:15 when I reached the lobby of Kane's building.

"Good evening, Ms Law." The man behind the desk smiled as I walked in, and I recognized him as the doorman from my previous visit.

"Tom, isn't it?"

His head dipped in acknowledgement, revealing a slightly bald patch on the top of his head. "That's right, Miss."

I took a few steps towards his desk, out of the path to the lift. "Very nice to meet you. Please, call me Naomi."

"As you wish." He bowed again despite my attempt to put him at ease. This level of formality wasn't something I normally encountered.

I tried another approach to break the ice. "Have you worked here long?"

He blinked at me, as if the question confused him. Or maybe he was just thrown off by the fact that I *asked.*

"For three years, Miss. Since the building opened."

"Wow. It looks new, but I didn't realize it was *that* new."

His shoulders relaxed as he seemed to realize I genuinely wanted to chat. "The building's inhabitants like it that way. A few have already moved out in order to go somewhere newer."

I shook my head at the idea. "The TV in the gym didn't have enough channels?"

A smile flickered across his face before he reined it back in. "Perhaps that was it. I stick to Freeview myself. Don't see anything wrong with it."

"You and me both. Do you get any down time on the job to watch anything?"

His eyes widened slightly, like I'd just asked him if he stole from the residents. "I'm afraid not. I need to be available at all times and I shouldn't keep you any longer, Miss. Mr Davis is already upstairs."

I recognized a dismissal when I heard one. "I'm guessing His Lordship doesn't like to be kept waiting?"

Again, he almost smiled, fighting to hold it back. I gave him a conspiratorial wink, not expecting a reply.

"Thanks, Tom. Have a good evening."

"And you, Naomi."

At least he used my name once. That would have to do.

Inside the lift, I swiped the keycard Kane had given me, staring at it in my hand while the lift raced upwards. Maybe I should have asked Tom if Kane regularly handed these out.

*Did I really want to know?*

The doors opened, and I nearly ran straight into Kane.

He stepped into the lift without looking at me, barely glancing up to press a button for one of the basement floors. His phone was in his hand, his attention fixed on the screen. "I saw you arrive on the security monitor. I assume you've already eaten. We should get going."

He really had been waiting for me, apparently.

Wearing his suit trousers and a button-down shirt without the jacket, he looked like he'd just come from the office, and his already-familiar cologne stirred something deep in my stomach.

He looked good. I could admit it. It had been five nights since the last time we had sex and I'd be lying if I said it hadn't been on my mind.

"How was your week?" I asked.

"Fine," he said, still focused on his phone.

*Mine was fine too, thanks for asking.*

Instead of saying it out loud, though, I let the silence sit. Things would go smoother between us if I did my best to adjust to what he wanted in the moment, and in this moment, he obviously didn't want to chat.

I already knew better than to expect Kane to behave like a boyfriend. We weren't dating; that had been made perfectly clear.

In the underground garage, I followed Kane to a black Porsche that, although I knew nothing about cars, looked expensive. Still without glancing at me, he got in the driver's side and shut the door, leaving me to fend for myself.

"Such a gentleman," I muttered to myself with a laugh as I headed for the passenger side, tossed my bag onto the back seat, and got in.

Kane was already busy tapping on the console screen while I fastened my seatbelt. As soon as the buckle clicked, he backed out of his spot, not wasting a second. "I have to make some calls and I'm not sure how long it will take. Have you got headphones with you?"

"They're in my bag," I answered, gesturing to the back seat where it was now out of my reach. With a sigh, Kane reached back and grabbed it, tossing the bag into my lap before driving us out of the garage and into the city streets.

*This is going to be a fun weekend,* my sarcastic inner voice commented, but externally, I simply thanked him and dug out the headphones, pulling up a podcast on my phone and plugging in before turning my attention to the world outside the car window.

Soon, the city gave way to countryside as we joined the M11 motorway, flying past the other cars in a way that belied the Porsche's smooth ride. If I weren't looking at the changing scenery, it would have barely felt like we were moving at all. Kane's eyes stayed fixed on the road ahead, his lips still moving as he conducted his business. With my headphones in, I couldn't hear a word he said and soon, my thoughts began to wander.

Liam and I used to talk about taking Michelle on a holiday to the coast. It was one of those 'someday' plans, the things we'd eventually get to, but neither of us owned a car and hiring one big enough for her wheelchair and everything else we'd have needed to take would have been expensive. Taking the train with all our luggage and accessories seemed like a hassle.

Now that there were no more 'someday's, I wished we'd just gone ahead and done it anyway.

Eventually, Kane turned off the motorway onto an A road, travelling several more miles before winding down some smaller country B roads while I watched the scenery out the car window. The open sky seemed to stretch endlessly above the flat terrain, and I turned to Kane to say something about it but stopped myself when I saw he was still talking.

At last, we turned onto a single-lane road and drove up to a gate which opened slowly upon our approach. From there, it only took another minute or so to reach a modern-looking two-storey house set in a wide, well-kept yard. The car came to a stop and I removed my headphones just in time to hear Kane tell whomever he was speaking to that we'd arrived.

"I'm going to transfer you to my phone, hold on a second."

He disconnected from the car's Bluetooth and got out of the car mid-conversation, without a word to me.

Too intrigued by our location to be offended, I let myself out and grabbed my bag, noticing for the first time that Kane hadn't brought anything with him. He must have kept extra clothes and necessities at the house for his visits, something which wouldn't have occurred to me since I'd never had a second home before.

Kane used his fingerprint to open the front door, leaving it open behind him for me to follow. Apparently, he did, in fact, remember my presence. When I walked in, he was settling onto a sofa in the lounge, still talking and giving no sign of finishing up anytime soon.

No welcome. No instructions.

Fine.

Without a chaperone, I decided to explore the house on my own, and after kicking off my shoes and leaving my bag at the door, I stepped through an open doorway at the end of the lounge into a large, open kitchen at the back of the house. The large windows in front of me instantly commanded my attention.

"Wow."

I breathed the word out quietly to myself as I took in the stunning view of the sea that greeted me. At first, I could only see water, sparkling in the evening sunshine, but as I stepped closer to the window, a beach appeared below us, so far below that the house must have been sitting atop a small cliff. The sun's golden hues made the sand sparkle.

My nose was almost pressed up against the glass before I realized there was a door that led onto a back terrace, and I quickly made my way outside. Comfortable-looking chairs and a table sat beneath an awning while the scent of salt and sea filled the air. In the distance, a gull cried, and a soft, warm breeze brushed over my face.

Any tension I felt from Kane ignoring me on the journey melted away as I stood at the railing, drinking in the sight, sound and smell of the coastline. For the first time in ages, I didn't feel the need to be doing anything to keep my thoughts in check. The soothing, gentle lapping of the waves along the beach quieted something deep inside me that I hadn't even noticed needed to rest.

Gradually, the sun dipped lower in the sky, shadows becoming longer, and still, I stood there, entranced by the beauty and peace of the place.

I'd almost forgotten exactly what had brought me there by the time the door from the house opened behind me and Kane appeared.

# Chapter Eight

~**Kane**~

Having a call scheduled during the drive to Norfolk was no coincidence. After the way the conversation at Naomi's flat on Tuesday morning turned so deeply personal, keeping things more business-like between us when we weren't fucking seemed like the best move. A long drive alone together made keeping my distance harder, so I put up a barrier before she could get too close.

I noticed her out of the corner of my eye in the car, smiling softly at the passing scenery, lost in thought, but I didn't ask what was on her mind. I didn't need to know. That wasn't part of the plan.

By the time I wrapped up my call, Naomi had disappeared. Her bag still sat by the door, which suggested she hadn't gone upstairs, but the house was silent.

"Naomi?" I called from the bottom of the stairs. No answer.

I scanned the kitchen, about to move on when I found it empty, when the wind stirred outside, lifting strands of blonde hair and revealing her silhouette through the glass doors. She stood at the edge of the terrace, eyes fixed on the water, her arms wrapped around herself as if the wind might carry her away.

I should have turned away. Should have left her to her thoughts.

Instead, I stared.

Her chin tilted up as if daring the sea to challenge her, she looked fragile and unbreakable at the same time. The sight of her, bathed in the fading light, made something tighten in my chest.

*Fuck, she's magnificent.*

The thought came so fast I didn't have time to shove it away.

Frustrated with my lack of self-control, I pushed the door open harder than necessary. "I'm going upstairs. Do you want me to show you the room?"

Slow and dreamy, as if waking from a trance, Naomi turned to face me. "You don't want to sleep out here? It's beautiful."

My jaw clenched, the idea of lying beside her beneath the stars more tempting than it should have been. "It gets cold at night," I said, voice sharper than intended. "Come on, it's late."

Without complaint, she followed me inside, slinging her bag over her shoulder as we climbed the stairs. The master suite wasn't as big as the one in Canary Wharf, but it was still bigger than Naomi's entire flat. The setting sun threw long shadows across the floor as I flipped on the light.

"If you want to unpack, you can use the left side of the wardrobe. The ensuite is yours. I'll use the other bathroom."

Without waiting for a response, I grabbed a pair of pajama pants from the dresser and walked out.

The truth was, I didn't trust myself to stay in that room with her. Not when I was already too aware of how the past week had shifted something between us.

She wasn't just a stranger I met in a bar anymore. I knew things about her now, things that made her real, made her *matter*, and that should have been my cue to end this arrangement before it got messy.

Maybe it wasn't too late. Maybe when I walked back into that bedroom, I'd tell her I was too tired, that tonight wasn't happening, and when we got back to London, I'd call the whole thing off. I kept that resolve as I returned to the room and found it still empty, Naomi still in the ensuite, and I grabbed my phone off the table, intending to set myself a reminder to speak to Natalie about making the donation to the charity and putting an end to this.

Then Naomi stepped out of the bathroom and every rational thought I had shattered.

Her nightgown, gold satin, clung to the curves of her hips, the hem brushing the tops of her thighs. The neckline dipped just enough to make my mouth dry, her hair falling in loose waves over her shoulders. She looked soft and sensual and completely unaware of the effect she had on me.

My phone slipped from my hand, landing on the mattress, forgotten, and I held out my hand. "Come here."

Though I'd been nothing but an ass to her all evening, Naomi didn't hesitate. Her expression softened into a smile as she walked towards me, placing her palm in mine. I pulled her close, gripping the curve of her ass as I guided her onto my lap, spreading her thighs around me. The nightgown rode up, exposing bare skin, warm and impossibly soft beneath my hands.

She let out a breathy hum when she felt how hard I was, shifting her hips against me in silent invitation.

We were on the same page, thank fuck.

I needed this. Needed *her*.

And if a small voice in the back of my mind whispered, *I don't deserve this woman,* I crushed that thought before it could take root.

Right now, she was here. Right now, she was mine. And I wasn't going to waste another second pushing her away.

Wrapping my hand around her neck, I pulled her lips to mine, the kiss rough and needy. My other hand slid the straps of her nightgown off her shoulders, encouraging the fabric to fall from her breasts and pool at her waist. Our lips still locked together, I lifted my hips from the bed just enough to tug my trousers down and free my cock. Understanding my intention without words, she rose onto her knees above me while I positioned myself under her, and a satisfied moan rumbled between us both when I tugged her back down onto my ready cock. It barely met any resistance, her pussy already wet and waiting for me though I'd done nothing to prepare her.

Holding her hip in place with one hand, I slid the other between us to rub her clit, driving her need higher while I gave myself a chance to catch my breath. My tongue continued to explore her mouth and Naomi's hips rocked against me, craving every bit of friction she could find. At last, I released my hold on her hip so she could begin to ride me properly, and she immediately did, not needing any encouragement and keeping her mouth locked on mine the entire time.

As her pace quickened, I finally broke our kiss to lean back, changing the angle so she could take me in even deeper.

"Fuck, that's good," I groaned, the movement of her pussy around my cock winding me tighter and tighter. Time ceased to matter; it could have been two minutes or ten until the tension broke, leaving me bathing in the satisfaction of release. All that mattered was her.

Thankfully, when awareness returned, I felt Naomi pulsing around me, letting me know she came too. With very little help from me, quite honestly.

Gingerly, Naomi stood up, disconnecting our bodies and returning to the bathroom for a moment to clean up while I pulled my trousers back up and got under the covers of the bed, on the side she'd designated as mine. It might not be much, but for me, this was about as much of a routine as I'd ever had with a woman.

It actually felt kind of nice.

Still basking in the satisfaction of my orgasm, I pulled Naomi into my arms when she returned to the bed. "The weather's supposed to be good tomorrow. We could go for a walk in the morning."

Her hand naturally found a spot on my chest as she settled into my side. "On the beach?"

"If you want. There might be a lot of people though."

She had been the one to specify that we not be seen together in public, a fact she seemed to remember as soon as I mentioned other people.

"Where else could we go?" she asked.

"There are a few public footpaths around that won't be too busy. One of them leads to a windmill, not too far away. We could try to find it."

She nestled into me a bit more. "That sounds good. Did you get your work taken care of today?"

"Some of it. I'll need to do more tomorrow afternoon, but I can take the morning off."

"Okay."

The word came out as a sleepy murmur, and I reached over to switch the light off on the panel next to the bed. It didn't take long for Naomi's breathing to even out, and once I was absolutely certain she'd gone to sleep, I placed a soft kiss on her forehead.

"Good night, Naomi."

**~Naomi~**

Kane's arm still encircled me when I woke the next morning. His body felt warm, solid and familiar, and for a brief, blissful moment, I let myself sink into it, eyes still closed, inhaling his scent.

Contentment bloomed in my chest, unexpected but very welcome.

It didn't last, though. Gradually, reality crept back in, and the moment of peace evaporated.

Memories from the day before flitted across the back of my closed eyelids. The coldness. The detachment. The way he ignored me for hours, treating me like an afterthought, until suddenly, he dragged me into bed, touching me like he *needed* me, whispering plans for the next day as if nothing had happened.

What was I supposed to do with that?

Frustration coiled in my stomach, making me restless, so I carefully slipped out from beneath his arm, moving slowly so I wouldn't wake him. He barely stirred as I tiptoed out of the room, my heart hammering for reasons I didn't want to examine.

I made my way down the hall to the main bathroom and ran a warm bath, sinking into the water in hopes it would settle my thoughts.

I wanted to tell myself it didn't matter, that we were just sleeping together, nothing more. But the inconsistency, warmth one moment and coldness the next, left me feeling constantly a step behind. If he would just pick a version of himself and stick to it, I could handle it. I could *adapt*. But this? This left me dizzy, uncertain, *off-balance.*

By the time I emerged from the bath, wrapping a towel around myself, I had no more answers than before. Kane still hadn't stirred when I returned to the bedroom, his breathing deep and even. I watched him for a moment, debating whether or not to wake him, but decided against it. He seemed to work constantly, including evening receptions and phone calls in the car, so maybe he didn't get the chance to sleep in often.

Instead, I pulled my nightgown back on and padded downstairs to the kitchen, wondering if I could find anything to make for breakfast. The moment I opened the fridge, I did a double take.

It was fully stocked: fresh fruit, eggs, meats, everything. Someone had clearly been keeping the house supplied in his absence. *How often does he come here? What does it cost to maintain an entire second home like this?*

Pushing those thoughts aside, I tackled breakfast: omelettes, bacon, fresh fruit, and coffee from the most unnecessarily complicated coffee machine I'd ever encountered. The rich aroma filled the kitchen, and sure enough, footsteps soon followed.

Kane appeared in the doorway, still shirtless, his pajama bottoms hanging low on his hips. His hair was tousled from sleep, his jaw darkened with stubble, and when he stretched, arms raised, muscles flexing, I had to force myself to look away.

"What's all this?" he asked, voice rough with sleep.

I busied myself with pouring coffee. "Breakfast. We'll need the energy if we're still going for that walk. Unless you don't have time?"

"Yeah, I've got the morning free." He yawned, rubbing the back of his neck before dropping into a chair. "Looks like the weather will cooperate."

It certainly did. Sun streamed through the windows as we sat down at the dining table and tucked into our food.

"How often do you come up here?" I asked, still curious about the second-home situation.

He shoved a forkful of egg into his mouth before replying. "Not as often as I should."

*Typical.* Just enough of an answer to keep me from asking more, but not enough to actually *tell* me anything.

I tried a different approach. "Who do you usually come with?"

Kane arched an eyebrow at me, his lips twisting into a cocky smirk I knew well from our time in Rome. "Are you jealous?"

My eye roll made him laugh. "I mean: do you bring friends or family? It's a lot of space for one person."

"Sometimes."

Another non-answer.

He was in a good mood, relaxed and at ease, but still, he dodged anything too personal. So, I let it go, shifting the conversation toward the surrounding towns. That, at least, he was willing to talk about. We fell into an easy rhythm, and by the time we finished eating, some of the tension I'd woken up with had faded.

When I rose and reached for the dishes, Kane stopped me with a hand on my arm. "The cleaners will be in later. Let's get dressed."

He didn't give me a chance to argue, clasping my hand and pulling me toward the stairs.

As I suspected, he had a wardrobe filled with clothes there, separate from his business attire in London. We both changed into light, casual clothes, coincidentally matching with his navy polo complementing my blue-striped top. I tried not to dwell on how *right* it looked, like we belonged together. Because we didn't, not in any way that really mattered.

Once ready, we grabbed sunglasses and Kane packed a couple of drinks into a small backpack that he slung over his shoulders. Together, we headed out, taking a trail that led inland from the coast.

For half an hour, we walked single file, him just behind me, speaking only when necessary. Occasionally, we passed other hikers, exchanging polite hellos, but between us, there was only silence.

Just as we came to a bridge leading over a small stream, I came to an abrupt halt and reached behind me to grab hold of Kane's arm. "Look," I whispered, pointing into the trees.

A small group of deer foraged along the stream's shore just ahead of us. They seemed oblivious to our presence, going about their business without a care for the two people tramping through their forest.

In London, the occasional fox or stray cat was the only wildlife I saw, which made this a rare treat. Mesmerized, I barely breathed as I tracked their graceful, near-silent movements as they drank from the stream and nibbled at the plant life nearby.

Kane moved closer, his chest brushing against my back. Slowly, his arms came around me, warm and solid, enclosing me in his embrace. We stood there in silence, breath syncing as the rest of the world faded away.

For the first time in days, I didn't feel any uncertainty. No tension. Just quiet understanding and a sense of rightness, that I was exactly where I was meant to be.

But just as suddenly, the deer's ears pricked at a distant sound, and they darted back into the trees, out of sight.

With them gone, the spell over me broke too, and I sighed, shifting on my feet as I prepared to resume our walk. Before I could step away, however, Kane caught my hand.

He turned me, pulling me flush against him, his other hand sliding around the back of my neck, his grip strong and possessive. My stomach flipped at the sight of the storm raging in his blue eyes in the second before his lips crashed against mine.

**~Kane~**

Naomi's obvious surprise when I kissed her couldn't compare to my own. I hadn't planned to do it. Hadn't even considered it as an option until my mouth was on hers.

After things got uncomfortably emotional with her earlier that week, I made a firm decision going forward: no kissing, no touching, no intimacy outside of the bedroom. We weren't dating. Affection that didn't lead directly to my physical satisfaction had no place in our arrangement.

And yet, there I was, breaking my own damn rule.

Maybe the scent of her floral shampoo cast a spell, or the gentle weight of her leaning back against my chest while we watched the deer. I could plead temporary insanity for doing it in the first place, but the moment I felt her respond, felt her lips parting and her breath mingling with mine, I should have stopped. Instead, I sank into it. Into *her*.

What the hell was wrong with me?

I pulled back, my pulse unsteady, and met Naomi's gaze. Confusion flickered in her deep brown eyes, mirroring my own. She didn't know what to make of this any more than I did.

"We're about halfway. This way." My voice came out rougher than I intended, and without waiting for a response, I turned and started walking, taking the lead this time.

Better to put some space between us. When I followed her, I could make out the faint outline of her underwear beneath her trousers, a view that was far too distracting. Now, at least, I had something else to focus on.

We reached the windmill about half an hour later. It stood at the edge of a grassy field, the sky a bright blue canvas streaked with wisps of white. The walking path curved away to the left, but I veered off, finding a spot in the long grass and sitting down.

Naomi lowered herself beside me, watching as I pulled out the bottles of water and snacks from my backpack.

"How did you find this place?" she asked, reaching for a handful of almonds.

"A date showed it to me. She researched the area before we visited."

I expected that to shut down the conversation and it worked, although not in the way I thought it would. Naomi didn't press, didn't pry. She just nodded and finished her almonds, washing them down with a sip of water before lying back in the grass.

Her eyes fluttered closed as the sun kissed her skin, turning it golden beneath its rays. Her chest rose and fell in a slow, steady rhythm.

I should have looked away.

Instead, I found myself leaning closer, drawn by something I couldn't name. Her lips parted slightly as she exhaled, completely at ease, completely unaware of the battle waging inside me.

A battle I was losing.

Before I could stop myself, I bent down and kissed her again.

Naomi responded instantly, her arms sliding around my shoulders, pulling me down with her. Heat surged through me as my hand found its way beneath her shirt, skimming the warm skin of her stomach before cupping her breast over the thin lace of her bra.

Even after having her several times now, the thrill hadn't dulled. If anything, it burned hotter.

Until a loud throat-clearing cut through the haze.

Lifting my head sharply, I locked eyes with a white-haired man standing a few feet away on the walking path. His disapproving glare was comically intense while beside him, a woman pointedly looked up at the sky, pretending not to see anything.

"Good morning," Naomi called out, sitting up with effortless grace.

The man huffed before he and his companion strode off without a word.

Naomi snickered. I smirked. Then our eyes met and we both broke into laughter.

The pressure I'd been fighting against all week broke and instead of overthinking or analyzing it, I just let myself enjoy the moment. And fuck if it didn't feel good.

Would it really be so bad if I did more of that?

Maybe there could be a middle ground somewhere between emotional entanglement and cold detachment. A way to enjoy Naomi's company without losing control.

After all, I set the rules of our arrangement. If I wanted to change them, I simply had to tell her so.

"Can we clarify something?" I asked once our laughter faded, my voice steady.

Naomi's expression turned curious. "Sure. What is it?"

"We both know this is business. Nothing serious, right?"

She nodded.

"So, if I kiss you, or hold your hand, or talk about things that don't lead to sex, it doesn't mean anything deeper than that."

Naomi studied me for a moment before reaching up and smoothing my hair back from my forehead with a soft, gentle touch.

"Kane." Her voice was quiet, but sure. "You don't have to worry that I'm going to fall in love with you. I know what this is. But that doesn't mean we can't be friends, too."

Something tightened in my chest at the word.

"I could always use another friend," she added. "And I'm starting to think you're not as much of an asshole as you pretend to be."

I huffed. "Careful. If you keep flattering me like that, it'll go to my head."

She grinned and I kissed her one last time, just a soft, brief press of lips, before another group of walkers appeared.

"This isn't the most private spot," I muttered.

"You're the one who chose it," Naomi pointed out, her eyes dancing with amusement. She glanced around once more before meeting my gaze again. "Do you want to head back?"

Being back at the house with no one to bother us sounded pretty damn perfect. "Let's go."

Beneath the wide Norfolk sky, we walked back the way we came, chatting the entire time.

# Chapter Nine

~**Naomi**~

Kane wanted to make a phone call when we got back to the house, so I wandered onto the terrace, breathing in the sea air and feeling far more at ease than I had the day before. At last, I understood why he'd been so distant: he'd worried I might be falling for him. Exactly why that idea filled him with such horror, I didn't understand, but since it wasn't the case, I'd happily set him straight during our walk. Now, everything felt lighter.

Honestly, I liked the idea of us acting like a couple while keeping emotions out of it. Along with physical intimacy, I'd missed the small, simple comforts of a relationship: going on walks, watching TV together, having someone nearby without the pressure of always impressing them. Getting that back without the weight of commitment? That sounded perfect.

The midday sun glinted over the sea, the water rougher than the day before, sending waves crashing against the shore. I could have watched for hours, mesmerized by the endless motion, but it only took a few minutes for Kane to join me. Warmth enveloped me as he wrapped his arms around me from behind, his chest solid against my back.

"I ordered lunch from a café in town. They'll deliver it in about half an hour," he murmured near my ear.

I leaned back against him, letting my head rest on his shoulder. "Sounds good. Do you still have to work this afternoon?"

"I do, but I don't need to start until after lunch. Which means..." His lips grazed my skin. "I have the next thirty minutes free."

His meaning clear, I turned in his arms and pressed a quick kiss to his lips. "What are we waiting for, then?"

With a teasing grin, I bolted inside, sprinting up the stairs. Kane was close behind, catching me at the bedroom door, and within moments, laughter faded into gasps and tangled sheets. He made me come twice before his phone buzzed, signaling the arrival of our food.

"We've got two minutes until they reach the house," he challenged, breathless. "Think you can finish me off that quickly?"

Never one to back down from a challenge, I slid down his body and took him deep into my mouth.

"Fuck," he groaned, fingers twisting into my hair. Less than a minute later, he climaxed with a shudder, his grip on me tightening before finally relaxing.

He threw on his clothes to answer the door, and by the time I made it downstairs, Kane had already arranged the takeaway containers across the counter. The breakfast dishes had vanished, and it only occurred to me then that the bed had been neatly made until we messed it up again. His cleaners were like magical elves, slipping in to do their work while we were away.

"What do you have to do this afternoon?" I asked as we ate.

For once, he didn't evade the question. "A progress call with a client about a new app we're developing."

"What does it do?"

He swallowed his bite before answering. "Searches for inconsistencies in data sets and allows for wide-scale cross-system corrections after a manual review."

I stared at him, waiting for further explanation, and when none came, I laughed. "You know, you could be talking complete nonsense and I wouldn't know the difference."

His lips quirked as he raised his drink. "Who says I didn't?"

When we finished eating, I put the leftovers in the fridge while Kane settled onto the sofa with his laptop.

"What's your plan this afternoon?" he asked over his shoulder.

"The beach is calling me for a walk." I'd been itching to explore since we arrived, and if Kane didn't need me, it seemed like the perfect time.

"It's supposed to rain tomorrow. Make the most of it," he advised. "Take a right at the end of the path, the views are better that way."

"I will. Thanks."

Bending over the sofa, I kissed him lightly before heading outside, a pleasant sense of contentment settling over me. The fresh sea air worked its magic instantly, soothing me as I followed the path down the cliffside.

The beach was dotted with families and walkers enjoying the sunshine, but after nearly an hour of wandering, I reached a quiet cove. Large rocks jutted out of the water, the shore untouched by footprints. With no houses in sight and no other people around, I climbed onto one of the rocks, tucking my legs beneath me as I listened to the waves lapping at the shore and basked in the warmth of the sun on my skin.

Eventually, my thoughts drifted to the man I left behind in the house. It had been almost two weeks since the night in the hotel bar in Rome, two weeks of ups and downs and shifting perspectives. When things were going well with him, it felt electric. When we weren't on the same wavelength, he frustrated me to no end.

He might not be easy, but I couldn't deny that over the past two weeks, I'd felt more alive than I had at any time over the past year. Even putting aside the promised donation to the charity, agreeing to this madcap scheme of his might be worth it in the end simply for pulling me out of the rut I'd fallen so deeply into almost without realizing it.

For the past year, I'd been drifting like a piece of wood caught in the sea's waves, putting up no resistance.

But now? Now, I wanted to swim.

"Are you looking for your prince?"

I turned with a start as the unexpected question broke through my reverie. A man stood a few feet away, tall and lanky, with dirty blonde hair and glasses. I hadn't heard him approach, but since no one else was nearby, he must have been speaking to me.

"What?"

He winced, rubbing a hand down his face. "That sounded better in my head. You looked like the Little Mermaid sitting there, like the statue in Copenhagen when she's deciding whether to kill the prince."

A strange but oddly endearing introduction. As someone who could certainly be awkward myself, I offered him a smile. "I get it."

He returned a tentative smile of his own. "You just looked deep in thought, that's all."

"It's a good spot for thinking."

He took a step closer. "It is. I come here a lot, but I've never seen you before."

It had been so long since a man approached me out of the blue that I couldn't be sure whether this counted as flirting. My friends said my walls were so securely and obviously in place, it usually discouraged anyone from getting too close.

Not this time, apparently. Had something changed? Did it have anything to do with Kane?

I kept my tone friendly but neutral. "It's my first time here. I'm staying with a friend nearby."

He glanced around, scanning the small cove for another person. "Where's your friend?"

"He had something important to do."

"I can't imagine what would be more important than spending time with you."

*That* was definitely flirting and I arched a brow. "Really?"

He groaned. "Too much? I swear I can do better."

Remembering my own stuttering attempt at flirting with Kane in Rome, I took pity on him. "It's fine, but I should be honest: I'm not interested."

He nodded, disappointment flickering across his face. "You have a partner?"

*Sort of?* Explaining Kane was complicated, so for the sake of simplicity, I held up my left hand, showing off the engagement ring.

His face fell. "I'm sorry. I didn't see it."

"It's fine," I repeated. "Have a nice day."

I'd probably been out long enough anyway, so I slid off the rock and turned back toward Kane's house.

The man jogged after me. "Let me walk you back. No reason we can't still have a conversation, right?"

I hesitated. He seemed harmless but I didn't want to offer any false encouragement. "It's pretty far."

"That's good," he said with a self-deprecating smile. "Gives me time to redeem myself."

His awkward charm won me over, and I let him fall into step beside me. After exchanging names and finding out his was John, we talked easily and I learned that he lived in London, worked as a data scientist, and came to Norfolk to visit his nan on weekends.

The conversation made the return trip feel shorter, and before long, Kane's house came into view. His silhouette stood on the terrace, facing us and I waved in greeting, but instead of returning the gesture, he turned sharply and disappeared inside.

John took notice of the exchange. "Is that where you're staying?"

"It is. Thank you for walking me back. I'll say goodbye here."

"My pleasure. It was nice meeting you, Naomi. Maybe we could meet up in London sometime? With your partner, of course."

Before I could figure out how to answer, John's eyes widened, his gaze locking onto something behind me.

Turning, I saw Kane striding toward us, his expression thunderous.

So much for the light, easy vibes from earlier. What was he upset about now?

"M-Mr. Davis," John stammered when Kane reached us.

My head snapped back to him. How did he know Kane?

Kane's voice was sharp. "What are you doing?"

John swallowed hard, suddenly pale, while I frowned before stating the obvious.

"I'm coming back from my walk."

Horror blanched John's face as he looked between us, his breath escaping in a deflating whoosh. "Is he... is he your... I... I didn't realize."

"Didn't realize what?" Kane snapped.

"That you and Naomi were... that she's your..." John trailed off miserably.

*Shit.* He must have assumed Kane was the partner I mentioned, and I didn't want *that* particular misunderstanding circulating among anyone who knew him. "Kane is my friend," I clarified. "Nothing more."

Somehow, Kane's expression managed to turn even darker, as if I'd said something wrong. These damned mood swings of his were going to drive me crazy.

I glanced between the two men, still trying to make sense of the situation. "How do you two know each other?"

Kane crossed his arms over his chest. "John works for me. Or he did, anyway."

John looked ready to collapse while I forced a bright smile. "Isn't that a coincidence? What a small world. It's beautiful here, so I can see why you would both choose to visit."

At last, John found his voice. "I had no idea she was your friend, Mr Davis. We were only talking."

When I nodded in confirmation, Kane exhaled sharply. "It doesn't matter. I'll see you on Monday. Let's go, Naomi."

Without another word, he turned toward the house and John took off so quickly back the way we came, I didn't even get a chance to say goodbye.

With a sigh, I followed in Kane's wake, determined not to let his behaviour go this time until he gave me a reasonable explanation for all of it.

~**Kane**~

With each step towards the house, I tried to calm the fire burning through my veins.

I'd lost control and I knew it. I watched it happen but I couldn't stop myself.

After my phone call, I stepped onto the terrace to take in the view and to see if I could find Naomi among the people on the beach. In the distance, I spotted her walking close beside another man, their heads tilted towards each other. She laughed at something he said and my chest tightened like a fist had clamped around it.

I didn't even remember making the decision to head down to the beach; I just knew I had to get her away from him. It wasn't until I got closer that I recognized John, and that felt like another blow.

She wouldn't go out in public with me, but she'd walk the beach with someone who worked for me? What the fuck was he even doing there, hitting on her right in front of me? He could deny it all he wanted but I saw the way he looked at her before he noticed me.

The only thing that stopped me from firing him on the spot was Naomi's reaction, her confusion confirming her innocence. In her mind, they were just talking. But *his* face when he turned and saw me told me everything I needed to know. He wouldn't have looked that horrified if he hadn't been trying his luck.

Could she really be that clueless? Didn't she know how irresistible she was?

Back at the house, I went straight to the kitchen, pulled out a bottle of Jack Daniels, and poured myself a glass. The whiskey burned as it slid down my throat, but it didn't drown out the frustration.

Naomi entered the room behind me, taking a seat at the counter as she watched me warily. Electricity still crackled between us, ready to ignite in another storm.

When the last mouthful was gone, she finally spoke. "What was that about?"

Just like that, my patience snapped.

"I was about to ask you the same thing," I shot back. "Did you forget that we agreed not to be with anyone else?"

Her brows tugged together. "I wasn't *with* anyone. We were just talking. I'm not allowed to talk to anyone else?"

"That wasn't all he wanted to do," I growled, pouring another glass.

"It was, actually," she said, her voice tight. "He did hit on me at first, but he backed off when I showed him my ring. You're overreacting."

My hand froze mid-air, ice slicing through my veins.

"You did what?"

The words left my mouth so cold that Naomi drew back, as if they'd chilled her too.

"I showed him my ring," she repeated, less confidently than before. "To show him I was taken."

"But you're not taken." My voice wavered, and I hated that it did. "Not like that."

"No, but it was easier than trying to explain whatever the hell this is."

She gestured between us, the motion stiff, almost defensive.

Although I understood what she meant, the answer still sat wrong in my gut. "We might not be public, but I don't want you pretending you're still engaged to another man."

Her hands curled into fists on the counter, frustration flashing in her eyes. "You said the other day that it didn't bother you that I wear the ring."

"I changed my mind." The words came out harsher than I intended, but I didn't stop them. "It *does* bother me if you're going around telling people you're engaged, because you're not. That's over."

The second the words left my mouth, I wanted to take them back.

Naomi visibly recoiled. Her face crumpled, her composure cracking, and to my horror, her eyes filled with pain.

"Trust me," she said, voice barely above a whisper. "I know."

*Fuck.*

"Naomi..."

I stepped toward her, but I didn't get the chance to say anything else before she slid off the chair and walked out of the kitchen. No slamming doors. No yelling. Just a soft, quiet click as she shut herself away somewhere else in the house.

And somehow, that was worse.

I drained my glass, but it didn't drown out the self-disgust clawing at my insides. It didn't stop my chest from aching.

Because I'd hurt her. Because I was a jealous, selfish asshole, lashing out at her over something she had every right to hold on to.

Of course she still had feelings for her dead fiancé. Any normal person would.

And why did I even care? I didn't want her in that way. Not the emotional, soul-deep kind of way.

So why did it sting when she told John we were just friends? Why did it feel like a knife to the ribs to hear her say she was taken, not by me but by *him?*

Maybe I was losing my mind. Maybe the work, the late nights, the lack of sleep had finally caught up to me, and I'd lost my grip.

Whatever the reason, Naomi had done nothing wrong and I needed to fix this. When my pulse finally slowed, I exhaled and went looking for her.

She hadn't gone upstairs and my office door was still open. So was the bathroom. The only closed door was the one to the downstairs bedroom. I hesitated for just a second before pushing it open.

Naomi sat on the sofa by the window, her gaze focused on the world outside. Though her cheeks were dry, telltale red marks still rimmed her eyes.

She'd been crying. Because of what I said. Because of *me*.

I really was an asshole.

Without a word, I sat down beside her. The cushion sank beneath my weight, her body shifting slightly toward mine but she didn't look at me.

After a moment's silence, I spoke as softly as I could. "I didn't mean that the way it came out."

She stayed silent for a beat too before sighing. "I know."

Although her tone was steady, something in it felt cracked.

"Sometimes, I think I've accepted that he's really gone. Other times... it's easier to pretend nothing's changed. But if I'm ever going to move on, I need to stop living in the past."

Her right hand drifted to her fourth finger, rubbing against bare skin, and my throat tightened.

She'd taken the ring off.

I didn't imagine for a second that it had anything to do with me. My cruel words might have been the catalyst, but deep down, I understood she'd done it for herself.

Wanting to acknowledge it, I reached for her hand, bringing it to my lips and pressing a kiss to the empty space on her finger. Her eyes closed, processing whatever she was feeling, but I had no idea what that might be.

Gruffly, I did my best to be supportive. "I can't imagine what this has been like for you, but you're stronger than you think. When you're ready to move on, you'll find someone special again. You're... pretty special yourself."

Compliments didn't come naturally to me, but I meant it. Hopefully, it sounded sincere.

She took a slow breath. "I don't know when I'll be ready."

"You don't have to know. There's no rush. And until you are, for the next few months..." I met her eyes. "You have me."

A small spark returned to her gaze. "That depends."

"On what?"

"On whether you can stop acting like a jealous boyfriend."

She'd hit the nail on the head and we both knew it, but I feigned offense anyway. "Jealous? Me?"

"No, of course not," she teased. "I must be imagining it."

The heaviness in the room lifted, the mood shifting as Naomi glanced around, clearly ready to change the subject.

"Why do you have this room here?"

Though I knew exactly what she meant, I played dumb. "Where should I have it?"

Her eyes rolled, which I took as a good sign. If she was busy finding me irritating, at least she wasn't swimming in sadness. "I mean: it's accessible. The wet room, the grab bars. Is it for someone who uses a wheelchair?"

It didn't surprise me that she'd picked up on those details, but with the way my emotions were already out of control, I didn't want to venture onto that topic.

I lied instead.

"It was like this when I bought the house. I haven't bothered to change it."

Thankfully, she accepted that answer and I stood back up, pulling her gently to her feet along with me. Once we were back in the hall, I closed the door to Abel's room behind me.

"Do you want to go into town for dinner? There's a nice steakhouse there."

Naomi's eyebrows lifted in surprise. "Wouldn't people see us?"

*Damn it.* I kept forgetting she didn't want to be seen with me. "We could order in, then."

"Or we could cook," she suggested. "You have tons of food here. The kitchen is fully stocked."

I must have looked unconvinced because she laughed, her mood lifting even further.

"Alright, *I* can cook, and you can be my assistant. I'm about to put you to work, Mr Davis."

For some reason, I didn't mind the sound of that at all.

**~Naomi~**

Kane surprised me in the kitchen. Based on the way he'd reacted to my suggestion that we make dinner ourselves, I expected him to be completely useless, but not only did he chop vegetables with some skill, he even threw some extra spices into the curry when he thought I wasn't looking.

Pauline had referred to him as a 'self-made' millionaire, implying that he hadn't grown up with money. Maybe he used to cook for himself. Maybe all that stopped him from doing it now was that he had better things to do with his time.

As much as I would have liked to ask him about it, any attempt I'd made to that point to get to know him on a more personal level had failed. Every time I asked him anything remotely personal, he gave the vaguest answer possible and changed the subject.

I didn't have it in me to fight him tooth-and-nail to extract those details, especially after the emotional upheaval of the afternoon, so I put my questions aside and simply enjoyed the camaraderie of cooking together.

With the sun still shining, we ate our supper out on the terrace in the fresh sea air. Kane looked handsome and relaxed, sipping on a glass of wine, his earlier jealousy forgotten, and when I put my first bite in my mouth, I had to stifle a groan of pleasure.

"Okay, what did you put in this? Mine never tastes so good."

His warm chuckle slid over my skin like velvet. "You noticed that, did you?"

"You're not quite as mysterious as you like to think," I teased, though it wasn't entirely true.

He didn't answer my question, but to my surprise, he gave me a more interesting reply instead. "My mum is a great cook. I took her to India a few years ago and she did a course there, so now, she fancies herself a curry expert. I might have picked up a trick or two from her."

He'd never mentioned his mum before, and try as I might, I couldn't imagine what kind of woman would have raised a man like Kane. Dozens of curious questions bubbled up inside me, but knowing he was likely to shut down if I got too personal, I tried a different angle instead.

"What else did you do in India?"

My efforts backfired when he returned to his typical, vague response. "I was there for work."

Undeterred, I tried again. "Do you ever get to travel for fun?"

"Not very often. Work keeps me busy."

Work obviously meant a great deal to him. Was it the money that motivated him? The image of success he'd built for himself? What did he get out of it?

The more I got to know the man, the more questions I had.

Before I could ask any of them, he turned the line of inquiry around on me. "What about you? Do you travel much?"

I shook my head. "No. A bit in Europe, but never abroad."

He nodded as he took another drink from his wine glass. "If you could go anywhere, where would you go?"

Taking another bite of my dinner, I said the first thing that popped into my head. "Well, Indian food is good, but Thai food is my absolute favourite. So, I'll say Thailand."

The corners of his eyes crinkled in amusement as he smiled. "Is food usually at the top of your priority list?"

When I shot him a dirty look, he laughed.

"Don't act so innocent. I remember the sounds you made with that chocolate cake in my flat."

Just the memory of that cake almost made me groan again. A second later, something clicked in my head. "Did your mum make that cake?"

He told me someone he knew made it, and just now, he mentioned his mum knew her way around the kitchen. His fingers tapped once against the stem of his wine glass before he caught himself and stilled. The brightness in his eyes faded like shutters closing over a window.

What on earth happened to him to make him so guarded over even the most innocent personal questions? And why did each time he shut me out only make me want to find a way past his walls even more?

Once again, he answered without answering. "I prefer carrot cake."

Choosing to let his obvious deflection go, I wrinkled my nose at his statement. "If there are vegetables in it, it's not a pudding."

"Oh, now you're a dessert snob? What's *your* favourite?"

"Oof, going right in with the hard questions." His smile returned in full force as I thought it over. "Probably crème brulée, but there are at least six honourable mentions."

"I don't think that's a Thai specialty," he pointed out. "Want to change your trip destination?"

"Why choose? I could have dinner in Thailand followed by dessert in France."

The crazy thing was that it probably *was* doable for someone like him. Not so much for me.

We lingered over supper long after our plates were empty, enjoying the wine and the sun and the beautiful view. Conversation flowed easily, light and teasing, but eventually, Kane's phone buzzed. With a sigh, he pulled it from his pocket and checked the screen.

"I need to make a quick call. Do you mind?"

"Of course not." Though he probably would have done it anyway, I appreciated that he asked. He *could* have some manners when he wanted to.

After carrying our dishes back inside, Kane went into the lounge to make his call while I tidied the kitchen. Even after I finished the dishes, he was still talking, and I peeked into the lounge to see him sitting on the sofa, phone in his left hand and rubbing the back of his neck with his right.

I might not be able to offer any assistance with his business call but a stiff neck? That, I could help with.

As he spoke, I walked over behind him, wrapped my fingers around his and moved his hand away from his neck. When he tried to turn his head, I gently pressed it back, my fingers finding the tight knots along his neck. His body tensed for a fraction of a second, just long enough to tell me that letting someone take care of him wasn't something he was used to, but he didn't stop me. Even when his voice caught as my thumbs pressed down on a tender spot, he didn't move away.

When his neck muscles felt looser, I moved down to his shoulder blades and then to his upper arms, only stopping when he said goodbye to the person on the phone.

"I can't tell if that was nice of you or mean," he murmured after hanging up.

"How was it mean?" I asked, trailing my fingers lightly through his hair.

"I was trying to concentrate and you made it very difficult."

The words were warm, letting me know he didn't actually have any complaints, and I moved around the sofa to take a seat next to him. "Does it feel better?"

His eyes gleamed, his gaze dropping to my lips. "It felt amazing, but now the rest of me feels left out."

"I'm sure we can fix that."

The words were barely out of my mouth before his lips found mine. Hands gripped my hips, pulling and twisting me until I sat on his lap, straddling him. I took full advantage of that position to pull his shirt off, bending down to kiss his neck before he could lift my shirt over my head. My hips rocked against his hardening cock while he undid my bra, yanking it down to suck one nipple into his mouth.

Apparently, a neck massage was all the foreplay he needed, and I wasn't about to complain.

We had to stand up to finish getting undressed, and once we were both naked, I pushed him back down onto the sofa, laughing at his grunt when his ass hit the fabric. Not willing to be outdone, he spun me around so that I faced away from him, spread my legs wide across his lap, and lowered me down onto his ready cock. A deep moan rumbled from my throat as he split me open.

Each time, it surprised me how good it felt. Each time felt different and new. Shouldn't I be getting used to it by now? How many times could my need for this man sneak up on me this way?

I gave up trying to understand it and simply gave in to the sensation instead.

We fucked each other roughly, his lips dragging along my back, his hands on my breasts one moment, on my clit the next, everywhere at once while I bounced on top of him, my body stroking his length with each rise and fall of my hips.

"So... fucking... good..." he panted from behind me, sounding almost as confused about that fact as I was. "Are you going to come for me, Naomi?"

I almost did just from hearing him ask the question. "Almost there. A little more..."

That was all the direction he needed, his fingers rubbing expertly against my clit until the world exploded around me. Pleasure crashed over me, my body clenching around him, and his hands went to my hips as he bucked up into me one more time.

As our bodies stilled, motionless except for the rhythmic contractions still echoing inside us, his arms wrapped around my waist, his cheek pressed against my back. His hum of satisfaction mirrored my own, at least for now.

But the dangerous thing about Kane was that I knew that satisfaction wouldn't last long. Soon, I'd be craving him again all over again. I was getting hooked on the way he made me feel, his touch and his intensity, but just like any addiction, it wasn't healthy in the long run.

Eventually, it would come to an end, and when it did, the crash of withdrawal was going to be hell.

# Chapter Ten

~**Kane**~

I'd been with a lot of women, no use in denying it, but nothing had ever felt as natural as it did holding Naomi on my lap, my cock still inside her, as we rode out the waves of our orgasms together. I could listen to her moans on repeat and never get bored of the sound.

*Why* it felt so different, I had no idea. I didn't usually dwell on questions like that. But with Naomi's body pressed against mine, warm and soft, a strange thought crept in: this felt... easy. After our argument that afternoon, it could have been awkward. *Should* have been awkward, even. Instead, everything else faded away as soon as we got our hands on each other, and in each trembling breath she took, I knew she felt it too.

"What do you want to do with the rest of the night?" I asked in an attempt to break the spell between us before I did something stupid.

Naomi sighed, lifting herself gingerly off of me. "I'm worn out from walking today. A film sounds good. Do you have a TV in here?"

She glanced around the room, which had no obvious sign of one, while I reached for the remote and pressed one of the buttons. A panel in the wall opened, revealing a rather impressive flat screen.

"Of course," she muttered as I smirked up at her. "Let me clean up while you choose something."

She headed off to the bathroom and I grabbed a blanket from the drawer beneath the coffee table. By the time she got back, I had a legal drama queued up, and she snuggled up to me beneath the blanket as we watched, both of us still naked.

We made it through about half an hour of the film before I had her pinned beneath me on the sofa, her legs wrapped around my waist. An hour later, we had to pause it again when Naomi pushed me onto the floor and rode me to another climax. By the time the film finally finished, we were both exhausted, and we walked up to my bedroom together, leaning on each other for support, and fell straight to sleep.

The smell of brewing coffee woke me in the morning, letting me know that once again, Naomi had got up before me. I had a quick shower but didn't bother putting any clothes on before joining her downstairs.

My bare feet made no noise as I entered the kitchen so I caught her unawares. Wearing her gold nightgown again, which she must have put on when she got up because we were both naked when we fell asleep, she reached up into the cupboard to pull down some dishes, causing the satin dress to lift just enough to reveal the curve of her rounded ass.

The sight immediately woke my cock up, and by the time Naomi turned and saw me standing there, gasping in surprise at my sudden appearance, it was already at half-mast.

She immediately burst out laughing. "Looks like you recharged overnight."

When I didn't join in her laughter, her smile faded, heat rising in her cheeks instead. "Put those down," I instructed, gesturing to the plates in her hand. "The table isn't ready to be set yet. I need it for something else first."

When I held out my hand, she stepped towards me and took it without hesitation. My hands went to her ass, lifting her up and perching her on the edge of the table. The height of it brought her hips into perfect alignment with mine, a fact she immediately recognized as I reached down and slid my fingers through her wetness.

*Fuck,* she was already wet. It seemed to be an almost permanent state with her, the same way I kept finding myself hard in her presence.

"How does that feel?" I teased, rubbing my fingers over her clit as she tilted her hips towards me, craving more. Before she could answer, I thrust two of them inside her, curling them until I found her g-spot. Her body was becoming second-nature to me, my fingers immediately knowing where to go.

"Wonderful," she gasped, bucking against my hand. "But not quite as good as your cock does."

That was more than enough invitation for me. Pressing her back onto the table, I spread her legs wide around me and drove my stiff cock into her slick pussy.

"Fuck, Kane," she cried, and the sound of my name on her lips only made me slam into her harder, each movement desperate in its intensity. Why did it feel like weeks since I'd been inside her instead of mere hours?

The table creaked with each punishing thrust, the legs dragging across the hardwood floor. Naomi gripped the edge of the table to keep herself steady, her head tossing from one side to the other, her blonde hair splayed beneath her and her back arching as her peak approached.

Knowing just how to push her the rest of the way, my fingers found her clit again, rubbing in a circle that got firmer with each stroke, and soon, her legs trembled around me. I let go too, the last few thrusts a jagged stutter as I emptied myself inside her.

Still panting, I helped her back up again, kissing her gently. "Good morning."

She huffed a shaky laugh. "Go put some clothes on or we'll never get anything done."

When I returned, she'd set the table and laid out another fresh meal, but as good as it looked and smelled, it didn't compare to the sight of her sprawled across the wooden surface, taking everything I gave her.

Would I ever be able to sit at this table again without that image crossing my mind?

Usually, women began to bore me sexually after a week or two, but Naomi was like a drug I couldn't get enough of. The more I had her, the more I wanted her.

The rain started coming down as we finished eating, so we decided to head back to London a little earlier than planned. Though she still hadn't told me exactly how her fiancé died, I figured if it *had* been a car accident, she might be uncomfortable in the inclement weather, so I slowed down considerably on the drive back.

We spent the rest of the day in my flat, rain dripping down the floor-to-ceiling windows as we watched another film and ate take-away from my favourite Thai restaurant, between a few more rounds of sex. Honestly, I'd lost count of how many times I'd fucked her over the weekend. She might have still thought I was crazy with the amount I was donating to her charity in return for her time, but she was worth every penny.

When my alarm went off on Monday morning, I found Naomi's side of the bed empty and cold.

On my bedside table, she'd left a note.

The tube was a little unreliable last week so I decided to get an early start. You looked so sweet sleeping, I didn't want to wake you. Too bad it doesn't last when you wake up. ;)

Thank you for the memorable weekend.

Naomi

The note was perfectly her: teasing but kind. I ran my thumb over the paper, rereading her words. 'Memorable' was an understatement. Most women blurred together after a while, their names and faces fading into the background, but not Naomi. She stood out in a way that should have terrified me. *Did* terrify me.

And yet, I found myself reaching for my phone to check my schedule for the week, looking for the first opportunity I'd have to see her again.

**~Naomi~**

Hiding my blush when my colleagues asked about my weekend might have been the best acting I'd ever done. All day, my mind kept flashing back to my body intertwined with Kane's, in the bedroom, in the living room, on the kitchen table. He was insatiable and I *loved* it. I'd never felt so powerfully sexy before.

Secretly, I found myself hoping he'd ask me to come over again that night. The thought of staying at home in my quiet flat and tiny bed held no appeal compared to the idea of being with him again.

However, when I eventually heard from him in the afternoon, an unpleasant emptiness settled in the pit of my stomach.

> Looks like a busy week for me. Friday should be free. Will confirm with you later.

*Friday?* Suddenly, the week stretched out endlessly ahead of me, dull and beige compared to the intensity of being in Kane's spotlight.

It couldn't be because he didn't *want* to see me, could it? We'd had our ups and downs over the weekend, but it all ended on a good note. At least I thought it did. Maybe he'd just had enough of me for a while?

And why should it matter to me, anyway? This was business, and he was essentially giving me four days off. I should be grateful for the break.

Not wanting to betray my sudden insecurities, I texted back as cheerily as I could.

> Hope it all goes well. Will wait to hear from you.

My thumb hovered over the 'x', debating adding a couple of kisses on the end, but I decided against it and just hit 'send' instead.

By Tuesday night, I'd started checking my phone every hour. Wednesday morning, I told myself to stop, but it was like an itch I couldn't scratch. Every time I looked, the screen remained stubbornly empty. Silent. And somehow, that silence felt louder than any words he could have sent me.

Wednesday evening, I headed to the pub with friends, and I'd barely taken a seat with my drink before Jolie grabbed my arm. "Naomi, I have the perfect man for you!"

An image of Kane's naked body popped into my mind and I quickly pushed it away. "Is that so?"

"Artistic, sensitive and penniless." She beamed at me. "That's your type, right?"

I had to laugh. That had been Liam, alright, and pretty much the complete opposite of Kane. "Who is he?"

"A new co-worker."

I fought against my wince. Jolie worked at an animal shelter, meaning her male colleagues were usually kind, soft-hearted... and often in their 50s or older.

"He's our age," she assured me before I could point that out. "He's working with us part-time to support his writing career."

That... actually intrigued me, I was surprised to find. I hadn't been interested in meeting anyone since I lost Liam, which was why I agreed to the situation with Kane. But over the past three weeks, not only had he reawakened my libido, he'd reminded me what it felt like to crave something more. Conversation. Companionship. A reason to check my phone with that flutter in my stomach that only came from attraction.

And that was the problem, wasn't it? Kane never promised me any of that. I was the fool hoping he might give it to me anyway.

Still, even if I *was* interested in meeting Jolie's friend, I'd committed to Kane for three months. In this case, I would have to pass, and Jolie's next statement gave me a perfect out.

"We're all going out on Friday night and I'm bringing you along."

"I'm afraid I can't. I have plans on Friday."

Like I'd just announced I won the lottery, all conversation at the table stopped, every head turning my way.

"What plans?" Eric asked.

"With who?" added Jen.

"Just something for work," I mumbled, hoping they wouldn't notice I'd now used that excuse two weekends in a row. "A donor I have to meet with. I can't get out of it."

"A business dinner?" Jolie clarified. "That's fine. Just come by afterwards."

"It might go quite late," I protested, more mental images of Kane and I together in his big bed doing their best to grab my attention.

"I can guarantee we'll be later," she promised. "No excuses! I'll be expecting you."

Since she obviously didn't want to let it go, I gave as much of a non-answer answer as I could to bring the conversation to an end. "I'll see what I can do."

When I got to work the next morning, I checked my email to find a message from Pauline waiting for me. Curiously, I peered over the top of my screen at my colleague sitting five feet away from me, but she was on the phone, ignoring me. I clicked into the message to see what was so important that she couldn't wait to tell me about it in person.

A link greeted me, and when I clicked on it, up popped the Evening Standard website with that day's 'celebrity' birthdays listed.

At the top of the list, with a featured photo, was 'eligible bachelor' Kane Davis.

The picture set off an annoying flutter of butterflies in my stomach. On day four without him, apparently I was suffering from a little withdrawal.

I leaned around the screen to peek at Pauline again, and though she was still on the phone, she gave me an enthusiastic thumbs-up sign.

"Call him," she mouthed while the person on the other end of her call kept talking. "Wish him a happy birthday."

Rolling my eyes, I retreated back behind my screen.

Thanks to Jane, everyone in the office knew I was in touch with Kane about a possible donation, and Pauline was still doing her best to play matchmaker. *If she only knew.*

However...

Maybe sending a birthday message wouldn't be the worst idea ever. He hadn't mentioned anything about his birthday, and if he had plans to celebrate it, I obviously wasn't invited. That was the agreement: no public appearances, no attachment, but it left a strange, hollow feeling in my stomach anyway.

Because we were friends now, kind of. Friends celebrated each other's birthdays. And I *did* hope he had a nice day, even if that day didn't involve me. I typed out a message but quickly deleted it and typed another instead. No... too formal. *Deleted.* The next one felt too casual. An hour later, I still hadn't sent anything, agonizing over what should have been a simple two-word message.

*Happy birthday.*

But actually, there was nothing simple about it. Because if I sent it, I'd be admitting that I cared, and if I didn't, I'd spend the rest of the day worrying he'd think I didn't.

In the end, I decided a text message of any kind felt too impersonal. A card would be better, since I could get a cheeky, silly one that suited our unorthodox relationship. But since I hadn't found out about his birthday until that morning, there wasn't time to post one.

However, I *could* drop one off. With the keycard he gave me, I could pop into his flat and leave the card there for him to find when he returned home from whatever event he had going on that evening.

*Yes.* That was the right decision, and once I'd made it, I could finally relax.

By the time I left work, I'd decided to pick up a couple of cupcakes as well as the card, and with my small bag of goodies, I hopped on the tube to Canary Wharf.

Tom was at his desk in the lobby of Kane's building, and he offered me a friendly smile when I walked in. "Mr Davis didn't mention you were coming by today."

"He doesn't know, actually," I confided. "It's his birthday, so I'm dropping off a small gift. Nothing fancy."

"I had no idea his birthday was today."

It wasn't just me, then. "I brought you a little treat too," I revealed, pulling one of the cupcakes from the bag.

The older man seemed genuinely touched, his eyes crinkling with his wide smile. "Well, thank you, Naomi. You're a ray of sunshine around here, and I'm sure Mr Davis thinks so too."

Although I had my doubts about that, I kept them to myself. "I'll be in and out in a minute," I promised as I headed to the lift. That was the plan: drop the card and cupcake and leave. But as the lift doors closed around me, sealing me inside, a nervous energy curled in my stomach. Was I overstepping? Kane had given me a keycard, but had he expected me to use it this way? Would he be pleasantly surprised by the gesture or annoyed?

Or worst of all... completely indifferent?

**~Kane~**

"Happy birthday."

Natalie gave me a warm smile when I arrived in the office, but it did little to combat my restless mood. My phone had been buzzing non-stop since I got up that morning; apparently, I'd been featured in some stupid society column and now everyone knew it was my birthday.

Normally, I'd spend the day at home with my family, but with multiple deals in sensitive stages of negotiation, taking time off wasn't an option. I'd be heading home on Saturday instead, which meant missing a night with Naomi. The thought of losing one of our nights together sat uncomfortably in my chest, heavier than I wanted to admit.

Each day without her put me on edge, and I avoided messaging her, knowing my bad mood could bleed through. My self-control was already hanging by a thread, especially since my birthday stirred emotions I preferred to ignore. I never made a big deal out of it, and I certainly had no plans to celebrate.

Which was why I ignored Natalie's greeting and went straight to business. "Send in the files for my nine o'clock meeting."

Throughout the day, I periodically checked my phone, skimming through the flood of messages without replying. There was only one name I wanted to see, but Naomi hadn't messaged me since Monday. Each time I checked and found nothing, the grey cloud hanging over me grew a little darker.

By the time my last meeting ended, exhaustion warred with restless energy. Staying in the office didn't appeal to me, but neither did going home alone. I considered calling a car and surprising Naomi, but given my mood, that seemed like a disaster waiting to happen. No, better to wait until tomorrow, as planned.

As if reading my mind, Natalie appeared in my doorway. "Any plans tonight?"

"No." I didn't look up from my computer.

"Not even with that new woman you've been seeing?"

That got my attention and my gaze snapped to hers in surprise. Natalie never pried into my personal life. When she first started working for me, we had a brief, purely physical fling. Since then, we'd occasionally hooked up between relationships, but it had never been anything more. We didn't talk about who we were dating.

But she wasn't stupid, and I'd given her enough tasks concerning Naomi lately that she'd obviously put it together.

"No," I repeated. "I'm taking some work home. I'll give you a list of files to prepare, and then you can go."

"Or I could come over and help," she offered. "I don't have plans either."

I studied her, trying to gauge her intentions. "I thought you were still seeing that earl's son."

She shrugged. "We broke up last week. Turns out I wasn't the only one he was seeing."

"Sorry."

"No big deal. His house was more of a turn-on than he was."

I huffed a quiet laugh despite myself.

"Seriously, though," she continued. "Nobody should have to spend their birthday alone."

That reminder gave me the final push I needed. On my own, my thoughts would spiral. Having her around would be a distraction, and she already knew my work inside and out.

"Alright," I agreed. "Let's grab the files and go."

The walk to my flat was short, and once we got inside, I ordered some take-away while we worked at the kitchen island. Naomi's presence there was still fresh in my memory: her laughter, the way she'd licked her lips while eating my mum's chocolate cake, the way she made my place feel... warmer.

Even now, she lingered in my thoughts, though I knew I shouldn't be thinking about her this much.

After we ate, Natalie shifted closer, scanning the document over my shoulder. Her breath skimmed my skin as she leaned in, and though she didn't say anything, I could feel the unspoken invitation. It would only take a word from me for something to happen between us.

Once, I wouldn't have hesitated. I would have taken what she offered, knowing we'd both walk away satisfied.

But now, every time I thought about touching her, Naomi's face appeared in my mind.

I'd promised her I wouldn't be with anyone else.

The thought sent a sharp pulse of frustration through me, but whether it was at the situation or myself, I wasn't sure. All I knew was that the longer Natalie sat this close, the harder it was to ignore my own damn body.

"I think I'm done for the night," I said abruptly, pushing back from the counter.

Natalie turned to me, her expression unreadable for a beat before she made her move, her hand sliding around the back of my neck, pulling me down as her lips crashed against mine.

Her familiar taste stirred up memories of past encounters, and my body immediately reacted, already revved up from my thoughts of Naomi. It took a few seconds for my brain to catch up and remind me that things had changed. It didn't feel the same.

I took a step back, putting some distance between us. "I *am* seeing someone," I reminded her. Even if that had never been an issue for us in the past, this time was different.

"But she's not here," Natalie pointed out, her gaze sliding down my body as she came to stand before me. The growing bulge in the front of my trousers was impossible to miss, and when she pressed her hand against it, I bit out a muttered curse. "Besides, it's your birthday. A good day to indulge."

"That's not... I don't want..." My protests fell on deaf ears as she fell to her knees in front of me, rubbing my cock through my trousers. *Fuck.* My hand gripped the edge of the counter, my eyes closing as I tried to fight my body's reaction. It didn't help. With every press of Natalie's fingers against me through the fabric, my mind imagined it was Naomi instead and I only got harder.

But it *wasn't* her, which was why I had to say no.

The word was on the tip of my tongue when a new voice spoke.

"Kane?"

Every muscle in my body locked.

As if I'd summoned her just by thinking about her, I opened my eyes to find Naomi standing at the kitchen doorway. A confused smile flitted across her face as our eyes met, and my stomach sank faster than a stone thrown into the Thames.

From where she stood, she could only see my upper half, the kitchen island hiding the woman on her knees in front of me. She held a brown paper bag in one hand, head tilted slightly as she waited for me to say something.

What the fuck was I supposed to say?

Before I could find the words, Natalie rose to her feet, her face flushed and her ponytail flipped over one shoulder, and Naomi's face immediately drained of colour. I could practically see the pieces falling into place in her mind as she took in Naomi's appearance and the direction she'd just come from. A flicker of something - hurt, perhaps, or maybe just disgust - flashed through her eyes before her expression went blank.

*Fuck, fuck, fuck.*

"Naomi," I finally managed to push out. "We're just reviewing some contracts."

I gestured to the papers spread across the island's surface, hoping it would lend a shred of credibility to the claim, but Naomi's expression only hardened. Without a word, she tossed the bag she'd been holding down onto the nearest countertop and turned on her heel, disappearing back out of the room.

"Naomi, wait...," I called out, but Natalie shook her head as we heard the soft ding of the lift.

"She's already gone, Kane."

I muttered another curse, running a rough hand through my hair. What were the fucking odds she would walk in at that exact moment? I'd been about to stop it. Nothing would have happened, but of course, it didn't look that way to her.

"Did you give her a key?" Natalie asked, her surprise clear in her tone.

I didn't bother answering. "You should go."

"Are you sure? She already knows I'm here, so we could at least finish."

The fact that she thought that would work on me said more about me than I cared to admit. "Go home, Natalie."

Her lips pressed into a tight line at the dismissal, but she did as I said, leaving me alone in the kitchen.

Meanwhile, I sank back down into my seat, feeling like absolute shit. That morning, I'd been mad at the world, but now, I only had myself to blame.

Grabbing my phone from my pocket, I sent Naomi a text.

> Please come back. Let's talk about this.

I had no idea what I would say, but I could at least try to explain.

Naomi didn't ignore me, but her reply also didn't make me feel any better.

> You said you want me to tell you when you do something that upsets me? I'm upset, Kane. Leave me alone.

Blowing out a long breath, I read and reread the words, looking for a loophole. Leaving her alone meant leaving her mad at me, but going after her would trample all over her request. Maybe I could give her some space for the night and attempt to apologize properly when she came over the next night?

Putting the phone away, my gaze landed on the bag Naomi had left behind. She never said why she showed up uninvited, but as I opened the bag and caught sight of the card and cupcake, my stomach twisted in renewed guilt.

She came for my fucking birthday.

Sat on the tube for an hour, completely out of her way, just to show she was thinking of me.

If it was possible for me to feel even lower than I did now, I couldn't imagine how. Still, I reluctantly pulled the items out of the bag, bracing myself for the worst.

On the outside of the envelope, she'd scrawled a short note.

> Sorry for sneaking in. See you tomorrow.

Obviously, she hadn't expected to find me at home, and more than anything, I wished she hadn't.

The card itself was plain and white, the message on the front written in a cartoony, black script.

*Birthdays come only once a year.*

Inside, it added: *Aren't you glad you're not a birthday?*

She'd signed her name with a kiss.

It was perfect.

And I'd completely ruined it.

With another deep sigh, I texted her again.

> I'm sorry. I'll make it up to you.

I didn't expect a reply, which was just as well since I didn't get one.

# Chapter Eleven

~**Naomi**~

I scrubbed at my face extra hard the next morning, hoping to erase all traces of the tears I shed the night before. Anger sustained me during the tube ride home, but as soon as I made it through the door of my flat, the floodgates opened.

*Why* I was crying, I didn't even fully know. Compared to the pain of losing Michelle and Liam, it seemed like a silly thing to cry over. Kane had moved on. And? Since he broke the terms of our arrangement, he'd still have to make the donation and I wouldn't have to see him again. It was a win-win.

So why did my stomach feel like it had been hollowed out with a dull knife?

And why did he text me that he would make it up to me? What was there to make up? What more did we have to discuss? From what I could see, things were well and truly over. A not-quite-three-week fling that had been fun while it lasted, for the most part, and now, I could move on.

In the afternoon, I sent Jolie a text.

My plans for tonight have been cancelled. What time should I meet you?

My phone buzzed almost instantly in reply, making me smile at her eagerness to play matchmaker. However, when I checked the message, it didn't come from Jolie.

> I'll be home by six, you can come by any time after that.

My eyes flitted in disbelief from the message up to Kane's name on the profile. He must be joking. Or, worse, he thought that he could just snap his fingers and I'd come running, no matter what else had taken place.

Not this time.

In a day or two, I'd get in touch to make sure he knew how to make the donation, but for the time being, I had no intention of even giving him the satisfaction of a response.

The reply from Jolie arrived a few minutes later.

> Fantastic! We'll be at the Ten Bells from six. You two are going to hit it off, I just know it!

My reply had significantly fewer exclamation marks, but I tried to stay upbeat.

> Sounds good. Looking forward to it.

I made a stop at home after work to get changed, making more of an effort than I usually would for a night out with friends. My jeans hugged my hips, the soft pink top I chose showing off a bit of cleavage. I wore my hair down, layering on my make-up a little more than usual, with high-heeled boots to complete the outfit.

By the time I reached the pub, the Friday night crowd had packed all the tables, but Jolie squeezed me in next to her when I found them, almost buzzing with excitement as she gestured to the man on my other side.

"Naomi, this is Theo. Theo, my friend Naomi that I was telling you about."

We weren't doing subtlety, apparently.

Theo ducked his head, hiding a smile. "I've heard a lot about you."

I had to laugh. "I can only imagine, but you're not under any obligation to spend the night chatting with me just to make Jolie happy."

At first glance, he definitely ticked most of my usual boxes. Shoulder-length brown hair with a trimmed beard, kind brown eyes, a little on the skinny side. The 'starving artist' type, my friends called it.

"Can I buy you a drink anyway?" he offered.

"Only if I can get you the next one."

The hours quickly blended together as we chatted, sometimes with the whole group and sometimes just the two of us. He was open and up-front about being at the point in his life where he wanted a serious relationship, which I appreciated, but my chest tightened when he mentioned wanting a family.

Liam and I had already been dating when I found out I wouldn't be able to have children. He supported me through it, riding the emotional rollercoaster with me, and it didn't change the way he felt about me, especially since he already had Michelle who required all his attention anyway.

But anyone I started seeing now would be coming in blind. At some point, I'd need to have the conversation with them, and I knew very well that for some men, it might be a dealbreaker. It wasn't something I looked forward to.

At least that had never been an issue with Kane.

The second his name popped into my head, I pushed it forcefully down, doing my best not to imagine the night we might have been having in his penthouse flat if he hadn't gone back on his word.

Besides, even aside from the potential issue my infertility might cause in pursuing a relationship with Theo, I just wasn't feeling it. He was nice, absolutely. Handsome, certainly. But when his leg pressed against mine, I waited for a tingle of attraction that never came. When his fingers grazed mine, instinct urged me to pull away. There was no heat. No excitement. No *need.*

Just the stark absence of everything I had felt with Kane.

Eventually, the group at the table dwindled to just a few people. When Theo went to use the toilet, Jolie pounced on me. "What do you think? He's great, right?"

"He seems really nice," I started, and she groaned.

"Don't say 'nice' like that."

"Well, he is, but he's also looking for something serious and I just don't think I'm ready for that yet."

"They all say that because they think it's what we want to hear," she argued. "I bet you anything if you tell him you're just looking for some fun, he would jump at the chance. And who knows? Maybe you'll find you want more too."

Once again, Kane's face flashed before my eyes.

When Theo returned, Jolie stood up to leave so I followed suit.

Theo helped me into my jacket. "Which way are you heading? Want to split a taxi?"

Jolie must not have told him we were in my neighbourhood. "Actually, I live pretty close. I'm just going to walk."

"Want some company?"

"She does," Jolie interjected before I could respond. "I hate her wandering around the city on her own."

I rolled my eyes at her protectiveness but didn't argue. It was literally only a few streets away, and I'd send him on his way once we got there.

As soon as we got out into the quiet of the street, my phone rang. It had buzzed in my pocket on and off during the evening, but the noise of the pub had drowned out the ringer. I took it out to silence it, noticing I had several new voicemails and messages.

It didn't take a genius to guess who they might be from.

"Do you need to take that?" Theo asked.

"It can wait," I replied, firmly shoving the device back into my pocket. "Tell me more about this novel you're writing."

He was still on the first chapter by the time we reached my house, and I cut him off with an apologetic smile.

"This is me. Thanks for walking me back. It was nice to meet you."

He took the hint that he wasn't invited in, but it didn't stop him asking a follow-up. "Can I ring you sometime?"

As I opened my mouth to respond, a familiar voice sliced through the night air from behind me.

"No, you bloody well can't."

**~Kane~**

Confusion filled the man's eyes as they darted between me and Naomi and back again. She still had her back to me, those tight jeans hugging her in a way that made my fists clench at my sides. Those boots, those curves... I could just imagine the thoughts running through that guy's head, and it made my blood run hot. How dare he think he had a chance with her?

"I'm sorry, who are you?" he asked, the question addressed to both me and Naomi.

"He's nobody," she answered stiffly. "And yes, you can definitely give me a call sometime. Why don't you give me your number and I'll send you a text?"

She pulled out her phone, and the second she tilted it toward him, something inside me snapped. Before I even registered what I was doing, my hand shot out, fast and reckless. My fingers barely grazed the edge of it but the force was enough to send it flying. The sickening crack of glass against pavement jolted through the still air, a sound as sharp as the anger flashing in Naomi's eyes when she finally looked over at me.

"What did you do that for?"

I couldn't bring myself to apologize, not when I would rather have it destroyed than have her put another man's number in it. Instead, I snatched up the broken device and shoved it into my pocket. "I'll buy you a new one."

"I don't want your money."

The man took a step back, still eyeing us both warily. "I don't want to get in the middle of anything here."

"You aren't..." Naomi started to say, but I cut her off with my own response.

"Good. You can go then."

"Are you okay here with him?" he asked Naomi, ignoring me.

She blew out a long breath. "I'm fine. He's an asshole, but he's not dangerous."

"Maybe you should stop seeing him then."

I could have sworn he *wanted* me to punch him in the face. By the looks of him, one single punch would have brought him to his knees. What could she possibly see in someone like him?

"I'm trying to. Thanks again for walking me home."

My chest tightened at her words, but at least the man finally took the hint and left us in peace. I scowled at his retreating back while Naomi turned to fully face me, her arms crossing defensively over her stomach.

"What are you doing here, Kane?"

That was exactly what I wanted to talk about. "You were supposed to come to my flat. You didn't show up, you didn't answer my texts or my calls. I was worried something had happened to you."

The relief I felt when I saw her walking down the street from the backseat of the car where I'd been waiting had been short-lived when I realized she wasn't alone.

She didn't seem fazed in the least by my admonishment. "Our agreement is over. You don't get to decide what I do anymore."

Over? What the fuck did she meant by that?

Taking a fortifying breath, I made a conscious effort to soften my tone. "What are you talking about?"

Her arms remained crossed, her entire posture defensive. "You broke the terms. That nullifies the agreement."

"Wait... because of last night?" Although I knew she'd been upset to find me with Natalie, and I was fully prepared to apologize, it never once crossed my mind that she would consider that a dealbreaker. "Nothing happened. You didn't give me a chance to explain."

"I'm not an idiot, Kane. I don't need you to explain what that woman was doing on her knees, or what went on after I left. You're the one who set the condition about not being with anyone else, so you can accept the consequences of breaking it. I'll expect you to make your donation to the charity as soon as possible."

She turned on her heel so fast her hair whipped over her shoulder, her boots clicking hard against the pavement. For a second, I just stood there, stunned by her words, until instinct finally kicked in. I caught up to her on the step when she stopped to pull out her keys and my fingers wrapped around her arm, firm enough to keep her in place.

"I know how things looked, and yes, she offered to get me off just before you came in, but nothing actually happened. I didn't sleep with her."

Her raised eyebrows suggested my explanation didn't impress her. "You got mad at me for talking to another man last weekend. Just now, you broke my phone because one wanted to give me his number. But you getting a blow job in your kitchen is just fine?"

"There was no blow job," I repeated. "She offered, yes, but I was going to tell her no. It was just bad timing that you came in when you did."

When her expression didn't shift, I tried to explain further.

"That was my assistant, Natalie, and sometimes we..."

"Your assistant?" She spat the word out as if it were bitter on her tongue. "So, you're *that* kind of boss? I should have guessed."

"That's not fair."

"Isn't it? From the first time we met, I could tell that you get off on having people under your thumb. Using your power to get people to do what you want without ever considering what they want. Did it ever cross your mind that she's a real person with feelings? That I am?"

The coldness in her tone stung me, the words just sharp enough to find their target. I let go of her arm, only now realizing that I'd still been holding onto it. "Is that really what you think of me?"

"What else am I supposed to think? You don't tell me anything about yourself. You don't let me in at all. I can only judge you based on the way you behave, and this is what I see."

When she turned to shove the key into the lock, I didn't stop her. I didn't move when she pushed it open, or when she closed it behind her and locked it, all without another word.

Left alone on her front step, I slowly turned back to the street, the silence suddenly deafening.

Naomi's stark assessment of my character might have been hard to hear, but it did contain some truth. I liked to feel in control, especially when it came to women. So much in life couldn't be controlled, so what was wrong with taking some ownership where you could get it?

But I wasn't simply on a power trip just for the hell of it. I hadn't forced Natalie into anything, and I didn't really believe I'd forced Naomi either. She wouldn't have agreed to our arrangement if some part of her hadn't wanted to. I just gave her a push towards acknowledging it.

All week, I'd been counting down to this night, imagining her beside me, under me, breathless, laughing, challenging me the way only she could. Making me feel grounded. Connected.

Instead, I was left with the echo of her anger and the click of a deadbolt locking me out.

If she followed through on her threat, if I never saw her again, would I ever get that feeling back again?

Why did it scare me so much that I might not?

Clearly, an apology wouldn't be enough. If I wanted her to resume our arrangement, I couldn't simply demand it.

Maybe... maybe I would have to finally give her something real.

# Chapter Twelve



**~Naomi~**

I spent Saturday morning hibernating in my flat, alternating between stewing over my argument with Kane and fighting a restless, hollow feeling I couldn't quite shake. Our arrangement was *definitely* finished now. The look on his face when I told him exactly what I thought of him, and the fact that he hadn't even tried to follow me inside afterward, confirmed it.

So, why did I still feel so unsettled?

When my buzzer rang at lunchtime, my stomach lurched, betraying me with the fleeting hope that Kane was downstairs. Which was ridiculous. I didn't *want* that, I had to remind myself.

Besides, it wasn't him anyway. Instead, I opened the door to a delivery man holding a package I wasn't expecting.

"I think you have the wrong flat," I said, eyeing the box as he handed me an electronic pen to sign his tablet.

He pointed at the name on the screen. "Naomi Law?"

"Yes, but..."

Still confused, I signed for the package and took it upstairs. When I opened it to find a brand-new phone, my heart momentarily stuttered.

I hadn't thought much about Kane's offer to replace mine, or even the fact that he took the broken one. But when I took this one out of the box, a sticky note with a PIN number was stuck to the screen. Entering it, I found all my apps and contacts already restored.

*I'll be damned.*

It didn't change anything about what had happened, and it *definitely* didn't make up for the way he acted, but I had to admit it was thoughtful in an unexpected way. He hadn't just replaced the phone; he'd made sure it was ready to go, as if nothing had been broken in the first place. The sheer efficiency of it impressed me. How the hell had he managed to do this so quickly?

A text message awaited me from the man in question.

> I'm meeting my parents for dinner tonight. If you want to join us, I'll tell them you're a colleague.

That was it. No apology, no mention of our argument, no explanation for why he suddenly wanted me to meet his family. Just an invitation that made no sense.

What did it *mean?*

My words from last night echoed back to me: *You don't tell me anything about yourself. You don't let me in at all.*

Was this his attempt to prove me wrong?

The more I thought about it, the more my curiosity grew. Who had raised Kane Davis? Did they see the same man I did, or something entirely different? There were parts of him that still didn't fit together: the ruthless businessman versus the man who backed the Abel Foundation, the one who kept everything bottled inside versus the one developing a way for non-verbal people to communicate.

The man who could be cruel one moment and oddly considerate the next.

Maybe meeting his parents would give me answers. Or maybe it would at least make the end of this whole thing feel less abrupt.

Before I could overthink it, I typed out a reply.

Where should I meet you?

His response took only seconds.

I'll pick you up at 5:30.

And bring me back home afterwards.

If that's what you'd like, yes.

I bristled at the implication that I might change my mind, but instead of arguing, I set my phone down and went to figure out what the hell one wears to dinner with the parents of the emotionally unavailable man who had been paying me to sleep with him.

Professional seemed like the safest option, since Kane planned to introduce me as a colleague. I settled on a yellow button-down blouse and black dress trousers, my hair twisted into a loose updo. Hopefully, his parents wouldn't ask too many questions about his business, since I still didn't fully understand what he did.

At quarter past five, I went downstairs to wait, and Kane arrived five minutes later, driving the same car we'd taken to Norfolk. I'd been expecting his usual car service, but I hid my surprise as I slid into the passenger seat.

Would he address our argument, or pretend nothing had happened?

"It'll take us about 45 minutes to get there," he said as he put the car in gear.

Apparently, we were going with the 'pretend nothing happened' option.

I turned my gaze to the window, determined not to speak first. He looked good, but I wouldn't tell him so. He smelled even better, his familiar cologne stirring my body to react as memories pressed in, ones I did my best to ignore.

We both stayed silent as he drove through the city, his attention fully on the road until we hit the A40 and traffic thinned out.

Resting one arm on his armrest while the other kept the steering wheel steady, Kane glanced over at me.

"The card was cute. And I enjoyed the cake."

Not quite an apology, but I recognized it for what it was: an opening.

"I thought you'd be out for your birthday," I said, keeping my eyes on the passing trees. "You said you had plans all week."

"I did. Every night except that one." He hesitated, his fingers drumming lightly against the wheel. Almost *nervously*. "I don't really celebrate my birthday. It's not a happy day for me, so I planned to be alone. I was going to do some work at home and Natalie offered to help. Obviously, things got a little out of hand."

"Obviously," I murmured.

He exhaled through his nose. "I really was going to turn her down."

I could feel his eyes on me, but I didn't turn to meet them.

"I know it didn't look like it," he continued, "but she took me by surprise. It had been a few days since I saw you, and my body thought it sounded like a great idea, even if I didn't."

The wry honesty in his voice might have made me smile under different circumstances.

"If you were that desperate, you could have asked me to come over. I thought that was the whole point of our arrangement."

I caught his grimace from the corner of my eye. "Honestly, it wasn't on my mind when she invited herself over. She'd just broken up with her boyfriend and wanted a distraction. I should've made it clearer that it wasn't an option, but it doesn't have any deeper meaning. I don't want her, Naomi."

Something in my chest loosened just a little.

"And this is a regular thing for the two of you?"

"In a way. We dated briefly after she started working for me. And before you accuse me of harassment again..."

I rolled my eyes, but the anger I'd felt the night before had started to ebb.

"...*she* came onto *me*. We figured out quickly that we weren't good for each other, but every once in a while, usually after she breaks up with someone, we hook up. It's physical, nothing more."

Wasn't that exactly what *we* had been? No emotions, no complications.

At least that had been the intention.

"If you already had someone to sleep with, no strings attached," I said slowly, "why did you need *me*?"

"Honestly?"

"Preferably, yes."

My dry delivery made him chuckle, and the sound of it lingered in the air for a beat before he answered the question.

"The sex is a lot better with you."

I turned my head toward him, searching his face for a hint of a joke, but his smile had faded. His jaw was tight, like he hadn't *wanted* to say that out loud. As if admitting it made him vulnerable.

Something warm curled in my stomach. I knew how good the sex was for me, and based on his reactions, I'd suspected he felt the same. But hearing him say it out loud, to know that it hadn't all been in my head, still felt good.

It also made me more curious than ever to get to the root of exactly what happened to this man to make him so jaded in the first place.

Before either of us could decide how to move on from there, Kane took the next exit, bringing us into a development on the edge of a large town.

"Where are we?" I asked as we drove along the quiet, respectable residential streets.

"Just outside of High Wycombe. This is where I grew up. Not in this house, but nearby."

My eyes darted back towards him in surprise. "We're going to their house?"

I'd assumed we would be meeting his parents in a restaurant or pub, somewhere a little more public. Being in their home felt... intimate.

Kane simply nodded. "It's easier that way."

Easier? In what way?

Again, I lost my chance to ask for more details as Kane pulled into the driveway of a good-sized bungalow with a big, neat yard. The front door opened before Kane had even turned the car off and a pleasant-looking middle-aged couple appeared in the doorway at the top of a... wheel-chair ramp?

Why was there a ramp? Was there a connection between the ramp and the accessible room at Kane's Norfolk house? Neither of his parents appeared to be wheelchair users, but appearances could be deceiving.

My questions kept piling up as Kane opened his door and got out of the car, calling out a greeting as he went. He didn't come around to open my side, so I let myself out and circled the car to join him.

From the front door, his mother's eyes lit up in delight as she caught sight of me, and my stomach immediately sank. Kane *had* told her I was just a colleague, right? No one got that excited about meeting their child's co-worker.

What exactly had I gotten myself into?

**~Kane~**

Though it wasn't easy, I kept my expression neutral as my mum's gaze flicked rapidly between me and Naomi, her excitement barely contained.

"Happy birthday, love. You didn't tell us you were bringing a guest."

There was an almost giddy edge to her voice, and I knew why. I never brought women home. *Ever.* Which meant she thought Naomi must be someone special.

I hadn't warned her in advance because I wanted it to seem spontaneous, like bringing Naomi along had been a casual, last-minute decision. It wasn't. I'd thought about it all damn day, and even then, I wasn't sure Naomi would go through with it.

"This is Naomi, a colleague of mine." My voice remained even and controlled. "We just finished a business meeting, and I figured since you'd have plenty of food, I'd bring her along. Hope that's okay."

Mum didn't acknowledge the explanation, beaming as she pushed past me to pull Naomi into a hug. "We're so happy to meet *any* friend of Kane's. He never brings people over."

"Colleague," I repeated firmly. "She's a *colleague*."

Neither of them paid me any attention.

My dad walked over, clapping a heavy hand on my back. "She's gorgeous," he *tried* to whisper, but it came out loud enough to be heard in the next town over.

I resisted the urge to pinch the bridge of my nose. "What's for dinner?" I asked, hoping to move things along before this became even more mortifying.

Mum, still holding Naomi's arm, started leading her into the house. "Is he this way at work? Always right to the point, no small talk?"

"We haven't actually worked together very long," Naomi demurred. "I couldn't really say what he's like."

"Well, I want to hear all about what you two are working on," Mum stated, and I had to smile at the panicked glance Naomi threw my way.

The kitchen was warm, filled with the savoury scent of simmering tomatoes and herbs. Mum had three different pots bubbling away on the hob, steam curling into the air. Rich and comforting. It smelled like home.

We were still missing one person, though. "Where's Abel?"

"In his room," Mum said. "Go say hi. Dinner needs a few more minutes."

"Perfect. We'll be back soon."

I led Naomi out into the wide hallway, my footsteps slowing as we neared Abel's door. Even though I'd invited her there *specifically* to meet him, I still couldn't quite explain why I was doing it.

Of all the rules I followed, keeping my home life separate from everything else was the one I *never* broke.

And yet, there we were, about to trample all over it.

I hesitated, my fist hovering over the door for a beat too long. Should I offer some kind of explanation first? Would that defeat the purpose?

As much as this was about revealing parts of myself to her, it would reveal things about her too. The way she reacted to the person behind the door would shape my opinion of her going forward, for better or worse, more than anything that had come before.

Better to just get it over with, I decided, knocking firmly. A moment later, a computerized voice replied, "Come in."

Pushing the door open, I stepped aside to let Naomi enter first.

Abel sat in his wheelchair, his communication device mounted in front of him. His head tilted slightly to the side, dark hair, an exact match to mine, framing his face in that way he liked. Personally, I'd never let mine grow that long.

His sharp blue eyes lit up when he saw me, but when Naomi followed, they went wide, a grin stretching across his face.

Naomi stepped closer without hesitation, her warm smile an instinctive response to his enthusiasm. "Hello."

Like a hawk, I watched her tone, her body language, scanning for discomfort or any sign of negativity.

Nothing.

Only curiosity and friendliness.

Abel's fingers moved stiffly over the buttons of his talker. "Hello," the robotic voice greeted. "Who are you?"

"This is Naomi," I answered. "We're working on something together."

She turned to me with a small frown. "Kane didn't tell me he had a brother."

Her tone was neutral, but I braced myself anyway. I'd heard it all before: pity, shock, casual cruelty disguised as curiosity.

"This is Abel," I said gruffly. "My twin."

"Twin?"

Genuine surprise flickered across her face, but I couldn't tell if it was the good kind or the bad kind.

I tensed further, mentally preparing for whatever came next. If she said the wrong thing, she might be making her own way back to London tonight.

However, once the revelation had a chance to sink in, Naomi leaned closer, studying Abel with playful scrutiny. "I don't believe it," she said at last. "You're much more handsome than he is."

Abel burst into joyous laughter, his whole face lighting up. Naomi waited patiently as he tapped at his talker. "I'm funnier and smarter too, but don't tell him that."

Naomi's laugh was deep and unforced. "It'll be our secret, I promise."

I exhaled slowly, tension I hadn't realized I held slipping from my shoulders. She was handling this well. Almost *too* well. What was the catch?

As she glanced around, her eyes landed on me again, brow furrowing slightly.

"Hang on... did your parents *honestly* name you Kane and Abel?"

I snorted. "They're completely insane. You'll see over dinner."

Abel tapped his device, smirking. "They always knew he was the evil twin."

Naomi laughed while I shook my head. That joke had been one of Abel's favourites for years. "That does it," she told him. "You're sitting next to me at dinner so you can tell me all your best stories about Kane. Deal?"

He nodded with a wide, lopsided grin, and my chest tightened with an unfamiliar sense of... happiness?

That was unexpected.

I cleared my throat in a bid to regain some kind of control. "Let's go and sit down."

More taps followed until: "I'm already sitting," Abel replied.

"Don't encourage him," I muttered when Naomi laughed again, but when I turned to head back to the hallway, I found I was smiling too.

In the dining room, Dad was setting the table and Naomi immediately offered her assistance. "What can I help with?"

Before I could protest that she was a guest, she had already followed him back to the kitchen, so I took a seat next to Abel, who maneuvered to the head of the table, tapping away.

"Is she your girlfriend?" he asked.

I shook my head, my eyes fixed on the doorway to make sure we weren't overheard. "No. Just someone I work with."

Another pause as he tapped. "So, I can ask her out?"

My glare made him laugh.

"I knew it," the computerized voice said while Abel grinned up at me. *He thinks he's so fucking smart.*

Mum and Naomi brought the food in while Dad poured drinks for everyone, and when we were all set, Naomi sat on Abel's other side, as she'd promised.

In typical fashion for a dinner with my parents, the topics of conversation veered wildly across the board. One minute, they were talking about their new bird feeder and the next, the recent election in South Africa. Naomi seemed to take it all in stride, listening with interest and contributing when she could.

More interestingly, I noticed that she would stop and turn to Abel anytime he started composing a sentence on his talker. She never rushed him or looked away when it took too long. I was so busy watching her, trying to guess what might be going on in her head, that I hardly contributed to the conversation at all.

No one seemed to notice. Everyone's attention was firmly focused on our guest.

Usually, Mum or one of Abel's carers would help him eat, but on the rare occasions we had guests, he wanted to do it for himself. I grimaced as he struggled to spear a piece of chicken with his fork, the plate moving away from him as he tried to push it down. If I did it for him, he'd get annoyed with me for interfering; experience had taught me that.

However, as if it were the most natural thing in the world, Naomi reached over and steadied the plate, holding it in place so he could get the chicken himself. She never even looked at him as she did it, her attention on the story Dad was in the middle of telling, and Abel continued eating as if nothing had happened.

When our plates were empty, Naomi tried to stand up to help Mum clear them, but Mum insisted she stay put. "I'm going to bring in some cake for the boy's birthday. Stay there."

Naomi's eyes lit up. "Is it your chocolate cake? I've never tasted anything so good."

Mum's lips parted in surprise, her gaze immediately darting over to me. "Well, when did you have a chance to try that?"

Immediately, Naomi realized her mistake and attempted to backpedal. "Oh, Kane brought some to the office one time."

Mum clearly didn't buy it, but she didn't push. "Well, I'm afraid it's not the chocolate one this time, but I hope it's just as good."

Based on the way Naomi devoured the lemon drizzle cake Mum produced, I didn't think she had any complaints. "You should go on Bake Off, or write a recipe book, Mrs Davis. This is amazing."

Mum's beaming face couldn't have looked more delighted.

Meanwhile, Abel struggled with the crumbly cake, and again, Naomi took the initiative. "You really don't want to miss any of this. Can I help with the last bit?"

When he nodded, she took the fork from his hand and helped to scoop up the pieces that had fallen, making sure none got left behind. As she raised the fork to his lips, a twinge of jealousy hit me square in the chest.

*What the hell?*

After dessert, we moved into the lounge, where Naomi took a moment to look at the pictures around the room, including one of me and Abel at my university degree ceremony.

"That's one of my favourites," Dad commented.

"I don't know, I kind of like this one better." She pointed at the photo from a childhood birthday party where Abel shoved a piece of chocolate cake in my face right before Mum snapped the pic.

Bringing her there for dinner had felt so monumental when I decided to do it, but surprisingly, it now felt almost natural to see her sitting among the people I loved most in the world, laughing and talking as if she'd known them for years.

Eventually, however, the evening had to end, and I was the one to break it up. "We need to head back to the city."

Abel groaned and Dad's face fell. Honestly, I'd started to think they liked her better than me.

"Are you sure you can't stay over?" Mum tried to cajole Naomi. "I make a mean fry-up in the morning."

I interceded before she could turn up the pressure too much. "Neither of us has a change of clothes and you only have one guest room."

Looking almost as reluctant as the others to have the evening come to an end, Naomi got to her feet, leaning over to whisper something in Abel's ear as she passed. He gave her a somber nod in reply, leaving me wondering what on earth they might be planning.

When we finally made it to the front step, Mum gave Naomi another tight hug. "I hope we'll see you again."

"Thank you so much for having me," Naomi replied, carefully *not* making any promises.

My hug followed, and Mum pulled me down to whisper in my ear. "If that woman really isn't your girlfriend, you better fix that straight away. She's perfect for you."

There was nothing I could say to that, not with Naomi standing right there, so I settled for, "Goodbye, Mum."

They all waved from the door as we drove away, and I glanced over at Naomi, trying to guess what might be going through her head.

After the last time I introduced someone to Abel, I swore I'd never do it again. Had breaking that vow been worth it? Did she truly accept Abel as he was, or was she just better at hiding her feelings than the others had been?

And why did what she thought of us both mean so much to me?

# Chapter Thirteen



**~Naomi~**

Kane exhaled deeply as we drove away from his parent's house, as though we had made a lucky escape. Personally, I didn't think it had gone that badly. In fact, I enjoyed myself much more than I expected to. His family was normal and down-to-earth, so much so that I found myself wondering how they managed to produce someone as unique as Kane.

Abel came as the biggest surprise. Kane had never dropped even the slightest hint that he had a twin brother. Pauline never mentioned it either, making me think it must not be common knowledge. Heaven knew she'd told me enough other random facts about him that a brother definitely would have made the list if she knew about him.

Kane's love for his brother was clear, not only in the way he behaved around him that evening but in the other things that dropped into place the longer I had to think about it. His commitment to the foundation, for one. The *Abel* Foundation. And his desire to enable non-verbal people to communicate would help his own brother along with countless others. The cause was deeply personal.

So, why did he keep Abel's existence so quiet? Embarrassment didn't seem like the right answer, not when his eyes shone with pride every time Abel made me laugh.

I waited as long as I could, giving Kane space to start the conversation, but the longer we drove in silence, the heavier the air inside the car became.

Finally, I tried a safe opening. "Your family is nice."

Kane gave a small nod, his fingers tightening slightly on the wheel.

"I like your brother a lot," I added, watching his profile carefully. "He's very funny."

"For someone like him, you mean?"

His sharp tone caught me off guard. I blinked, recalibrating, but kept my voice even. "I mean funny, full-stop."

A muscle in his jaw twitched, followed by another long beat of silence.

When he glanced over at me, his eyes were dark and unreadable. "Aren't you going to ask me what's wrong with him?"

It felt like he'd just placed a landmine between us, waiting to see if I would step on it. I had no idea what he wanted me to say, but I could only answer honestly. "No, I'm not, because there's nothing wrong with him."

Kane's lips curled into a sneer. "Don't do that."

"Do what?"

"Pretend like you don't see his disability. You're not blind."

His bitterness seeped into every syllable, setting my nerves on edge. Instinct told me we were on dangerous ground, but I didn't fully understand how we ended up there.

I exhaled slowly, keeping my response measured. "Of course I see it. I just don't think there's anything wrong with it."

Apparently, that was the wrong answer.

Kane let out a sharp breath, his grip on the steering wheel going white-knuckled. "So, you think he's meant to be that way? That it's all he deserves?"

His voice cracked slightly on the last word and my stomach twisted.

"Don't put words in my mouth," I said softly. "I work with people with disabilities, remember? All kinds. I've seen people dealing with things no person should ever have to live with, and I've met plenty of people much more challenged than Abel is. I assume he has cerebral palsy?"

Kane swallowed hard and nodded.

"And the accessible room in your Norfolk house is for him? Why didn't you just tell me that when I asked?"

His jaw tensed and his Adam's apple bobbed as he struggled with the answer.

"People are uncomfortable with him," he said at last. "They don't want to be around him, and I don't want to expose him to that."

My chest ached at the way his voice tightened, the way he carefully framed his words to sound like logic rather than pain. But I saw it now: he wasn't hiding Abel, he was trying to protect him.

"Most people don't mean anything by it. They just aren't used to it. I know the looks that Liam used to get when he took Michelle places, and she was just a little girl. People are afraid of what they don't understand."

"That doesn't make it any better," he muttered.

"No, not really," I admitted. "But you can't let it bother you. Who cares what they think?"

"I care." His voice had grown gruff and he cleared his throat roughly. "They have no right to judge him. He's amazing. He could have done so much."

"He can still do great things," I offered, but Kane shook his head, not letting me finish.

"It's not the same. Don't you see? He could have been *me.* By the luck of the draw, I was born first, and the doctors didn't realize he didn't have enough oxygen. If they got him out first, he would have been okay. He would have..."

His voice caught mid-sentence. He stopped, swallowed, and tried to start again but the words wouldn't come. I took in the sheen in his eyes, the rapid blinking and the deep, uneven breaths and quickly realized this went far beyond frustration. This was grief, and it had very little to do with me.

He'd been carrying this around for a long, long time, and travelling seventy miles an hour in a car wasn't the place to address it.

I shifted slightly in my seat, peering at the sign in the distance for an upcoming exit. "Pull off here."

"No, I don't need..."

"Kane." I cut him off, my tone brooking no argument. "Take the exit."

He hesitated, grip tight on the wheel, but at the last second, he did as I asked. At the roundabout, he pulled into a petrol station and killed the engine. The moment the car fell silent, his shoulders fell too, his body seeming to cave in on itself.

I unbuckled my seatbelt and turned to face him fully. "I know you're not going to listen to me, but this was not your fault. It's not anyone's fault. Sometimes things just happen, and it sucks. It fucking sucks, but beating yourself up about it doesn't help anyone. It doesn't help Abel, it doesn't help your parents, and it definitely doesn't help you."

His lips squeezed tight together, like he wanted to argue with me but knew that if he did, he'd lose control.

I didn't care about that. I wanted him to let it out, since he'd clearly been keeping it bottled up for far too long. "What? Tell me what you're thinking."

"It *is* my fault. It should have been me."

My heart cracked beneath the certainty in his words and the pain in his tone. Tears sprang to my eyes as I shook my head as firmly as I could. "That wouldn't have been any better."

"For him, it would have been." His face began to crumple in front of me and my chest tightened to the point of pain. "I work as hard as I can to take advantage of the chances he never had. I try to live enough for the both of us. But it's never enough. It will never *be* enough."

His next breath came out ragged, and I felt the moment he gave up fighting it. I immediately reached for him, wrapping my arms around him before he could decide to push me away.

In the end, he didn't even try. His face pressed against my shoulder, his arms locked around my waist, and his entire body shook with deep, silent tremors while tears streamed silently down my face.

I didn't say anything. Didn't try to tell him it was okay, because it wasn't.

Although his brother was still alive, he grieved for the person Abel might have been and the future he would never have. And beneath all of it, guilt circled like a shark drawn by the scent of blood, the kind of guilt that could eat a person alive.

Mix that together with a need to protect his brother from a world that could be casually cruel at the best of times, and suddenly, so many things about Kane made sense. The need for control. The walls he put up. The devotion to his work.

I understood it all within that silent embrace, and I simply held him because no words could fix it. No logic could erase the weight of what he'd carried for so long.

I held him because I knew how he felt, and because I'd been there before.

I'd held Liam after Michelle's death, felt the weight of his guilt, and no matter how hard I tried, I couldn't help him. Maybe I wouldn't be able to help Kane either, but now that he'd finally let me in, I no longer wanted to walk away.

Maybe we both needed to heal, and maybe, together, we might be able to figure it out.

**~Kane~**

I couldn't remember the last time I cried. And the last time I cried *in front of someone?* Not since I was a boy. But when Naomi made me pull over, when she encouraged me to say things out loud I usually kept buried deep inside, it felt like a dam broke.

I should have been embarrassed, but when we finally pulled away from each other, I saw her tear-streaked cheeks, and rather than shame, a strange sense of calm settled over me. She wasn't judging me or humouring me. Somehow, she felt it too, and for the first time in a very long time, I didn't feel quite so alone.

Reaching into the glove box, I found some tissues and handed a couple to her before scrubbing roughly at my face with one of my own. Clearing my throat, I turned the car back on, pressing my palms once more into my eyes to ease the sting there.

"Are you okay to drive?" Naomi asked softly.

"I'm alright. It's getting late, we should keep going."

She didn't argue, and we drove in silence for a few minutes, the weight of what just happened resting between us but not in an uncomfortable way. When she reached over and placed her hand on my thigh, the soothing warmth of it simply felt... right.

So, I started talking. Unprompted. Unscripted. From the heart and whatever popped into my head.

"This is why I hate my birthday. It feels wrong to celebrate the day I was born, the day *we* were born, when it ruined Abel's life."

"Even when you were younger?" she asked softly.

"Especially then. Mum used to have joint birthday parties for us but no one ever wanted to come. Their parents would make them, but I could tell they didn't want to be there because they didn't feel comfortable around him. That they didn't see him as being the same as them."

Naomi shifted in her seat so her body angled towards me more, giving me her full attention. Thankfully, she left her hand on my leg, since I liked it there.

"Did you go to the same school?"

"Yeah. There was a special school in the next town over but Mum and Dad weren't impressed when they visited. People assume Abel has learning difficulties because he can't speak, but he doesn't. He's smarter than a lot of kids I went to school with. So, they pushed for him to be at school with me, which meant I heard the way people talked about him. Maybe it's better now, but twenty years ago, kids were assholes."

"I don't think it's all that different now, unfortunately," she mused. "What did you do when you heard them talking?"

I huffed out a scornful laugh. "Mum told me to ignore it but of course, I didn't. I almost got excluded for punching a kid in the face once. Knocked out two of his teeth."

Naomi winced, but I caught a glimpse of the smile she tried to hide. "He was lucky to have you."

The word rubbed me the wrong way. "He's never been lucky a day in his life."

She tensed, as if she anticipated another argument, but I was done fighting for that night. I offered an olive branch instead.

"But I know what you mean. I tried to look out for him. I never told him about the girl he had a crush on in sixth form who I caught doing an imitation of him behind his back."

Naomi swore under her breath, and I had to smile.

Buoyed by her support, I told her something I'd never told anyone before.

"The last time I dated someone seriously was in university."

"Oxford?" she guessed.

"Cambridge."

"Naturally." She flashed me a teasing grin to lighten the mood, as if sensing what I had to say next would bring it down again. "What happened?"

"We were together for over a year before I brought her home to meet my family. Her family lived closer and went out more, so we always ended up with them, but when we graduated, we started talking about moving in together in the city, and I finally felt ready for her to meet Abel. I felt I knew her well enough by then to predict how it would go."

"And how did it go?" Her words were so soft, I could barely hear them over the engine's hum.

"I thought I'd prepared her. I told her about him, what he could and couldn't do, but when she met him, she completely withdrew. She didn't get too close to him, wouldn't be alone in a room with him. She barely said a word on the drive home, and two days later, she broke up with me. Said she didn't want to have kids that would end up like him."

"Seriously?" Outrage filled Naomi's voice, strong and sharp. "She didn't know CP isn't genetic?"

"I don't know what she thought, honestly, but the fact that she looked at the most wonderful person I've ever met and saw him as something to be feared made her so ugly to me, I was glad to never see her again."

The indignation and horror I felt that day tightened my chest again, all these years later.

"I can't decide if I hope she has a child with additional needs, so she has to learn the truth for herself, or if I hope she never does because I wouldn't wish that kind of parent on anyone. You know she's one of those people who would say they don't care whether their child is a boy or a girl, as long as it's healthy. But what if it fucking isn't healthy? Doesn't that mean she wouldn't want it?"

My anger built with each word, and Naomi squeezed my thigh, offering a silent show of support. I knew I didn't need to explain any of this to her, but it felt important to say it anyway.

"My dad never loved Abel any less than he loved me, and I'll love my own kids no matter what. I can't be with someone who feels otherwise, and the fact that I couldn't tell she was that kind of person, that I spent a year with her and didn't pick up on it, made me doubt my own senses. It made me wonder if the kind of person I would actually want to be with even existed."

"So, you closed yourself off," she guessed, phrasing it not as a question but as a statement. "You stopped giving people the chance to disappoint you."

She summed it even better than I could have. "Pretty much. People fucking suck."

Her soft laugh didn't carry much humour in it. "Yeah, they really do sometimes."Discussing my past hadn't been easy, but for the first time since that breakup, I didn't feel like I had to keep my guard up. Naomi didn't recoil from anything I said. She didn't pity me. She simply listened. She sympathized. She *stayed.*

Somehow, distracted by our conversation, we'd arrived back in the city almost without me realizing it. It didn't take long to reach Naomi's flat. When I pulled up outside it, leaving the car idling, she glanced up at the house but didn't make any move to get out of the car.

"It's pretty late. Do you want to stay here tonight?"

Hope flickered in my chest as my eyes met hers. With everything else that happened that night, I'd almost forgotten this whole day started with me trying to make amends for what happened with Natalie.

"Does this mean our arrangement is back on?"

She quickly shook her head. "No. I'm done with that."

*Oh.* The disappointment that crushed down on me nearly took my breath away.

"However."

Like I was on a roller coaster, my spirits lifted again. "However?"

"You can still come in if you want to. Maybe we can come to a new kind of arrangement."

Reading between the lines, I thought I understood. She was inviting me in, not just to be her bed, but to her life. Not a contract, but a relationship, and though not even a month ago, I would have run at the sound of that, I didn't want to anymore.

I just wanted her.

When I reached over to turn the car off, Naomi's eyes sparkled with both relief and excitement.

Did she honestly think I'd say no? She clearly had no idea just how much this night had meant to me?

Inside, we barely got the door locked before we were wrapped around each other. I inhaled her kiss like someone who'd been deprived of oxygen, and she devoured me just as hungrily. Somehow, knowing we were doing this not because either of us had to made it feel new. Not that either of us had required much coercion in the first place, but knowing that she was choosing to be with me after seeing me at such a low point, more emotionally vulnerable than I'd let myself be with anyone in years, gave every kiss and caress new meaning.

Something profound had shifted between us, and I knew she felt it too.

We stumbled towards the bedroom, shedding our clothing along the way. Fully naked, Naomi lay down on the bed, arms beckoning me to join her, and I'd never seen anything more irresistible in my entire life.

And I didn't resist her. My body covered hers, fingers intertwining as I kissed her lips, her neck, her breasts. I didn't let go of her hands as her legs wrapped around me and my cock found her entrance, pushing into her with no guidance. Her wet core welcomed me eagerly, our hands squeezing and clutching each other as I rocked within her. Slow and intimate, it had never felt exactly like this before, and I never wanted it to end.

"Kane," she moaned as I nuzzled into her neck, sucking and licking it as her hips bucked against mine, drawing me in deeper.

"Tell me," I grunted back. "Tell me how it feels."

"It feels..." she trailed off on a gasp, her breath stuttering. "Like you were made to be inside me."

I groaned in appreciation. "Fuck, yes. I love being inside you. I love the way you *feel* from the inside. I love..."

I trailed off as it hit me that the next word on my lips was about to be *you*.

I couldn't say that now, during sex. It would sound cheap, and I didn't want it to come across that way.

But to my very great surprise, I found that the idea of saying it to her didn't scare me as much as it should have.

"Yes?" she prompted breathlessly, reminding me that I hadn't finished my sentence.

"I love the way it feels when you come with me inside you," I told her instead, pushing harder into her with each phrase. Her moans spurred me on even more, thrusting into her even faster, pleasure building for both of us, until, with one final gasp of my name, she came.

Her body clenched around me and I shuddered into the most intense orgasm I'd ever had.

We stayed there, locked together, hands still linked, until our breathing returned to normal and the world finally seemed steady again. And as reality returned, something settled inside me, an acknowledgement that I was *allowed* to want this.

With one final kiss, I released her and rolled over onto my back, bumping into the wall next to me with a solid thud. "You have *got* to get a bigger bed," I groaned.

Naomi simply laughed, and when she returned to the bed after cleaning up, she nestled in beside me as if it were the most natural thing in the world, her fingers lightly stroking my chest until I fell asleep.

# Chapter Fourteen

~**Naomi**~

Kane's arm was draped over my waist when I woke in the morning. I lay there for a moment, my back to his chest, feeling the steady rise and fall of his breath. It would be so easy to stay like this, to close my eyes and pretend we were just another couple waking up together, no history and no complications.

But that had never been who we were.

Carefully, I eased out from under his arm and tiptoed to the bathroom, muffling a yawn. There was no way to silence the toilet flushing, though, or the gasp I let out when I caught sight of my reflection. A large, purplish-red love mark bloomed on my neck.

*Damn it.* Looked like I'd be wearing turtlenecks all week.

My first instinct was irritation, until I thought back to how good it had felt, the way his mouth had burned over my skin, marking me as his. A slow heat unfurled in my belly as the memory played out.

Maybe I didn't mind so much after all.

The sex had been incredible, as always. Maybe even more so than usual because, for once, it hadn't come with any unspoken expectations or power plays. Last night, I'd asked him to stay simply because I *wanted* to, and he had stayed for the same reason.

That was new.

I wasn't naive enough to believe it meant Kane had suddenly abandoned his playboy ways. And I wasn't entirely sure I was ready to be in a relationship, especially not with someone as volatile as him.

But I liked him. More than I probably should.

I liked the way he was starting to let me see the man beneath the arrogance, the one who carried more weight on his shoulders than he let on. The more he opened up, the more I suspected we might be exactly what the other needed, at least for now.

How long that would last, I had no idea, but I didn't want to overthink it.

*One step at a time, Naomi.*

When I slipped back into the bedroom, Kane had rolled onto his stomach, one arm sprawled over my side of the bed. I grabbed a long T-shirt and found my phone in the trousers I'd discarded last night.

As I hoped, a message from Abel was waiting. I slipped him my number as we left the night before, hoping we could keep in touch.

> Just checking in to make sure you got home okay and my brother isn't holding you somewhere against your will.

I chuckled softly as I sat down at the dining table to reply.

> Yes, and no. Does he seem like the kidnapping type to you?

> Definitely. The last woman he brought home was never seen again. I'd be careful if I were you.

My chest tightened as I read the message, remembering what Kane told me the night before. Abel obviously meant it as a joke, which meant he didn't know the reason Kane and his girlfriend broke up. I wondered if he had any idea how much his brother tried to protect him, and how much he beat himself up for his failings.

> You better hope he's not a criminal since you share the same DNA. You might find yourself accused of all kinds of things!

I was still smiling when the floor creaked in front of me, and I glanced up to see Kane standing in the doorway, sleepy-eyed and gloriously, completely naked. My thighs clenched at the sight of him.

"Who are you texting that's making you smile like that?" he mumbled.

"Jealous?" I teased, setting my phone down.

His lips curved. "Not when you're looking at me like that."

He stretched out his arms, the movement shifting the lines of his toned body in ways that made my mouth dry.

"How did you sleep?" I asked, attempting to keep my mind off the way his muscles flexed.

He rolled his head from side to side. "Not bad, considering the accommodations."

"I'm sorry I didn't buy my bed with you in mind."

"You *should* be." His lazy grin made my stomach flip. "We'll stay at my place tonight."

It wasn't a question, and before I could respond, he turned and walked into the bathroom, missing the way my mouth fell open.

I could have protested. I probably *should* have protested, but the truth was, I wanted to go, so why fight it?

I got dressed while Kane showered, slipping into a dress I knew he'd like. My shower wasn't made for two, but as I listened to the water running, I found myself thinking about the last time we'd shared one at his place.

Maybe I'd convince him to take another later.

By the time he joined me in the kitchen, he was back in the previous day's clothes, his eyes darkening when he saw what I was wearing.

At this rate, we were never going to make it out of my flat.

"Coffee or tea?" I asked, attempting to distract him.

"Why don't we go out somewhere?" he suggested. "A late breakfast?"

When I blinked at him in surprise, his lips twisted into a smirk.

"If our arrangement's over, that means your stipulation about not being seen in public no longer applies, right?"

Well, he had me there. I still didn't love the idea of ending up in the gossip pages, but he wasn't fighting me on the end of our agreement, so I could make a few compromises too.

"There's a place around the corner that does a great full English. Nothing fancy, but it's good."

"Sounds perfect." He pressed a kiss to my temple before heading to the door, throwing me off-balance yet again.

Outside, I shivered against the spring morning air. The sunshine through my window had been deceptive and it felt colder than it looked out. Kane casually wrapped an arm around me to warm me up, and as we settled in at the cafe to eat our breakfast, he pulled out his phone.

"Do you have any annual leave left for this year?"

"A bit." More like all of it, actually, but he didn't need to know that. I'd needed the distraction of work to keep myself going, but after the work trip to Rome and our weekend in Norfolk, taking some time off actually sounded kind of appealing. "Why?"

"I've got a busy week, but if I wrap things up, I could free some time next week." He glanced up. "Thought we could go somewhere."

'Somewhere'? With him? I had no idea what he was talking about and my confusion must have shown on my face because his trademark smirk settled across his face.

"I told you I'd make it up to you, remember?"

*Make it up to me.* So, this was about settling a debt between us? One last hurrah? A final trip together before we both moved on with our lives?

I swallowed down the sudden tightness in my throat. "That sounds nice. What are you thinking? Back to Norfolk?"

The memory of his kitchen table there sent a flush of heat through my body and from the way his lips curled, I suspected he might be thinking of it too. "No, I think somewhere warmer. I'll do some checking."

"Nothing too crazy," I warned. "I'll pay for my flight and hotel..."

"Can you take the whole week?" he interrupted.

*A whole week.* A proper holiday, with a man I couldn't seem to get enough of.

It sounded dangerously appealing.

"I'll check with my boss tomorrow, but tentatively, yes, I can make that work."

His eyes flickered with something unreadable before he nodded and put his phone away.

Once we finished eating, we went for a walk in Ealing Common since the sun had grown a bit warmer, then returned to my flat to get back into his car for the ride to his place, even though he still hadn't actually *asked* me if I wanted to go.

After parking in the underground garage at his building, Kane pulled me towards the stairs rather than the lift. "Let's go visit my office first. Maybe you can actually figure out what I do there."

I wrinkled my nose at his teasing, making him laugh. "Will anyone be there on a Sunday?"

"Only security. I have a feeling they'll let me in."

"I actually hope they don't, just so you stop being so smug about it."

We laughed and chatted on the short walk to his office building, one of the many high-rise buildings scattered around Canary Wharf. His company occupied the 16th floor, with a sleek, modern office that felt very similar to his flat.

"Did you use the same interior designer for both places?" I had to ask.

He shrugged. "When you find something that works, why change it?"

The whole floor impressed me, but when we got to his personal office, the whole of our charity offices could have fit inside it.

"This is excessive, just so you know," I had to point out before gesturing to his chair. "Can I try it out?"

"Go ahead." He stayed by the door, smiling as I sank down into the comfortable leather and reclined.

With my hands behind my head, I crossed my feet on top of his desk. "How do I look?"

Rather than answering, he turned around and drew the blinds before locking the door.

My blood instantly began to thrum in my veins, anticipation building as I lowered my feet back to the floor. "Why do I feel like I've just been called to the headmaster's office?"

Kane licked his lips as he stalked towards me. "If your headmaster ever did the kinds of things I'm about to do to you over this desk, he deserves to be locked up."

"Actually, *she* never…"

A gasp eclipsed the end of my sentence when he reached me and yanked me firmly off his chair, pushing me up against the edge of his desk as he tugged up the bottom of my dress.

*Fuck, yes.*

My body throbbed for him as one hand kneaded my ass, the other busy with pulling down his zip. He didn't even bother to take my panties off, simply pushing them to the side to slide his fingers inside me. When he found me wet, he muttered a soft curse of his own.

"Every fucking time, Naomi. You're so ready for me."

"Always," I had to agree.

His fingers withdrew, drawing a whine from deep in my throat, but the emptiness didn't last long. His cock took their place, filling me harder and fuller than his hand ever could.

This was nothing like our tender lovemaking the night before. Rough and urgent, he thrust into me over and over. My nails clawed at the surface of his desk, my moans mingling with his grunts as we both gave into this powerful, primal need.

"Fuck, Kane," I gasped, barely able to speak as he rammed into me. My arms shook from the strain of holding my position. "I need…"

"I know," he cut me off, biting down gently onto my shoulder as one hand reached around to find my clit. The friction, the passion, the all-encompassing desire crescendoed into a shattering orgasm that had my body buckling within his iron grip.

With one last muttered gasp of my name, Kane's thrusting stuttered and his cock pulsed inside me, his hold only loosening when all the shuddering stopped.

*Holy fuck.*

Just when I thought it couldn't get any better, he pulled *that* out of the bag.

With a deep exhale, Kane sank back into his chair, drawing me down onto his lap, my back still pressed against his front. His lips traced softly over the place he'd bitten, his breath a whisper against my skin.

"Now I can think about that all week when I'm stuck in meetings at this desk," he whispered. "I'm going to spend the whole week hard."

My chest shook with laughter as he held me tight against him. "Is that the first time you've done something like that in here?"

His hesitation was all the answer I needed, and I quickly remembered what he'd said about hooking up with his assistant. Of *course* it wasn't his first time. I knew exactly what kind of man Kane Davis was; he'd never tried to hide it.

I pulled myself to my feet, adjusted my dress and tucked my hair behind my ear, my body still thrumming with the memory of him.

"I'm getting kind of hungry. Since you probably aren't planning to cook, we should get going and put an order in."

Kane didn't move. "Naomi, I don't want you to think..."

"I don't think anything," I quickly assured him, turning back to flash him a bright smile. "That was fun and I like being able to picture where you work. Thank you for bringing me here."

He hesitated, eyes on me like he still wanted to say something, but when my smile held firm, he nodded to himself as he stood back up, tucked his cock back into his trousers, and led the way back out of his office.

**~Kane~**

Naomi's hand nestled in mine as we walked back to my flat, her grip warm and steady. She pointed out little details on the street as we went: quirky signs, a flower growing between cracks in the pavement, the way the light hit a shop window just right. Things I'd never noticed despite walking this route a thousand times before.

She didn't seem upset, and weeks ago, she'd promised to tell me if she was. But I'd felt the way her body stiffened in my office when she realized I'd definitely fucked around there before. The tension was brief, barely noticeable, but it lingered in my mind. For the first time, I regretted some of those encounters with women whose names I'd long since forgotten.

I hadn't let anyone get close since breaking up with my university girlfriend. Selling my first company within six months of graduating had changed everything. That kind of money brought a revolving door of people happy to be with me without actually knowing me. If they started asking too many questions, I moved on. Some of them were probably good people, but I never stuck around long enough to find out.

With Naomi, it was different.

I didn't know exactly what changed that night in Rome, but I didn't want to keep pretending nothing had. She'd become special to me, and while there might have been other women over my desk in the past, she was the only one I wanted to remember.

How the hell was I supposed to tell her that? I didn't have a fucking clue, but taking her away for a week seemed like a good place to start. A week alone, away from distractions, might give us the time and space to figure out what this was. What *we* were.

All I really knew for certain was that I didn't want to let her go.

In the lobby, Naomi waved at the doorman. "Hi, Tom."

He beamed back at her. "Good evening, Naomi. Thank you again for that cake the other night, it went a treat with my tea."

"That shop is my favourite," she replied. "Though I think I like the caramel ones even better than the chocolate. What's your request next time I go?"

"Well, you don't need to, but I would never say no to anything with lemon."

My eyes volleyed between the two of them, trying to process what was happening. When did they become so chummy? I'd lived there for years and had never had a conversation with him that didn't consist of me asking him to do something for me.

"Got it," she assured him. "Have a good night."

"You too." At last, he turned to me, his professional mask slipping back into place. "Mr Davis."

I followed Naomi into the lift, shaking my head. "Do you make friends with everyone you meet?"

She'd completely won over my entire family the night before, based on the texts Mum sent me earlier, and now, I found out she'd been buying my doorman cakes.

She tsked at me. "It costs nothing to be kind, and even if it did cost something, you could afford it. Maybe you should try making friends a little more often."

"I made friends with you," I reminded her, pressing her back against the lift wall as my lips found hers in a lingering, hungry kiss.

When dinner arrived, we ate at the island in the kitchen while I tried to explain some of the deals I was working on over the coming week. Though she tried her best to follow along, I could see the exact moment her eyes began to glaze over. I switched to stories about my family instead, and those kept her much more entertained.

"Where does your family live?" I asked, realizing I had no idea.

"Devon." She licked her spoon clean from the ice cream I'd ordered from dessert. Naomi definitely had a sweet tooth, much more than I did, and I loved the way her whole face softened in pleasure over something so simple. "Mum and Dad had me quite late in life so they're retired now, enjoying the quiet, coastal life."

"Brothers or sisters?"

"Nope. Only me."

*Huh.* Maybe that explained why she made friends everywhere she went, since she was almost on her own in the world. Whereas I always had my tight-knit family to fall back on and had never felt I needed more than that.

After dinner, Naomi suggested a shower, and even though I'd had one that morning at her flat, I was happy to oblige. Especially since she was much more interested in getting dirty than getting clean.

By the time we climbed into bed together, sated and sleepy, I couldn't remember a day where I'd felt quite so comfortable in my own skin. Naomi lay on her side, her breathing slowing into something steady and familiar.

In just under a month, this woman had carved out a place for herself in my home, in my head, in my fucking bloodstream.

All that was left was my heart, and its defenses were getting weaker every day.

**~Naomi~**

As usual, I woke up before Kane. His alarm was set for 7:30, but I needed to leave before that, so I got ready as quietly as possible and left him a note to say goodbye.

The thought of not seeing him all week left me feeling deflated, but the promise of our upcoming holiday made it easier to bear. As my body bumped and jostled with the rhythm of the tube carriage, my mind wandered to... other movements. Specifically, how many times we could have sex in a day if we had nothing else to do. Kane *always* seemed up for it. I was beginning to wonder if the man was even human.

No matter how the trip ended, if he truly intended it to be the farewell tour he'd hinted at the day before, at least we'd make some memories.

I resolved to do my best to live in the moment and enjoy it for what it was.

My mind still lingered on thoughts of tropical beaches and tangled sheets when I walked into the office, only to be met with an eruption of applause.

I jolted to a stop, glancing behind me in case someone important had arrived after me, but the doorway was empty. They were clapping for... me?

*What the hell?*

Jane stepped forward first, hands clasped in delight, eyes shining. "You're a miracle worker, Naomi. We're so lucky to have you."

I looked to Pauline, searching for context, but she beamed back at me just as brightly.

"I am?"

Jane laughed, dabbing at her eyes. "Mr Davis rang this morning with his additional donation."

*Oh.* A wave of relief hit me as understanding finally dawned.

During our argument on Friday, I told him I expected the donation to be made as soon as possible. It hadn't come up again since, but this was clear proof that our agreement was well and truly over. Kane was tying up loose ends so we could both move on.

"He really wanted to make sure the project got funded," I said, my own excitement beginning to match the energy radiating off my colleagues. "I'm so happy it worked out."

"Well, it'll pay for the project *and* a lot more besides," Jane exclaimed. "For the first time in the charity's history, we have more money than we know what to do with! Not that that'll last long, of course. I already have some ideas."

Laughter rippled through the room, but something about her words didn't sit right with me. There shouldn't have been any money left over. We'd only ever discussed the additional funding needed for the project.

"Exactly how much did he donate?" I asked, a strange sense of unease creeping in.

Pauline let out a squeal. "As if you don't know!" She was practically vibrating with excitement.

Jane's smile faltered slightly when I didn't react the way she expected. "Wait. You really don't know?"

I shook my head. "We discussed a number, but perhaps it wasn't the final one."

Jane took a breath, as if bracing herself before delivering the punch-line. "Was that number a million pounds?"

I nearly choked. "*Million?*" The word came out strangled. "He donated a *million* pounds?"

Jane nodded furiously, and the room burst into renewed cheers.

I forced a smile, but inside, I was reeling. Why would he do that? Guilt? A final grand gesture before walking away? The amount he originally offered was already more than fair, but this went beyond generosity.

Jane launched into her plans for the extra funds, and while I tried to stay present, my mind kept circling the same question.

What was Kane playing at now?

It took well over an hour before the giddiness in the office began to settle and we returned to work. I collapsed into my chair, staring blankly at my computer screen for several minutes before pulling out my phone.

> Everyone is so excited. We can't believe it. I don't really know what to say.

I didn't expect a quick reply since he'd warned me how busy his week would be, but only a few minutes later, my phone buzzed.

> You don't need to say anything. The charity deserves it, I hope it helps. Did you get the time off for next week?

The donation still didn't make sense, but I pushed it aside for now.

> Not yet. I'll ask now.

Given Jane's current state of euphoria, I probably could have asked for the next year off and she would have agreed. I was back at my desk in under a minute.

It's approved.

Great. Natalie will send you some places to choose from.

The idea of his assistant arranging our holiday, now that I knew the precise nature of their relationship, grated on me, but I also knew just how busy he was. *Live in the moment,* I reminded myself. No stressing about the future *or* the past.

Later that afternoon, I received a message from her with a few resort options in the Algarve, the Canaries, and Turkey. No mention of the compromising situation I found her and Kane in, and definitely no apology, not that I really expected one.

All the trips were within a reasonable budget, thankfully. Apparently, he *had* heard me about paying my own way after all.

Lanzarote looks perfect. Should I send the money to you? What about the flight?

You can settle everything with Mr Davis after the trip. He said not to worry about it for now.

*Mr Davis.* So professional. Did she call him that when they were fucking, I wondered?

Jealousy curled in my stomach but I forced myself to ignore it. Soon, I'd be as bad as Kane, getting jealous over someone who wasn't really mine in the first place.

That night, I went through the resort pictures again, imagining us curled up together in bed or lounging by the pool. Although, as soon as I imagined Kane in his swimming trunks, my thoughts immediately drifted to the bedroom again. If this was going to be the last week we spent together, I wanted to make sure I got my fill of him.

Kane himself texted me before bed.

> Lanzarote's a good choice. Don't worry about packing too much. Bring your passport, toiletries, and some shoes. I'll take care of the rest.

I eyed the message suspiciously before replying.

> What are you up to?

> Just have some things I want to see you in. It's completely selfish, I assure you.

The drooling emoji he added made me laugh out loud, and all the mixed feelings from earlier in the day - the uneasiness around his donation and the jealousy over Natalie - faded away.

All week, he continued to text me at regular intervals. Nothing big, just checking in or sharing random thoughts, but it felt different to how things were before. More open. More willing to let me in.

The visit with his family and our talk afterwards definitely seemed to have changed things for the better, and with each message that made me smile, I wished a little more that it didn't have to end at all.

I had to let my parents and friends know about my holiday, but I kept things intentionally vague, sending out a message en masse. "I'm going away with a man, but it's really new and I don't know how long he'll be around."

The responses I got were all filled with genuine delight.

"I'm so happy to hear you're putting yourself out there, Naomi."

"You deserve to have some fun. Have the best time!"

"I thought something seemed different about you lately. I hope he's a good one."

The one person I couldn't fool was Pauline. "It's Kane Davis, isn't it?" she asked gleefully when the others were all out at lunch one day. "I had a feeling about you two."

Finally, Friday arrived, and I showed up to the airport with my small carry-on bag, hoping Kane hadn't forgotten his promise to bring clothes for me. What if it was some kind of trick so I wouldn't have anything to wear and we'd have to spend the whole week inside the hotel room?

Actually, that didn't sound all that bad.

However, I didn't have to worry. When I got to the check-in counter, I spotted him immediately, standing next to two matching suitcases. I wasn't the only one who noticed him either. More than a few travelers gave him appreciative glances, but the moment he saw me, his focus sharpened. His smile was slow, lazy, and confident, an expression that sent a pleasant hum through my veins.

"Now, there's a sight for sore eyes." He wrapped his arms around me, dropping a light kiss on my lips without a care for the people around us. "Looking forward to this?"

Flushing under the public display of affection, I nodded. "It's been a long time since I went away just for fun."

"Me too."

Back in Norfolk, when we talked about travelling, he said his trips were always for work.

"Do you need to do some work while we're away?"

I braced for the answer, half-expecting him to say he'd need a few hours each day for calls.

Instead, he shook his head. "I told everyone I'm off the grid. Not checking my phone at all. Come on, let's get going."

He handed me one of the wheelie suitcases so he could grab my hand with his free one, and pulled me towards the check-in counter. The *first class* check-in counter.

"What are you doing?" I whispered. "Our seats are in economy."

Kane seemed unbothered. "I'm a frequent flyer so I get some perks. Priority check-in is one of them."

Sure enough, the woman at the counter didn't bat an eye when she took our passports and luggage. We also got put through a priority queue at security, and once inside, Kane steered us towards the airport lounge with huge, comfortable armchairs and a buffet of food and drink.

I'd never seen *this* part of the airport before. "All this is part of your perks?"

He nodded, shooting me a sly smirk. "There's even a shower in the back if you want to pass the time together that way."

The dirty look I gave him only made him laugh.

We helped ourselves to some food from the buffet, and no sooner had we finished eating than a man in a smart uniform approached. "Mr Davis, Ms Law, your flight is ready to board."

We were escorted straight to our gate, and I wanted to apologize to everyone waiting in the queue as the man marched us straight to the front.

Kane held out his phone with our boarding passes for the gate agent while I looked back at the waiting crowd, frowning as something caught my attention. There were an awful lot of Asian passengers on this flight. Far more than I would expect for one travelling between Britain and the Canary Islands.

Taking a step back, my eyes darted up to the departure screen above the gate.

*Hang on a minute.*

"Kane? I think we're at the wrong gate."

"Hmmm?" He didn't turn around as he passed over our passports.

"This flight isn't going to Lanzarote," I tried again. Why did the man from the lounge bring us here? Why wasn't the gate agent saying something?

With our passports back in hand, Kane returned his phone to his pocket and looked back at me over his shoulder, smug self-satisfaction written all over his face. "Isn't it?"

The penny finally dropped. No one had made any mistake, except for me in thinking that Kane had respected my request to book a trip I could afford.

Even though I already knew the answer, I asked him anyway: "Why does it say the flight is going to Bangkok?"

# Chapter Fifteen

~**Kane**~

Somehow, I managed to keep a straight face when Naomi asked why the flight board said Bangkok.

"Because it's helpful for the passengers to know where the plane is going."

She smacked my arm, which, admittedly, I deserved.

"What did you do?" she demanded as I began to walk down the bridge leading to the airplane.

"You told me in Norfolk that if you could go anywhere in the world, you'd choose Thailand," I reminded her. "So, we're going to Thailand."

"But... you can't just... you said..." she sputtered, trying to keep up with me and lodge her complaint at the same time. "You sent me the options and I said Lanzarote. You said it was a good idea!"

"Because I knew you would argue with me if I suggested this. Now, you have no choice but to let me make your dreams come true."

Better to ask for forgiveness than permission, I always thought.

"That's not true," she tried to claim as we stepped on board the plane. When the flight attendant saw our seats, her smile brightened and she directed us to the front of the plane.

"What's not true? That you would have argued or that you have no choice?"

Naomi didn't reply. Her steps had slowed to a full stop when we reached the first class pods, her mouth hanging open in surprise.

I pointed to her seat. "You're in this one."

Still looking stunned, she sank down into her seat while I put my carry-on bag away and took off my suit jacket. By the time I took my seat and smiled over at her, I expected her excitement to kick in.

Instead, her frown had deepened. "Kane, I can't afford this."

"I don't expect you to pay for it. I want to treat you. It's all taken care of."

I'd never met a woman who wouldn't happily spend my money, but Naomi looked the opposite of happy as she continued to argue. "You should have asked me."

"I wanted it to be a surprise."

I truly didn't understand her reaction. This was a much better trip than the one she'd chosen.

"A surprise," she repeated slowly. "Just like my clothes for this trip. And the donation to the charity?"

What did the donation have to do with anything? "That was me keeping up my end of the deal."

"No, our deal was for £400,000. Not a million pounds."

The edge in her tone rubbed against my already raw nerves. I didn't need a big show of gratitude, but making it sound like I'd done something wrong pissed me off. "You can't find a use for it?"

"That's not the point. I don't like..."

She trailed off there, but I needed to hear the end of that sentence. "Don't like what?"

From the way her lips pursed, I could tell I wouldn't like what she said next, and I was right.

"I don't like feeling like you're trying to buy me."

For a long moment, those words hung in the air between us, weighing down on my shoulders and slowing the heavy thud of my heart.

"That's not what I'm doing."

"Isn't it?" Her gaze was steady and searching. "Isn't this just another way for you to keep control? To get me to do whatever you want me to do?"

My jaw clenched. That wasn't fair.

"It's controlling to help kids who need treatment? Or give you a *nice* holiday instead of a week in some cheap, crappy hotel?" I snapped. "It's my money. If you want to tell me what I can or can't do with it, maybe that's *your* control issue."

The moment the words left my mouth, I regretted them.

The last trace of excitement disappeared from her eyes and she inhaled sharply, her expression closing off. "I've been looking forward to that 'cheap, crappy hotel' all week. I thought it would be great because I'd be there with you. But I guess your enjoyment is really all that matters."

Before I could reply to that, she got up and walked back down the aisle, speaking to one of the flight attendants who pointed her to the toilet. Frustration boiled over and I slammed my fist against the armrest. This wasn't how I planned for any of this to go.

I thought she'd be thrilled at the change in destination and the unexpected luxury. And why wouldn't she be over the moon about the extra money I donated?

Even after a month of getting to know her, there were things I just didn't understand.

Maybe I needed to make more of an effort to figure them out.

Taking a breath to exhale my frustration, I tried to put myself in her shoes. Yes, this trip was objectively better than the one she planned, but while she thought we were making plans together, I took over. Although my intentions were good, they were still *mine*, and she wanted a partnership.

Taking another person's opinions into consideration would be a change for me, but when it came to Naomi, I was willing to try.

By the time she returned to her seat, the plane was filling up fast, so I leaned over to her, hands up in surrender. "If you really want to go to Lanzarote instead, we can go. I'll find a flight, and I'm sure that hotel will still have some rooms left. I can't imagine there are *that* many people who want to go there."

Naomi's eyes rolled, but I could see the beginnings of a smile pulling at her lips. "You're so ridiculously arrogant."

"I know." I flashed her a smile that doubled as a peace offering. "Do you want to go? We'll have to get off before they close the doors."

She glanced back over her shoulder, as if she were really considering it, but ultimately, she shook her head. "You've already paid for all this. It would be a waste not to use it. But don't go booking any ridiculous excursions without talking to me first, okay?"

"Got it. Cancel the skydiving."

I pretended to make a note on an imaginary notepad, and Naomi smacked my arm, a real smile breaking through.

"I mean it. I don't need you to spend a ton of money to have a good time. I'm here because I want to be, not because of any agreement and not because of your money. I want to spend time with *you*. The rest is background."

Something in my chest pulled taut at those words, a feeling I couldn't quite explain. I did my best to cover the unexpected reaction by making a joke. "So, the next time I want to surprise you, I should ask you first?"

She wrinkled her nose at me. "Exactly. Now, what the heck is all this stuff for?"

She gestured at the pod around her, and we spent the rest of the time before take-off exploring all the perks of her seat. When the flight attendants came around with the menus for dinner, Naomi's genuine surprise delighted me. Everything was new and exciting to her, and I loved experiencing it through her eyes.

We chatted for a couple of hours until we got tired, and when I showed her how to fully recline her seat to sleep, I could have sworn she went to sleep with a smile on her face.

When I woke up several hours later, Naomi was already up, watching the map on her TV screen.

"Are we there yet?" I mumbled.

Her smile had only grown more radiant overnight. "Nearly. Another hour or so. What are we doing when we land?"

"Whatever you want." From now on, we'd make all the decisions together. "We're staying in Bangkok for two days so you can eat as much food as you like and then we're going to Koh Samui for five days. It'll be private and quiet, just like you wanted."

Sadly, the hunger in her eyes was obviously for the Thai food that awaited us and not for me.

Personally, while I knew we'd have fun in Bangkok, I couldn't wait to get to the beachfront villa on Koh Samui. There, if nothing went drastically wrong before then, I'd decided that I would tell her that I wanted more from this relationship. That I wanted it to *be* a relationship, a real one.

A little voice in the back of my head whispered in self-doubt - *What if she doesn't want more? What if she doesn't see you as partner material?* - but I forced myself to ignore it. Surely, after a week together, I would know for sure. I had nothing else to do but figure it out.

She'd had me under her spell since the night we met, and I wanted to know for sure she was mine.

Then, it really would be the perfect trip.

**~Naomi~**

I couldn't believe we were actually in Thailand.

After my initial shock and discomfort at the surprise change faded, I had to admit it was sweet that Kane remembered our conversation about travelling to Thailand and made it happen. Sure, I still didn't love how he went about it, but when I remembered that he was accustomed to doing things his way, without needing to take anyone else's preferences into account, I could understand it. He thought he was doing a nice thing, and when he realized I felt differently, he offered to make it right.

His willingness to learn meant something.

So, I let go of my reservations and embraced our new reality instead. We only had this week left together, in an incredible, exotic location, and I wanted to make the most of it.

With the time difference, we arrived just after noon local time and headed to the hotel first so we could drop off our bags and get changed. When I walked into the room, my jaw dropped again.

"Kane, this place is massive! We're not even going to be here other than to sleep."

"Might as well sleep in comfort," he said with a shrug. "And you haven't seen the bathroom yet."

Shooting him a suspicious look, I headed for the bathroom door, gasping in surprise when I saw what lay behind it. It wasn't just a bathroom, it was a *sanctuary* with a rainfall shower the size of my entire bedroom back home, sleek marble counters, and more buttons than a spaceship.

"What do you think?" Kane murmured, coming up behind me, his arms looping around my waist. His voice was low, teasing, and resonant with hunger. "Should we try it out?"

I tried not to sound *too* eager. "Well, we do need to freshen up after that flight."

His laugh told me he wasn't fooled by my excuse, but I didn't really care.

Half an hour later, we finally took our hands off each other long enough to get dressed. Kane handed over my suitcase, giving me my first look at the clothes he brought for me. They were soft, luxurious, and beautiful, higher quality than anything I'd ever owned in my life. And of course, it all fit me perfectly.

"What did you do, measure me in my sleep?" I asked while I dressed in a pretty white blouse and floral skirt.

"I have my secrets," was all he would say.

Out in the city, we wandered the streets for hours. If we passed a shop that looked interesting, we went in. If we passed a food stall that smelled good, we tried it. At a park, we fed the ducks, and at a temple, we joined the locals in a prayer.

For hours, I forgot to be cautious. I let myself be swept up in the energy of the city, in the warmth of the air, in *him.*

"When's the last time you went exploring without a plan?" I asked as we meandered back toward our hotel long after sunset, my hand tucked securely in his.

"Never," he answered quickly. "But surprisingly, I didn't hate it."

Neither did I. If anything, I loved it. The anonymity of being there, with no one recognizing Kane, no one caring about who he was, made everything feel lighter. More *real.*

Kane touched me constantly. If he wasn't holding my hand, his arm was around my shoulders or curled around my waist. When we stopped to look at something, he stood behind me, pulling me back against him like he couldn't help it.

It would have been so easy to read into it, to believe it meant more, but I knew better. Our conversation back in Norfolk played on repeat in my mind, reminding me that he wanted the comfort and familiarity of a relationship without the entanglement.

He hadn't said anything about that changing, so I couldn't let myself forget it.

Because if I let myself hope, if I let myself *fall*, it would be so easy to get lost in him.

So easy to shatter when it ended.

I'd lost someone I loved before, and I barely survived it. I wouldn't go through that again.

By the time we reached the hotel, my feet ached and I felt like I'd never be hungry again. Kane turned to me in the lift, his hands sliding around my waist as he leaned in for a kiss.

I groaned, pushing him away with a laugh. "I ate *way* too much. I don't think I've ever felt less sexy."

His expression fell into utter devastation, making me giggle.

"And now you're *mocking* me," he complained, his voice rich with faux indignation. Taking my hand, he pressed it against the front of his trousers, letting me feel just how affected he was. "Are you really going to leave me like this?"

Heat curled through me at the evidence of his need. It made me feel powerful and powerless at the same time. Because I *wanted* to see the way his breath hitched, the way his eyes darkened, and the way he came undone when I touched him.

"Maybe I can put one more thing in my mouth tonight."

He immediately brightened, and I laughed again as the lift doors opened and I pulled him back to our room. A stool next to the bed was the perfect height, so I sat, reaching for his belt. He groaned at the contact when I slid his boxers down, his hard cock eager for attention. When I looked up at him, his eyes burned with an intensity that made my stomach flip.

Kane's hands threaded through my hair as I took hold of him in my hand and licked my way up his shaft. His touch felt supportive rather than controlling, like he needed to hold onto me rather than directing my actions. Once I had him nice and wet, one hand began to stroke him while I peppered kisses along the hard lines of his stomach and down his inner thighs. I was in no hurry, soaking in his heavy breathing and grunts as I continued to play with him until he'd grown almost impossibly hard.

Normally, I'd have no issues with him coming in my mouth, but I hadn't been lying when I said I was uncomfortably full. So, I decided on a different incentive for him instead.

Letting go of him for just a second, I pulled my shirt off over my head and removed my bra. His lips parted, eyes heavy with lust, Kane reached down to cup one breast in his hand.

"I'll never get tired of looking at these."

Batting my eyes up at him, I wrapped my hand around his cock again and began to pump faster than before. "Why don't you see how they look painted with your cum?"

"Fucking hell." His eyes widened in surprise but only for a moment. Need quickly took over, his hands returning to my hair, gaze fixed firmly on my chest. His cock somehow swelled even more within my grasp, his balls tightening just before warm strings of white liquid shot across my neck and breasts.

His hips stuttered, his breath coming in pants, but his eyes never once wavered from the sight below him.

Since I had his full attention, I ran my finger through his release, rubbing it into my skin, and he groaned in approval.

"That might just be the best thing I've ever seen on you."

He leaned down, forehead resting against mine before he placed a kiss there instead. His hand joined mine on my chest, smearing his cum even more, soaking it into my pores.

It felt like he wanted to brand it into me, like he wanted me to *remember* this.

He didn't need to worry.

No matter how this week ended, I already knew I would never forget Kane Davis.

**~Kane~**

Naomi fell asleep quickly, her exhaustion from the long flight and the day's exploring winning out, but I wasn't so lucky.

Moonlight, or maybe just the city lights, filtered through the curtains, casting soft shadows over her face. She looked peaceful, her breath slow and steady, her body completely relaxed, and as I watched her, something tightened in my chest.

She was breathtaking like this. Almost as beautiful as when she laughed, her face lighting up in pure delight. Almost as devastating as when she looked at me with dark, hooded eyes, my cock in her hand just an hour ago.

Everything about being there with her, *having* her, felt so fucking *right*.

I wanted to wake her up and tell her so, tell her how much she meant to me. Tell her that even though trusting someone like this still scared the shit out of me, for *her*, I was willing to try.

But every time my hand twitched toward her shoulder, every time my lips parted to say her name, something stopped me.

*What if she didn't feel the same?*

The thought pinched that tight feeling in my chest so hard, it made it hard to breathe.

From the beginning, she'd made it clear she didn't want a relationship, but a lot had changed since then. I'd changed. *We* had changed. It didn't seem like a stretch to imagine her feelings had shifted too.

But what if they hadn't?

In business, I never made a move until I was certain. I went after what I wanted relentlessly, knowing that *everything*, and everyone, had a price.

But this wasn't a deal, not like it had been in the beginning. I couldn't buy her love. Couldn't negotiate her into staying.

I closed my eyes, inhaling deeply, trying to force the tension from my muscles. *Give it time.* Maybe, before the end of the week, there would be a moment when everything just fell into place, when I'd know what was in her heart, the same way I knew when a deal was about to close.

And if not? Then I'd pull out all the stops on our last night.

Either way, I wouldn't go home without getting an answer because the uncertainty was already driving me insane.

The next morning, Naomi was up early, eager to make the most of our last full day in Bangkok. We spent the day exploring: riding the sky train, weaving through traffic on motorcycle taxis, visiting temples and markets and palaces.

But my favorite part was *her*. Watching her take it all in, watching the way her eyes sparkled when she found something unexpected. Letting go of everything but this moment.

That evening, I led her to the river, pretending the private boat tour I'd arranged in advance was a last-minute idea. "I think these are available to hire. Should we get one?"

She lit up instantly. "Really?"

I shrugged, playing it cool. "When's the next time you're going to be here?"

She planted an exuberant kiss on my cheek. "I'd love to."

The cruise was perfect. A local chef prepared our dinner and lingered to chat with us afterward.

"I actually have a brother who just opened a Thai restaurant in London," he said. "I can send him a message now if you'd like a reservation for when you get home."

I turned to Naomi, raising an eyebrow.

Her smile faltered, shifting into the fake one I hadn't seen in a while. "Why don't you give us the name and we'll check it out when we get back?"

He handed me a business card, and I tucked it into my wallet, ignoring the slow, creeping tightness in my chest.

What did that mean? Was she not interested in the reservation, or did she not want to make any plans with me past this week? Was she already planning her exit?

Before I could figure it out, she tugged on my hand. "Can we go out on the deck?"

I followed her, the warm night air wrapping around us as I pulled her back against my chest. The lights of the city shimmered on the water, and for a few minutes, we stood in comfortable silence.

"This is wonderful," she murmured, her head resting against my shoulder. "Thank you for bringing me here."

I wanted to ask what else was going through her head, if her thoughts were as conflicted as mine.

Instead, I let my hands slide down her sides. "Are you ready to go back to the hotel? "I don't want to waste any more of our nights here."

Her shoulders tensed slightly, just for a second, before she turned, cupping my face and kissing me with quiet urgency.

"I don't want to waste it either," she whispered.

In the hotel lift, Naomi made the first move, pressing herself up against me, her hands running down my chest to the waist of my trousers while she kissed me. My hands immediately went up her skirt. It was no coincidence that I'd only brought her skirts and dresses to wear on this trip.

We'd barely stumbled into the suite before she had my zip down, her hand diving into my trousers to press against my cock. "So hard," she moaned.

"Anytime you're nearby," I told her honestly. "Are you ready?"

"Always," she murmured back, kissing my jawline as her hand wrapped around my length.

Fuck it, we weren't making it to the bed.

Grabbing her ass, I lifted her off the ground, her legs wrapping around my waist as I pinned her against the back of the door. Both of us still fully dressed, I pulled my cock out and pushed her panties to the side, pressing deep into her.

The door rattled with every thrust, Naomi's moans echoing in my ear. "God, Kane, you're so deep."

I slammed into her again. "I want you to feel all of me. I want to feel all of you."

Her legs began to shake around me. "I do. I feel..."

The rest of that thought got swallowed by her orgasm as she tightened around me. Seeing the ecstasy on her face and feeling her inner walls squeeze me tighter, I came too. Both of us panted heavily as we came down from our highs, the room once more taking shape around us.

"At least we made it inside the door," she laughed breathlessly when I finally lowered her to the ground.

"You're definitely getting fucked in that bed before we check out in the morning," I warned her, making her squeal as I squeezed her ass.

And if I felt the tiniest bit of disappointment that the conversation didn't go any deeper than that, I pushed it down. The sign to have 'the talk' with her hadn't come that day, but we still had five more days to go.

# Chapter Sixteen

~**Naomi**~

The next morning, we were on another plane heading to Koh Samui. The short flight felt like no time at all with Kane sitting beside me, his fingers laced through mine, rubbing my hand with his thumb while we talked.

When we landed, a chauffeur stood waiting with the name Davis on a sign, and he soon dropped us off at a stunning little house built into the side of the cliff.

"Is this a hotel?" I asked. It looked much more like a private residence.

"Yes and no. It's a resort, but the property is made up of individual villas. This one is ours."

Nothing could have prepared me for the building's interior. Consisting primarily of one large bedroom, it had floor-to-ceiling windows on three sides, giving us a panoramic view over the sea. A terrace off the front of the building had a small dining area and a private infinity pool.

Kane pointed down to the beach below us when we stepped outside, a little cove surrounded by rock cliffs. "That's our private beach. There are steps to take us down."

"Kane, this is incredible."

Truth be told, it was a million times better than the hotel in Lanzarote where I thought we'd be spending the week, but I didn't admit that out loud.

"What do you want to do first?" he asked.

As tempting as the pool and the beach were, it was the bed my eyes landed on, and Kane grinned.

"You read my mind. But first, you need to get changed."

"Changed?" I repeated, following him back inside. "For what?"

He didn't answer, pulling his suitcase in from the door where the chauffeur had left it. From one of the front pockets, he pulled out two pieces of lingerie: a black one-piece teddy and a two-piece red set.

"If I had my way, you'd wear nothing *but* these for our whole stay. Which one do you want to try first?"

He looked like a kid in a candy store, so eager that I had to laugh.

"You choose," I offered, and his eyes lit up even more. After a moment's indecision, he handed over the black one and I ducked into the bathroom to put it on, sensing he wanted me to make an entrance.

As I slid the high-quality, and no doubt very expensive, fabric over my skin, I caught a glimpse of my reflection in the bathroom mirror. Who would have imagined, six weeks ago, when I got dressed for that night in the hotel bar in Rome, that I would find myself on another continent, being spoiled by the man I met that night. And he *was* spoiling me, pulling out all the stops to make this trip as memorable as possible.

But I hadn't missed the way he hesitated when the chef on the boat asked us about making reservations at his brother's restaurant in London. He left the answer to me, and then out on deck, he talked about making the most of the nights we had left.

We were ending our time together on a high point, but we *were* ending it. That was becoming clearer to me with every passing day.

And so, I let myself be spoiled, knowing the memories would need to get me through some lonely nights ahead.

By the time I opened the door, Kane had already stripped down to his boxer-briefs, his cock straining against the fabric. He really was *always* ready. His eyes devoured me as I walked out and did a little spin, the heat in his gaze feeding my rush of power.

I felt sexy and desired, and if that wasn't quite the same as loved, it wasn't half bad either.

"Is it what you hoped for?" I asked. My voice had gone husky with desire, and I knew he heard it too.

Heat flared in his gaze as he answered, "So much fucking better."

He prowled forward, pulling me into a hungry kiss, but when I tried to pull him towards the bed, he paused.

"I want you on top of me, just like the night we met."

That memory, sparking to life between us, made me even hungrier for him. I could barely wait as he pulled his underwear off and climbed onto the bed. The lingerie came with popping fasteners between my legs, and I snapped them open, keeping the bustier in place so he could enjoy the view as I climbed on top of him.

He filled me as perfectly as always, and I rode him slowly at first, savouring each touch as his hands explored me through the lacy material. In this beautiful location, on the other side of the world, it was easy to imagine nothing else mattered except the pleasure the two of us could create together. Nothing mattered but his groans beneath me as I moved faster, our eyes locked together.

"Fuck, Naomi, you're so beautiful."

Those murmured words, just before his eyes closed, sent a shiver through my body that soon exploded into my orgasm.

We were beautiful together.

The next few days passed in a blur of sex and water and food. Our villa came with a butler who brought us breakfast each morning and dinner each evening. We spent time on the beach, me wearing the bikini he'd brought for me and him in his swimming trunks, though just as often as not, they'd end up on the sand since there was no one around except the two of us.

We kissed in the sea, him fingering me until I came as the waves gently rocked us. We skinny-dipped in our private pool, trying to keep the moans quiet as we pleasured each other just in case someone happened to walk by the road in front of the house.

And of course we spent time in the bed, in and out of the lingerie.

Five days passed like an amazing dream that I never wanted to wake up from.

And it *was* a dream, I had to keep reminding myself. An illusion. This man was sexy and smart and fascinating, and surprisingly tender when he wanted to be, but he was *not* mine. He wasn't in love with me, hadn't said a word about wanting anything more than this week, and every time the sun set brought us one day closer to the day it would all end.

I had to keep that in mind so it wouldn't hit me so hard when it happened.

The last night of our stay, he produced one more surprise. "Could you wear this for dinner tonight?"

The beautiful beach dress had a deep neckline and a long skirt with a slit nearly up to the hip, pretty and sexy in equal measure.

I fingered the soft fabric in appreciation. "Are we going somewhere?"

He shook his head. "No. Why don't you take a shower and get ready?"

He was clearly up to something, especially since he didn't offer to join me in the shower, but I didn't ask questions. I took my time, enjoying the warm water and the fresh scents of the hotel's body wash before slipping into the dress and doing my hair and make-up, and finished off by adding some pretty jewellery that I bought in Bangkok.

By the time I emerged, Kane had already dressed in a white button-down shirt and navy trousers, looking even more devastatingly handsome than ever. Funny how the more time I spent with him, the better looking he got.

But what really took my breath away was when he let me to the terrace, which had been completely transformed during my time in the bathroom. Fairy lights looped along the awning, casting a glow over the white tablecloth and fresh flowers adorning our usually-bare table. A bottle of wine and a few trays of food already awaited us.

"What's all this?"

"Something special for our last night." He kissed my hand and led me to my seat, like a fairy-tale prince in a storybook.

"I wish we didn't have to go," I whispered, almost to myself, as I sat down in the seat he pulled out for me.

"Me too. This week has been... wonderful." His voice caught slightly on the last word, and I glanced over at him in surprise. He didn't acknowledge it as he continued to pour the wine. "However, all good things have to end."

That reminder sank into my chest like a lump of lead. I knew this would be our last night together, but hearing him say it out loud hurt more than I expected it too.

Thankfully, when he pulled the lid off the first tray and brought over a bowl of fresh pad thai, I was temporarily distracted. We still had that night, with good food, good wine, and almost certainly good sex, so I wouldn't waste any of it moping.

Mango chicken followed the pad thai, and we talked easily throughout the meal. Kane's attention stayed focused on the sea beyond us though, barely glancing at me at all.

Not long after we finished, someone knocked at the door and Kane jumped as if he'd been expecting it. He returned a moment later with another tray.

"I believe this is what you wanted for dessert," he said as he placed it down in front of me.

The sight of the perfect crème brulée made my throat swell up unexpectedly, taking me back to another dinner that night in Norfolk when we cooked together and talked about travel.

He'd given me everything I mentioned wanting that night.

He'd left nothing to be done another time.

"Cheaper than stopping in France on the way home," he told me with a wink as he sank back into his seat.

I forced a smile, all the muscles in my face feeling tight. "It's perfect. Thank you."

Eventually, all the food and the wine were gone, and Kane stood up, holding out his hand. "Let's go down to the beach before it gets dark."

We wandered down the dirt path barefoot, our feet sinking into the sandy beach at the bottom as we watched the sun set over the water. Kane stood behind me, his arms around my waist, in what I'd started to think of as 'our' position.

"Naomi."

He said my name so softly, I thought I might have imagined it, but when I tried to turn around to face him, his arms tightened around me, holding me in place.

"Yes?"

He took a deep breath, his chest stuttering against my back in a surprising show of nerves. His fingers flexed against my stomach, then stilled.

Maybe he thought I would be like those other women he told me about, the ones who tried to cling to him when he was ready to move on.

The ones foolish enough to lose their hearts to a man who didn't want it.

"Our time together has been.... not what I expected."

Was that a good thing or a bad thing? From his tone, I couldn't tell, but I did know it sounded like the start of a goodbye.

"It helped me to see just how much I'd closed myself off emotionally, how I'd let the past dictate my future."

This was the basics of giving feedback: open with something positive before getting to the negative. I knew it from my time as a teacher, and surely, Kane the CEO knew it too.

"Six weeks ago, I couldn't imagine wanting a relationship, but you've opened me up to that possibility. Thinking that there might be someone out there I could build a life with, have a family with, doesn't seem so crazy anymore."

At the word 'family', the weight in my chest grew even heavier. Of course he would want that, and even if I could give him the other things he wanted, that was the one thing I'd never be able to provide.

It was sweet he was trying to let me down so easily, such a change from how cold he'd been in the beginning.

And it was that kindness, that unexpected consideration that prompted me to speak. He didn't have to beat around the bush. I knew exactly what I was getting into from the very beginning and I had no reason to complain. If anything, I'd gotten more out of it than I expected too. Before Kane, I couldn't imagine opening my heart again, but I'd done it. I'd let Kane in, farther and deeper than I ever intended to.

It wasn't his fault that he didn't feel the same, and I didn't want to drag this out for him any longer than I needed to. I would let him off the hook, so he would know there were no hard feelings and nothing to regret between us.

"I'm so glad, Kane." My voice sounded surprisingly steady given the frantic thumping of my breaking heart. "I know how hard it can be to be open to finding someone. It's an important step, and I really hope you find her."

His arms tensed around me even further, tightening to an almost painful grip. "What?"

I tried to turn again, but he still wouldn't release me. "Someone to build a life with, have a family with," I repeated. "I hope you find the perfect woman for you. You have so much to give."

It felt like he'd stopped breathing behind me, his body almost impossibly still. "What about you?"

The fact that he cared about me finding happiness too showed just how far he'd come since we first met. Maybe, once the sting of all of this had faded, once the bitter taste of loss left my mouth, we could even be friends.

"I'll be fine. We both knew what this was, right? I had a great time, and this trip has been amazing. I'll always remember it."

Those words should have absolved him of any lingering guilt he might have felt, but rather than embracing them, Kane's hold on me suddenly disappeared. By the time I turned around to see why, he'd already started walking away.

The sand swallowed the sound of his footsteps, but I still felt each one, like little earthquakes beneath me.

Did I say something wrong?

**~Kane~**

What a fucking fool I just made of myself. There I'd been, trying to tell Naomi that I wanted to be with her, that I *loved* her, for fuck's sake, and she cut me off to tell me I'd find somebody else. To remind me that we never promised anything to each other, but we'd always have this trip to remember.

Tears stung my eyes for the second time in weeks as I climbed the trail back to the house, ignoring the sound of Naomi's voice calling after me. I couldn't turn around. Couldn't bear to see the concern on her face when she'd just ripped my heart out and handed it back to me with a smile.

I needed air. Distance. A way to shut down the ache spreading through my chest like poison.

Stupidly, when she tensed in my arms when I mentioned having a family, I thought it was in anticipation. I thought maybe the idea excited her like it excited me.

Instead, it turned out to be a repeat of the night we met, when she walked out of my room without a backward glance.

*We're done here, right?*

Did I imagine it all? The connection between us and the way she looked at me? The way she laughed when I whispered something in her ear? The way her fingers curled around mine even when no one was watching?

When I reached the villa, I slipped on my shoes and kept walking out the front door and down the resort road. I replayed every second of the last week as I walked, searching for signs that I'd misread her, that she'd never wanted me the way I wanted her, but came up blank. It felt like we were on the same page. No arguments, no misunderstandings, just the two of us enjoying our time together and enjoying each other.

I planned the dinner with the menu she'd suggested back in Norfolk and I found the perfect spot on the beach afterwards. I'd pictured the scene a dozen times: her happy tears, the joy in her smile when she told me she loved me too and she wanted me just as much as I wanted her. The way she'd kiss me, and how I'd pull out the blanket I'd hidden earlier so we could make love on the beach beneath the stars.

I even imagined taking her home when we got back to the UK. I imagined my parents welcoming her with open arms and Abel's knowing grin.

It all seemed so real. So *close*.

But it hadn't been real because it was never *us*. It was just *me*.

And she could never, *ever* know how deeply I'd deluded myself.

Thank fuck I waited until the final night of our trip. We only had to suffer through one more night of awkwardness before we went home and I never had to see her again.

Back to normality. Back to the way things were before Rome, before I met her, before I thought there might be someone out there who made the idea of *more* sound appealing.

There had been nothing wrong with *less*. Nothing wrong with fucking my way around London without getting attached, taking what women offered me so freely and giving them a good time in return.

Maybe I felt numb back then, but I'd take numb any day over the painful sting of rejection.

By the time I returned to the villa, my emotions were back under control and I'd planned my escape. Naomi was sitting on the terrace and she jumped up when I walked through the door.

"Kane, what's wrong? Are you okay?"

The concern written across her face was genuine, but I didn't let it sway me. I'd steeled myself in preparation. "Something we ate didn't agree with me. You feel alright?"

She blinked in surprise. "Yeah, I feel fine. Where did you go?"

"To the main lodge to see the medic. He gave me some tablets, so it's a little better now, but I'm going to try to get some sleep. Hopefully, it'll pass before the morning."

A flicker of doubt crossed her face, but she didn't challenge my explanation. I went into the bathroom to get ready for bed, and when I came out, she'd turned down the bed and put a glass of water and a plastic bucket next to my side of the bed.

"In case you need it," she explained, grimacing in sympathy. "Can I get you anything else?"

"No. I'm good. Good night."

I lay in the dark, pretending to sleep as I listened to her breathing beside me. Pretending I didn't care that she wasn't curled up against my side like she had been every other night.

Pretending I hadn't just lost something I never really had.

I maintained the facade of food poisoning into the morning, and we barely spoke on the way to the airport. Inside, I went straight to the ticket desk.

"Checking for upgrades," I told her. In reality, I moved my seat, getting as far away from her as I could.

In Bangkok, we got even worse 'news': the flight was overbooked and I'd been bumped to a later flight.

"I'll wait with you," she immediately offered. "We can both take the later one. I'm not abandoning you when you're sick."

"Don't be silly. You need to get back and get some rest before work on Monday."

"I can take another day off," she insisted.

"It's really not necessary. I'll check into the airport hotel and try to get some more sleep before my flight. I'm terrible company anyway. It's better this way."

"Kane."

Concern filled her voice, but even hearing her say my name felt like a knife jabbing straight into my gut. I couldn't take any more of it, so before she could say anything else, I called over the VIP agent to escort her through security and make sure she got to the boarding gate. I slipped him a significant tip to make sure she got there with no delay.

I turned away as soon as they reached the security line, not sticking around to wave goodbye.

That had been torture, from start to finish, but at least it was over now. No more humiliation. No more pain. No more *feelings* of any kind.

I needed a fucking drink.

In the airport lounge, I ordered not one but two drinks and pulled out my phone to see what I'd missed over the last seven days. The messages went by in a blur as I scrolled, looking for something to distract me until the alcohol kicked in.

An old hookup's name popped up and I hovered my thumb over the message field before tapping out a few words.

You free tomorrow?

I stared at the words, trying to summon any sense of excitement at the prospect, but none came.

I deleted the message.

Interspersed with work messages were texts from some of my friends. 'Acquaintances' was probably more appropriate than 'friends' to be honest. These were other rich, young, single men that I hung out with at industry and social events, but knew next to nothing about on a personal level.

Who's the babe, Davis?

> You've got to bring her to my birthday party.

> I call dibs when you're done with her.

The messages on their own were nothing out of the ordinary amongst us, but in this case, I had no idea what the fuck they were talking about.

I didn't figure it out until I got to an email from Natalie with my daily media briefings. She always highlighted any mention of me or the company in the media, and there they were: a dozen photos of me and Naomi. Kissing at Heathrow. Holding hands on the streets of Bangkok. Even one on the deck of the fucking boat cruise we took.

Someone must have seen us at the airport in London and tipped off the local paparazzi in Bangkok. I'd been so wrapped up in Naomi, I hadn't noticed the lenses tracking us.

Unable to look away, I scrolled through the photos again. Naomi looked gorgeous, relaxed and happy. No wonder my friends were drooling over her. I'd never minded setting them up with any of the other women I dated, but the idea of Naomi with any of them made me want to tear my skin off.

And in every shot, I looked equally happy, more often than not with my eyes fixed on the woman at my side.

*Fucking idiot.*

I downed the first drink in one long gulp.

Even Mum had seen the photos. Her email had a link to the article with a smiley face and the text 'just colleagues?'.

Fucking perfect. Now I would have to break it to her that despite going on holiday together and looking ridiculously cosy, Naomi still wasn't my girlfriend.

Could this get any worse?

I swallowed down the second drink too, welcoming the burn in my throat as a temporary distraction from the pain in my chest.

"That's the face of someone who doesn't want to be getting on a flight home," a British voice said above me, and I raised my gaze from my phone to find a pretty blonde woman smiling down at me.

I shoved the phone back in my pocket, resisting the urge to throw it across the room instead. "I've been delayed."

She raised an eyebrow at the empty glasses in front of me. "Long delay?"

"Three hours, with a layover thrown in."

"London through Abu Dhabi?" she guessed.

I nodded, not even bothering to wonder how she would know that.

"Me too. Want some company while you wait?"

The old Kane would have said yes in a heartbeat. He'd already be thinking about quiet corners he could find to fool around in while they waited.

Instead, I thought of Naomi.

Of the way it felt to have her hand in mine. The way she smiled in those photos.

The way she ripped my heart out without even trying.

The ache in my chest sharpened, and I forced a smirk that felt foreign on my face.

"Have a seat."

# Chapter Seventeen


**~Naomi~**

I knew Kane was lying the moment the plane took off.

I'd suspected it earlier, between his abrupt departure from the beach, the way he shut down completely, and the half-hearted excuse of food poisoning. I wanted to believe him, I really did, but things didn't add up.

He wasn't pale. He wasn't clammy. He showed none of the symptoms of someone too sick to even talk to me. The taxi ride to the airport didn't seem to bother him, and once there, he never made any desperate dashes to the bathroom. He even ate breakfast on our flight from Koh Samui to Bangkok.

Although I wasn't sitting next to him, I asked the flight attendant to check on him, explaining that we were travelling together and I was worried. The answer came back the same every time: "He's fine, Miss."

And yet, he never brought up what happened on the beach. The conversation felt unfinished, like something had been left unsaid, but I couldn't even pinpoint why.

In Bangkok, when we were separated, he didn't hug me goodbye. He barely looked at me, and when I turned to wave, he had already vanished.

The knot in my stomach tightened.

This wasn't illness. Something else was bothering him.

And when my flight took off with first-class half-empty despite Kane claiming it was overbooked, I knew for sure.

Kane lied to me.

But why? What had I done that made him so desperate to get away from me?

I sank back into my seat, staring at the clouds beyond the window, retracing our last day together to try to figure it out.

Everything had been perfect until dinner. Even then, nothing felt *wrong*. Kane had been a little on edge, but not upset, which meant whatever changed happened after.

Happened during the conversation on the beach.

Doing my best to examine things neutrally, I played it back in my mind, word for word.

He said our time together had been unexpected. That it opened him up to the possibility of a *real* relationship.

That he wanted a family.

And I... I assumed it was a rejection.

Having braced myself for it all week, I thought he was acknowledging that the trip was a beautiful, fleeting moment, one I should be grateful for but never expect more from, because he was ready to move on.

But now, sitting there with twelve long hours ahead of me, I forced myself to ask the question I had been too afraid to consider before.

What if, when he talked about wanting a relationship, he meant he wanted it *with me?*

My heart thumped painfully against my ribs.

The word 'family' had blinded me so much that I never even let myself *consider* that he might have been trying to tell me something else entirely.

Because Kane didn't know I couldn't have children. I never told him.

So, when he said he wanted a family, he wasn't pushing me away. *Not yet.*

But I...

*Oh, God.*

I told him he'd find someone who *could* give him those things. I practically handed him my rejection wrapped up in a bow.

All along, I thought *he* was the one walking away when I was the one who pushed him.

No wonder he left. No wonder he lied.

He wasn't sick. He was *hurt.*

Eyes burning, I pressed my fingers to my temple, wishing I could hit rewind on the last 24 hours. *How did I get this so wrong?*

It had been right in front of me, and I was too wrapped up in my own fears to see it. Kane Davis *wanted* a relationship. With *me.*

And whether we called it that or not, we'd been in one for weeks.

Which left me with one vitally important question to answer: did I want that too?

I let the question settle in my chest, let it seep into every corner of my heart, knowing instinctively that the answer had already been decided.

I hadn't wanted it at first, not when we met. He was arrogant and impossible and made me want to scream half the time. His money, his easy charm, and the way he moved through life like nothing could touch him set off warning bells in my head, telling me he couldn't be trusted.

And yet, in the weeks since then, something had shifted.

I *saw* him now. Not just the self-destructive, reckless playboy, but the man underneath: the one who loved his family, who planned an entire trip just to make me happy, who had *tried* to open up to me, despite how foreign it was to him.

And I'd hurt him, because I was too scared to trust *myself* with the possibility of more.

A shuddering breath escaped me, drowned out by the hum of the plane's engines.

*I care about him.* More than I ever intended to, perhaps more than I ever *should* have, but I couldn't deny I did. If I didn't, I wouldn't feel like my chest was caving in.

It wasn't what I went looking for that night in Rome, but one of Liam's favourite sayings was that life was what happened when you were busy making other plans.

And Kane happened to me, whether I was ready or not.

And for the first time, I wasn't afraid of it.

There were still things I needed to tell him: about my infertility, about Liam, about the ways I had failed before and how much that fear still held me hostage.

Kane had given me pieces of himself that no one else got to see and I needed to do the same.

Because I *wanted* to be with him.

And I was stuck on this plane for another twelve hours with no way to tell him so.

My fists clenched in frustration as I stared out at the endless blue sky and sea of clouds. I couldn't do anything about it now, but the moment I landed, I was going to fix this.

**~Kane~**

By the time my flight finally took off, I was drunk.

Not just buzzed, not pleasantly numb, but *obliterated*.

The blonde from the lounge helped me board, letting me lean on her just enough to keep me upright so the flight attendants wouldn't question it. She dumped me into my first-class seat and leaned in close, her lips brushing my ear.

"I'll come say hi once we're in the air."

I merely grunted. Speech was beyond me. My head spun, my chest ached, and the only relief was closing my eyes and passing out.

When I woke, the alcohol haze had lifted just enough for the pain to settle in. My head throbbed, my stomach twisted, and my chest still fucking hurt.

I reached for another drink from the mini bottles at my seat, swallowing it in one go. It burned down my throat, but not enough. Nothing would be enough.

Right on cue, the blonde appeared.

"Good to see you're still alive," she teased, her face swimming before my eyes. "I booked some time in the shower spa. There's enough room if you want to join me."

She walked off, hips swaying.

Had she told me her name? I couldn't remember.

I didn't want her, not even a little bit, but the woman I *did* want was thousands of miles away and no longer an option.

The old me wouldn't have hesitated. He wouldn't have *felt* anything. And maybe, just maybe, if I did what he would have done, I could kill whatever part of me was still clinging to Naomi.

I forced myself to my feet, gripping each pod to keep from swaying, and stumbled my way down the aisle. By the time I reached the shower, I was already regretting it, but when I landed against the door with a thump, it swung open. Two hands yanked me inside, and her mouth was on mine before the door clicked shut.

I couldn't taste anything except the alcohol I'd been drinking. Maybe that was for the best.

Her hands moved lower, unzipping my trousers and reaching inside, and I squeezed my eyes shut, *forcing* the fantasy. If I imagined hard enough, if I ignored the wrongness curling in my gut, maybe I could make myself believe it was Naomi touching me.

Only then did I start to get hard.

"You're just as impressive as I've been told," she purred. "How do you want to do this?"

I didn't want to hear her voice, that was for fucking sure. Didn't want to *see* her. I turned her around, pressing her against the sink, and shoved a towel into her mouth before she could ruin the illusion. She probably thought it was so we wouldn't get caught, but I didn't care about that.

With her blonde hair, I could keep up the pretense that it was Naomi's body I slid into. I needed to believe, just for a second, that Naomi *hadn't* turned away from me. That she wanted me as much as I wanted her. That I wasn't alone, fucking empty and pathetic, running from something I didn't even know how to name.

I held onto that fantasy like a lifeline, but when I came, the illusion shattered.

Nausea rose in my stomach, my throat squeezing tight. What the fuck was I doing? I didn't want to be there with some random woman. I didn't want *this* at all.

I stumbled back, barely remembering to zip my trousers before pushing out of the room.

A flight attendant stood outside, offering me a knowing smile when the door locked again behind me, but I didn't return it.

The plane seemed to sway around me as I staggered back to my seat. I landed hard, put my headphones on, and stared blankly at the screen in front of me, trying to forget the last five minutes even happened.

When the blonde walked past a few minutes later, she trailed a hand over my shoulder and I nearly recoiled. Disgust curled in my stomach, not so much at her as at myself.

*Pathetic.*

By the time we landed at Heathrow, I was a wreck: hungover, jet-lagged, and exhausted. I dropped into the waiting car and pulled out my phone.

Naomi's name lit up my screen.

> Hope your flight was okay. I missed you. Can we talk? I don't have any plans today, I can come to you. Let me know when you're home.

I stared at the message far too long, the ache in my chest clawing deeper.

I wanted to see her.

I wanted to forget she ever existed.

In the end, I did nothing.

At home, I showered, scrubbing the flight and the scent of another woman's perfume off my skin before collapsing into bed.

Sleep swallowed me whole.

A gentle hand stroked my hair and I shifted, eyes still heavy, half caught in a dream.

"Hey."

The soft voice, familiar and warm, nearly made me smile, until reality crashed back in.

I sat up with a start, shaking my head to clear the last traces of sleep.

Naomi sat beside me: beautiful, real, and still not fucking *mine*.

My heart pounded as I cleared my throat. "What time is it?"

"Nearly five." She smiled softly. "I thought I'd wake you or you'd be up all night. The jet lag is real."

I blinked at her, trying to get my bearings. It took me a moment to remember she still had the keycard. Of course she could walk right in.

*Idiot.*

"How long have you been here?"

"A few hours," she admitted. "I saw your flight had landed, so I headed over and you were already asleep when I got here. I was going to wait until you woke up, but you were really out of it."

She still hadn't got to the information I really wanted to know. "*Why* are you here?"

"You didn't answer my text," she said, as if that explained everything. "I made some food. Are you hungry?"

On cue, my stomach growled. I'd been so focused on drinking my pain away on the way home, I couldn't be sure I'd eaten anything at all.

"Come on," Naomi encouraged me, getting to her feet though I hadn't agreed to anything. "I'll go put together a plate."

She strode out of the room and I found myself watching her go, my body reacting to her the way it always had. Even humiliated, I still wanted her.

After using the bathroom, I made my way to the kitchen where Naomi had laid out two plates, the savoury aroma of the stir-fry making my mouth water as I took a seat.

"Not quite as good as what we've eaten the last week, but I did my best," she said, clearly trying to keep things light, but as my head cleared further, I noticed for the first time that she seemed almost nervous.

What was that about?

I couldn't take the wondering any longer, so I asked her straight out: "Naomi, what are you doing here? What did you want to talk about?"

She swallowed hard, her eyes darting down to her untouched food before coming back up to me. "I wanted to talk about our conversation last night. Or the night before, I guess. On the beach."

"I know which one." The words came out flat, and she winced.

"The thing is... I think that I may have misunderstood you."

That was not what I expected her to say, and in spite of myself, in defiance of any sense of self-preservation, I leaned forward. "What do you mean?"

"I'm still not entirely sure I do understand, so how about I tell you what I heard, and you can tell me if I'm right or not?"

Reliving that conversation in my head had been bad enough; reenacting it with her sounded like torture. And yet, she'd come all the way over to talk to me about it, suggesting there was something she thought I didn't know. I could at least listen.

"Go ahead."

She took a deep breath, as if she needed some extra fortification for whatever she was about to say. "Okay. So, you said that spending time with me opened you up to the possibility of being in a proper relationship. Did I get that right?"

Repeating my foolish declaration seemed like an act of cruelty, but I'd agreed to hear her out, so I nodded.

"With someone that you could see yourself having a family with," she added.

Was that a question? I nodded again just in case, embarrassment striking all over again at just how ridiculous I'd been.

"And because of that, I assumed you meant you wanted those things with someone other than me. Was that right?"

For a long moment, I could only stare at her blankly, unable to make any sense of what she just said. Why the fuck would I have been talking about someone else? She couldn't have honestly believed that, could she?

Sure, I'd never declared my feelings to anyone before, but I couldn't have fucked it up *that* badly.

Naomi's fingers twitched around the cutlery in front of her as she waited for me to answer, eyes full of trepidation.

And in the face of her nervousness, the hollowness in my chest at last began to ease, the emptiness filling with a hope that I thought had been completely extinguished.

Was this for real? Did she actually want to be with me, but thought for some reason that I didn't want her?

It seemed impossible, but it was so much better than any alternative that I jumped on it like a lifeline, declaring my intentions as plainly as I possibly could.

"I meant *you*, Naomi. I want to be with *you*."

**~Naomi~**

My head fell into my hands, a groan vibrating deep in my throat as Kane confirmed my suspicions.

I'd been crawling out of my skin since I got home, so desperate to talk to him that I almost stayed at the airport to wait for his flight to arrive. When he didn't answer my text, I came over anyway, the same way he did when I ignored him back at the start of our relationship. What was good for one was good for the other, I figured.

And now he'd just confirmed that he *was* talking about me during that conversation on the beach in Thailand. The weight of my mistake settled on my chest like a stone.

The man had been trying to pour his heart out to me and I'd walked away like a fool.

"I'm so sorry, Kane. I thought you meant you were talking in general terms, about some hypothetical future partner, and that's why I said what I said. It honestly didn't cross my mind at the time that you were talking about me."

He looked at me as though I'd grown an extra head. "Why would you have thought I meant someone else?"

That was the million-pound question, wasn't it?

I swallowed hard, forcing myself to meet his eyes. "Well, to start with, you talked about the holiday being the end of our agreement, your way of making things up to me. I thought that meant you didn't want to see me anymore after we got back."

He shook his head, as if he could rattle my logic into place. "And nothing that happened between us the whole week convinced you otherwise? You didn't feel the connection between us?"

"Well, I did, but I thought it was just me. In Norfolk, you said..."

He cut me off before I could repeat his words. "That feels like a lifetime ago. Things have changed. Don't you agree?"

Something close to a smile had started on his face, a glimmer of hope flickering in his eyes, but I wasn't done yet. I still had to tell him the biggest reason I'd been so sure he meant someone else, and I had to do it now, before I lost my nerve.

"You talked about having a family."

The smile froze, his brows knitting in confusion. "And?"

"And... I can't have children. It's a long story, but it's not possible for me."

A slow blink was the only shift in his expression. Not shock, not disappointment, just processing. "What?"

"I had to have a procedure... the details aren't important, but the point is, I can't. So, when you said you wanted that, I assumed it would have to be with someone else."

Silence stretched between us, thick and uncertain. My stomach twisted as I searched his face for any sign that this changed things for him. Would this be a deal-breaker? Would he realize this wasn't what he wanted?

Finally, he spoke. "I didn't know that."

"I realized that on the way home." My shoulders lifted in an apologetic shrug. "I told you we didn't need to worry about birth control but I never explained why."

He exhaled, rubbing a hand over his jaw, still absorbing my words.

I hurried to add an escape clause. "I understand if this changes things for you. If a family is something that you really want, with your own biological children, I'm not the right person for you. And that's okay."

Kane's head shook slowly from side to side. "Naomi, I'm not thinking about kids right now. When I said that, I meant at some point in the future. All I was trying to say was that I want you to be my partner. And if we were together, and years from now, we decided we wanted that, there are other ways to go about it. It doesn't change a thing about the way I feel about you."

The breath I'd been holding escaped in a shuddering exhale. "You really mean that?"

His gaze didn't waver. "Of course I do."

The ache in my chest loosened, replaced by something warm and terrifyingly hopeful. My pulse thundered in my ears as my mind clung to his words, replaying them over and over.

He wanted *me*. Not some imaginary future with some hypothetical woman. *Me.*

"How *do* you feel about me?" My voice trembled, but I needed to ask. After making such a mess of things on the beach, I didn't want there to be any more misunderstandings. "You never actually told me."

Kane slid off his stool, leaving his untouched dinner behind, and closed the distance between us. Gently, he cupped my face in his hands, tilting my head up so I was looking directly into his eyes.

"I love you, Naomi." His voice was steady, sure. "You're perfect for me."

For a moment, I forgot how to breathe. The world around us seemed to still, narrowing until all that existed was him, his hands on my skin, his words settling deep in my chest.

"I..." The word caught in my throat. A laugh bubbled up, shaky and disbelieving. "Really?"

As soon as it slipped out, I winced. He just told me he loved me, and *that* was my response?

But Kane only smiled. "Really. Let me show you just how much."

I still had more to tell him about Liam. I still had to tell him I loved him too. But before I could say any of it, he leaned down and kissed me, and all I could think of was how much I'd missed him, how afraid I'd been of losing him, and how I never wanted to be apart from him again.

His mouth never leaving mine, he picked me up and carried me back to the bedroom.

He took his time, devoting attention to every inch of me, exploring my body like he'd never seen it before. He brought me to shattering orgasms, first with his mouth, then with his fingers, and finally, with his hard cock, filling me as perfectly as it always did.

Afterward, we lay tangled together, unwilling to let go. My limbs were heavy, my body exhausted, but I had never felt more whole. Kane pressed a soft kiss to my temple, his breathing even, his hold on me unrelenting.

Against all odds, despite the way we started and the way it had almost ended, we'd made it through.

As sleep began to pull me under, one last thought drifted through my mind:

*I still haven't told him I love him.*

The words were on the tip of my tongue, but my body refused to move, refused to shift so I could look him in the eye when I said it. So instead, I murmured it softly into the still air of his room.

"I love you too."

The way his arms tightened around me told me he heard it, even if he didn't say a word.

# Chapter Eighteen



**~Naomi~**

The alarm went off way too early the next morning.

Thailand already felt like a distant memory, washed away by the grey London morning outside my window. Reality was back, and with it, the demands of work, routine, and normal life.

Well, *almost* normal.

Kane stirred beside me, his arms still warm around my waist as I kissed him goodbye. It was a lingering kiss, the kind neither of us wanted to break first.

"Come back tonight," he murmured against my lips.

I smiled into one last kiss. "Try and stop me."

He promised to order dinner for us, something to celebrate our return home and our new relationship status, and I left his flat floating on a cloud.

Even the grumpy Monday morning commuters couldn't drag me back down. I weaved through the crowd, a ridiculous smile stuck to my face. The impatient sighs, the coffee spills, and the push and pull of the Underground bounced right off me.

At work, Pauline barely looked up from her screen before smirking. "I see you had a great trip."

I played dumb, holding up my arm for inspection. "Good tan, right? We had amazing weather."

She giggled, but her next words caught me off guard. "I actually meant the photos, but the tan is nice too."

I froze half-way to my seat. "What photos?"

Pauline's eyebrows shot up. "You haven't seen them?"

"Apparently not." It usually wasn't a good sign when something had been going on behind my back. "Photos of what?"

Rather than answering, she clacked away at her keyboard, and a second later, an email popped into my inbox.

As soon as I clicked on the link, my stomach dropped.

"Billionaire bachelor Kane Davis on holiday romp with mystery woman," the headline screamed in bright, bold letters.

Below it, a series of photos followed: Kane and me in Bangkok. His arm around me. Me stuffing my face with street food. Us kissing.

It made absolutely no sense.

"Where did they get these?"

Pauline had come up beside me while I squinted at the photos. "Paparazzi," she said with a shrug, as if it were an everyday part of life. "You didn't know you were being followed?"

"I had no idea," I admitted.

My mind reeled as I scrolled through the photos again. My world had always been small, just my friends, family, and work. Now, suddenly, complete strangers cared about what I did? They were taking photos of me?

The article hadn't mentioned my name, and none of my friends had messaged me about it yet., but the photos were clear. It wouldn't take much for people to put two and two together.

Had Kane seen them?

I sent him a quick text as soon as the office settled into its morning rhythm.

There are some photos of us in the papers.

His reply came back so fast, he must have already had his phone in his hand.

Saw them. You look great.

A small laugh escaped me. Of course that was his response.

It doesn't bother you?

I'm used to it. Does it bother you?

I hesitated, thumbs hovering over my phone.

I'm not sure. I'm not used to anyone besides my friends and family caring about what I do.

There was a brief pause before his next message came through.

Speaking of family…

My mum saw them.

I bit my lip, remembering how adamantly he had insisted that we were "just colleagues" when I met her.

Are you in trouble for lying to her?

She's too busy being thrilled about it to be mad. We're invited back for dinner this weekend. Are you free?

Something warm and sweet curled in my chest. Kane really wasn't playing around; now that we were officially together, he wasn't hiding it.

I'd love to. I better get back to work now, but I can't wait to see you later.

I can't wait more.

This openly affectionate version of Kane would take some getting used to, but my smile stayed in place long after I put the phone away.

**~Kane~**

I felt lighter than I had in years as I put the phone away. I'd completely forgotten to tell Naomi about the photos, and I was glad she didn't seem too upset about them. Now that I knew she'd never intended to break up with me in the first place, the photos inspired pride rather than sorrow. She looked amazing in them, and I wanted everyone to know she belonged to me.

The way everything resolved still felt like a dream. Her revelation about not being able to have kids came as a surprise, but I was also surprised by how little it bothered me. Having kids had always been one of those I just assumed I would do sooner or later, but it didn't matter to me at all whether those kids shared my DNA. If it came down to having my own biological kids with someone else or being with Naomi, the choice couldn't be clearer.

Because she loved me.

I'd replayed her whispered confession over and over in my mind, letting the memory sink into my bones.

Who the hell knew three little words could make such a difference?

The morning flew by getting caught up on what I'd missed during my week off, meeting with the heads of each of my teams for updates. Nobody commented on my uncharacteristically good mood, but I noticed a few side-eyed glances exchanged when they thought I wasn't looking. I couldn't care less. Nobody had ever been as happy as I was that morning.

When I finally got a break at two o'clock for lunch, Natalie brought in my food with a grim look on her face.

"Who died?" I joked as I swiped the coffee from her and took a long swig.

Her lips didn't even twitch. "I think you need to get your PR guy on the phone."

For the first time all day, my smile faltered. "Why? What's going on?"

"You're trending on social media."

*What the fuck?* "I am, or the company is?"

I couldn't think of any reason either of us would be making news that day.

"You, personally. *Very* personally."

Well, that didn't sound good. "Send it to me. I'll call Scott if I need him."

She went back to her desk and sent me some links. I clicked on the first one as I took a bite of my sandwich, still utterly confused.

The link led to an account that appeared to belong to a woman. In her profile picture, huge sunglasses covered her face, but her bright blonde hair looked vaguely familiar.

> Joined the mile-high club with @kanedavis97 between Bangkok and Abu Dhabi. Fun and flirty beforehand, not even the time of day after. Are all CEOs such a**holes? Ladies, weigh in. #milehigh #kanedavis #player #tenminutestand"

The sandwich turned to ash in my mouth.

*Fuck.*

I gripped the edge of my desk, my stomach plummeting.

*Fuck. Fuck. Fuck.*

The plane. The woman. The alcohol. The self-loathing that hit me after.

I had pushed the whole thing out of my mind, burying it under exhaustion and regret. I'd actually managed to forget about it completely.

I couldn't ignore it now.

The next link featured hundreds more posts, not all about me but all riding the wave. Stories of men treating women like trash after casual sex. Some about CEOs, some about billionaires, and every single one of them tagged with my fucking name.

"Natalie, get me..."

"He's on line two."

I snatched up my desk phone to see what we could do for damage control.

"Is it true?" Scott asked as soon as I said hello. "The initial post. Is it true?"

I gritted my teeth. "Yes, more or less."

"Alright. Since we can't deny it, you've basically got two options. You can respond with an apology, or you can wait it out until it goes away on its own. I'd personally recommend option two. I don't think engaging on this topic is going to win you any fans."

I exhaled sharply, rubbing my temple. "Option three: I hack the app and delete it?"

He laughed, sounding considerably more upbeat than I felt. "If anyone could do it, I bet you could, but it wouldn't help. People have screenshots. It's out there, mate, and you can't put it back in."

We ran through some long-term strategies, ways to subtly repair my image over time, without making it obvious I was trying to.

"In the end, I wouldn't worry too much about it," he concluded. "No offense, but you've kind of already got that reputation anyway. It's not like you were a saint before, and it's not like you were cheating on anyone. Just lie low for a bit and let it blow over."

*It's not like you were cheating on anyone.*

The words slammed into me like a freight train, stealing my breath. That was the real problem: not the press and not my reputation, but *Naomi*.

She forgave me for Natalie, but that was nothing compared to this. Nothing even happened with Natalie. This time...

This time, I had no such excuse.

I fucked that woman and Naomi was going to find out.

Even if I wanted to hide it from her, I couldn't. It was already too big, already spreading. She'd find out sooner or later, and if she didn't hear it from me first, it would be even worse.

I grabbed my phone from my pocket, my fingers itching to call her. Nothing new had come in since our last series of texts, so she didn't seem to have heard about it yet, but this wasn't a conversation we could have over the phone.

Briefly, I debated sending a warning and asking her to avoid social media, but that would only set off alarm bells. If someone sent me a message like that, I'd be on Google in two seconds.

No. I had to tell her face-to-face, the first chance I got.

But how the fuck was I supposed to explain it?

How was I supposed to look into her eyes, less than twenty-four hours after I told her I loved her, and admit that I hooked up with a stranger on a plane on the way back from *our* holiday?

I had no idea, but I also had no choice.

The afternoon stretched endlessly ahead, a slow, torturous countdown to the moment I would have to shatter the best thing that had ever happened to me.

And there wasn't a damn thing I could do to stop it.

**~Naomi~**

The office was unusually quiet that afternoon.

Michael and Simon were at a hospital meeting, Jane was out with a donor, and Pauline had left early. The volunteers manned the phones, leaving me with an unusual stretch of uninterrupted time. Perfect for a quick break.

I leaned back in my chair, stretching out the tension from a day of sitting at my desk, and clicked open my web browser.

Since my relationship with Kane would soon be public knowledge, if it wasn't already, I figured I should tell my family and friends before they heard about it somewhere else.

I drafted a short, matter-of-fact email, containing the relevant information without going into too much detail. I explained that I met him in Rome, he worked with computers, and we'd just been on holiday together. Those were the important bits. Kane's 'celebrity' status couldn't matter less to me.

Just before I hit send, however, it occurred to me that it might be nice to add a photo, now that some of the two of us existed. There had been a nice one of us walking hand-in-hand in Bangkok in the article Pauline sent me, but when I went back to find it, I'd already deleted it. I'd even emptied my trash that morning, clearing my computer of all the emails I'd received over the past week that I didn't need to respond to.

Apparently, I'd been a little *too* efficient. Still, it couldn't be that difficult to find it again.

Or so I thought, until I Googled Kane Davis and hundreds of results flooded my screen. *You've got to be kidding.* I scrolled through a few before realizing they were almost all related to his business. I needed news items, so I clicked on that tab again, and there it was: the exact article Pauline sent me that morning.

My mouse hovered over the link, ready to click, when another article just below it caught my eye.

Bearing today's date, the headline read: "Kane Davis hashtag exposes bad behaviour among City's high flyers."

My face scrunched up as I squinted at the words, trying to parse some kind of meaning from them. What the heck did that mean?

I clicked on the link to find out.

A picture of Kane's face immediately popped up, the face I'd kissed just a few hours earlier, and affection swelled in my chest as I took in his familiar features.

That warm, fuzzy feeling didn't last long.

"After CEO Kane Davis was called out for leaving user @b0mbsh3ll high and dry - or wet as the case may be - after a shower tryst on a recent flight, other users have been chiming in with their own stories of City magnates who like to love 'em and leave 'em."

More details followed, but none of it registered as I scrolled further down, only stopping when I got to the post in question.

I read it once. Then again. A third, fourth, and fifth time, and still, my brain refused to fully take it in.

A few things, however, couldn't be ignored.

Mile-high club.

Bangkok flight.

Posted yesterday.

A cold wave rolled through me, stealing the air from my lungs.

It couldn't be true. It *couldn't* be.

I gripped the edge of my desk, staring at the words, waiting for them to rearrange themselves into something that made sense.

This kind of thing must come with the territory of being so well-known, I tried to tell myself. People took secret photos of him on the streets in Bangkok. They probably lied about him on social media too. He had a crazy life.

That was all it was. He would tell me so himself if I asked him.

I felt certain of it.

*Almost* certain.

Somewhat certain?

The longer the question lingered, the less sure I became. It seemed impossible he wouldn't be aware of this post. She'd tagged him in it, for crying out loud. He had people who checked the media for him, analyzing every mention of him and his business.

So, why wouldn't he have mentioned it to me? A simple text to say, 'hey, there's a crazy story going around right now, but don't worry, it's not true'?

The only reason I could think of why he hadn't sent me a text like that would be if the post *was* true after all.

And as soon as I allowed the possibility to cross my mind, as soon as I pictured how cold and distant he'd been with me at the airport in Bangkok, how hurt he was and how he shut down, I knew it deep in my bones.

This wasn't a lie. *He did this.*

He made up an excuse not to fly home with me, had sex with someone else on the plane, then came home and told me loved me.

Nausea rose in my throat, the bile building so fast I had to press my hand to my mouth to stop it from coming out.

Was this what being in a relationship with him meant? Every time he felt neglected, he could rely on his assistant for a blow job to cheer him up? Every time we had an argument, he'd find some stranger to fuck?

I knew Kane's reputation from the start, had seen the photos of him with dozens of different women. He'd even told me flat out that he didn't do relationships, and somehow, stupidly, I convinced myself that it would be different with me. He would change for *me.*

How naive could I be?

My love hadn't been enough for Liam, and it wouldn't be enough for Kane either.

I squeezed my eyes shut, my pulse roaring in my ears. The last 24 hours had been a roller coaster, and I wanted to get off now.

This was all a mistake.

When I forced my eyes open again, the email I'd composed to announce my new relationship still sat there, waiting to be sent.

I hit delete instead.

**~Kane~**

Restless energy crawled under my skin as I paced the lounge of my flat, the lobby security feed on my TV as I waited for Naomi to arrive.

Every minute in the office had seemed like an hour, and once I got home, it felt like time stopped entirely.

I hadn't heard from her for the rest of the day, which I took as a good sign. Surely if she had seen anything, she would have texted me. She would have called. Since she hadn't, she must not have seen it.

I would take any smell blessing where I could get it. At least I'd have the chance to be the one to tell her, even if I still didn't have a clue how to do that.

At last, she appeared on the screen. Her face remained hidden from the camera thanks to the angle, but I recognized the back of her head immediately, and Tom's smile when he greeted her confirmed it couldn't be anyone else.

I exhaled deeply, relieved that I didn't have to wait any longer, even if I knew the conversation that lay ahead could very well destroy us both.

I drifted towards the kitchen door, checking that everything was still ready for the dinner I'd ordered for us, as if a perfectly cooked meal could soften the blow of what I had to say. But when the lift opened and Naomi stepped out, she didn't even glance my way. She immediately turned left, walking down the hall towards the bedroom and away from me.

"Naomi?" I called after her, assuming she simply hadn't noticed me. "Over here."

When she didn't respond or turn around, an uneasy feeling, even stronger than the anxiety I'd been carrying around all day, settled deep in my gut. I strode as quickly as possible after her, reaching the door seconds after she did. In that time, she'd already yanked the wardrobe door open and was pulling her clothes off the hangers, methodically and without emotion, and stuffing them into a bag.

My throat closed up, my heart stuttering inside my chest.

*No.*

She must have seen it after all. I knew it deep in my soul, but I asked the question anyway.

"What are you doing?"

At last, she looked over at me, but while I braced myself for anger or betrayal blazing in her eyes, the gaze that met mine was completely neutral. Almost blank.

As if she felt nothing towards me at all. Like I had already ceased to exist in her world.

My stomach knotted, any words I might have said drying up before I could speak them. I'd never seen her look that way, and when I said nothing, she turned back to pull the last few things out of the wardrobe, all without a word.

Her silence was worse than anything she might have screamed at me.

When she turned to go, I still stood in the doorway, blocking her exit.

"Please get out of the way."

Her tone was mechanical, containing no more emotion than her lifeless expression did.

I didn't move. I couldn't even if I wanted to. My body felt frozen to the spot, limbs too heavy to command. The weight of what I had done pressed down on me.

"Naomi, I'm so sorry."

The words came out in a whisper. Even my voice felt out of my control. I was suffocating beneath my guilt and grief.

"Sorry that I found out, you mean."

The finality in her voice sliced through me.

"I was going to tell you..."

She cut me off with a shake of her head. "You could have told me last night, or this morning. Any time before the rest of the world found out."

"It was the furthest thing from my mind last night. I forgot all about it until I saw the post."

Although my words were true, I didn't blame her for the disbelief that clouded her features, the first emotion she'd shown since arriving. "You *forgot*? That's the best you can come up with?"

"I know it sounds ridiculous, but it's true. I barely even remember it happening. I was drunk and hurting and I wasn't thinking."

She nodded, and for a brief, hopeful second, I thought that meant she understood. But her nod meant something else entirely.

"That's what I figured. You weren't thinking, so you fell back on your instinct, your nature. Because that's who you are."

"That's not what I meant."

I finally managed to gain enough power over my legs to take a step forward, but Naomi took advantage of the space my movement created to slip past me, out of the room.

I spun around, stumbling after her.

"Whether you meant it or not, it's the truth, Kane." She didn't look back as she marched down the hall. "Just like you weren't thinking when you had your assistant on her knees in the kitchen. Apparently, your reflex reaction is to lower your trousers at the first sign of trouble."

I wanted to argue that Natalie was a different story, to remind her that nothing had happened then, but it wouldn't help my case. I had to stick to what was important.

"I thought you broke up with me," I tried to explain, stretching forward to grab her arm and breaking her stride before she could reach the lift. She couldn't leave, not like this.

"So, it's my fault."

Again, she said it flatly, not as a question but as a conclusion she'd already reached.

"Of course not. I'm not blaming you, I'm just trying to explain where my head was at."

"It doesn't matter."

Those three words felt like a stab to the heart, each syllable twisting the knife a little deeper. Of course it *mattered*. It was the only thing that mattered, that she knew I hadn't meant to hurt her. It only happened because I truly thought we were over and I wanted to drown my pain.

I would take that pain back a thousand times over if she would just look at me with the same love in her eyes that had been there that morning.

She tugged her arm free from my grasp, but instead of continuing her escape, she looked me up and down, her eyes still blank and distant.

"Did you at least use protection?"

My face fell before I could stop it. The thought hadn't even crossed my mind until she said the word, and though my memory of the event was fuzzy at best, a condom didn't feature in any of my drunken recollections.

Naomi didn't need me to answer. She could see the regret written across my face, and hers hardened in response.

"So, not only could you have got this stranger pregnant, but you came home and slept with me a few hours later without telling me about it. Without thinking about me at all."

Guilt coursed through me as she started walking again, and in one last desperate attempt to stop her, I ran ahead to reach the lift ahead of her, blocking the exit. If I let her walk away like this, she might never give me another chance. I couldn't risk it.

I needed her to scream and shout, to show me she felt *something*, even if it was fury. Even if it was *hate*. Anything but the way she was shutting me out.

"I fucked up, Naomi and I'm so, so sorry. You can't imagine how much I wish I could take it back. It meant absolutely nothing. I love you and I want to be with you, only you. It will never, ever happen again."

I waited for her to look up at me, to look up from the spot on my chest she'd decided to focus on, but her gaze stayed resolutely down as she shook her head.

"I don't believe you, Kane."

The words stung me as much as if she'd struck me. She sounded so completely certain of it, her tone leaving no room for argument.

I tried to argue anyway.

"You *have* to believe me, because it's the truth. Tell me what to do to prove it to you, and I'll do it. You're all I want."

Pain flashed across her face, the first crack in her mask of indifference. "No, I'm not. I'm not enough for you. I'm not enough for anyone."

How could she possibly say that? How could she even think it? "You're more than 'enough'. You're everything to me."

As ridiculous as it would have sounded to the person I was two months ago, the words were achingly true.

And she still didn't believe me.

"If I was enough, you wouldn't have done this." A small whimper left her lips, and although I'd wanted her to show some emotion, to feel *something*, the broken little sound nearly brought me to my knees.

"It had nothing to do with you," I tried to reassure her. "This is entirely my fault. I'm a fucking idiot; that's the only reason it happened."

She shook her head again, her whole body beginning to shake. "If I was enough, he wouldn't have left. It keeps happening, so it has to be me."

*What?* "Who wouldn't have left?"

Her eyes finally met mine, and the pain swimming in them took my breath away. It was so *raw*. So deep. "What?"

"You just said he wouldn't have left you," I repeated. "Who are you talking about?"

Her eyes closed, a tear slipping down her cheek as they did, and I knew that whatever it was, she hadn't meant to say it. But she had, and now I needed to know what it meant, and why she looked like she could fall to pieces any moment.

When the answer finally came, I wasn't ready for it.

"Liam," she whispered. "I wasn't enough for him either."

Her fiancé? What did he have to do with anything?

"He died," I stated, the words coming out harsher than I meant them to in my confusion. "He didn't leave you on purpose."

"He did," she insisted, more tears spilling over her eyelashes.

"Naomi, that doesn't make any sense. It's not like he killed himself."

A sob tore from her throat, an almost inhuman sound that made my whole body go cold.

Because it could only mean one thing, and it made me an even bigger fucking asshole than I ever imagined.

"Naomi." Her name scratched my throat as it came out, my vocal cords tight and strained. "Did he kill himself?"

# Chapter Nineteen

~**Naomi**~

With Kane's final question, a dam burst open inside me.

I'd been fighting so hard to hold myself together, to keep from letting Kane see my anger and hurt, but once he asked about Liam, I couldn't hold it back any longer. All my strength evaporated and my legs gave way.

Before I could hit the floor, Kane's arms wrapped around me, crushing me against him. I didn't want to touch him, my disgust over what he'd done still strong, but I didn't want him to let go either. My arms clung to him desperately as he picked me up and carried me to the sofa in the lounge, sitting down with me on his lap, never relaxing his grip.

Anger tangled with the pain that always surfaced when I thought about Liam, and together, they dragged me under. My lungs fought for air, my breaths jagged and uneven.

I'd never cried over Liam in front of anyone. I knew if I started, I wouldn't be able to stop and it would be just like it was now: messy, loud, and desperate. Even though I could hear my sobs echoing around the cool, minimalist room, I could barely believe the noise was coming out of me.

Kane didn't say a word. He didn't try to calm me down or tell me things would be okay. He simply held me, his hand gently cupping my face against his chest as my tears soaked into his shirt.

His silence grounded me in a way I hadn't expected.

Minutes passed, maybe longer, before my body finally started to settle. My sobs faded to sniffles and my breathing became steadier. Only then did Kane tilt my chin up to meet his gaze.

His blue eyes were red-rimmed, as if he had been crying too.

"What happened?" he asked softly.

I shook my head, out of instinct, out of self-preservation, out of the anger and disappointment I still felt over what he'd done.

Kane's grip on me never wavered. "Please tell me. You let me share my guilt and pain with you and it helped so much to talk about it. It might help you too. Take your time. There's no rush."

His voice was hoarse, rougher than I'd ever heard it.

I closed my eyes and focused on breathing. Each inhale and exhale was like a lifeline, pulling me out of the darkness, and Kane was my anchor. I hated that I needed him on this night of all nights, that his presence was the only thing keeping me from crumbling completely.

And yet, when I finally spoke, it was almost without thinking.

"Liam had a daughter. Michelle. I told you about her."

"Yes," he confirmed, the word barely a whisper.

"She had epilepsy. It was part of her condition. She had a couple of big seizures that wouldn't stop on their own. We'd end up in A&E and she'd be admitted for days, but she always bounced back. Then, one night, she had one while we were sleeping."

I swallowed hard.

"Liam went to wake her in the morning, but she was already gone. The sound he made... I didn't know a person could make a sound like that. It shattered him."

Pressure built behind my eyes again, more tears threatening to fall, and I took some controlled breaths, doing my best to keep them at bay. Kane's breathing hitched, but he stayed silent.

"Liam tried to go on. He arranged her funeral. We cleaned out her room. He went to therapy. I knew he was in pain but I thought he was getting better. I thought I could help him through it. But one night, I found him crying in her empty room in the middle of the night, completely broken. He felt that he'd failed her. That it was his fault that she was gone. I tried to convince him otherwise, to tell him that he had done everything he could and it was no one's fault. I thought I got through to him. He seemed to calm down, and he told me he was going for a walk, to clear his head. And he never came home."

My chest tightened painfully, a whimper forcing its way past my lips.

"The police came that afternoon and told me they found him. He stepped in front of a train."

Kane's entire body tensed beneath me. He sucked in a breath, as if the words had physically hit him, but I wasn't done. I couldn't stop now.

"I should have known," I choked out. "I should have seen it. I should have..."

Kane's arms crushed me to him, as if he needed the contact just as much as I did. "No," he murmured against my hair. "You were right when you told him it wasn't his fault. And it wasn't yours either."

A fresh sob wrenched from my chest.

"Life just fucking sucks sometimes," he said, echoing the words I had once said to him about Abel. "But I know you, Naomi. You did everything you could. If Liam were here now, I know he would tell you that. I bet he'd give anything for another chance with you."

His words cracked something inside me.

Fresh pain surged through me, but along with it, some of the guilt started to loosen, bleeding out like an old wound finally being cleaned.

We sat there for a long time. When the tears finally dried, Kane didn't move. His arms remained around me, warm and secure, and despite every reason I had to be furious with him, I felt safe.

Finally, Kane let out a long, slow exhale. "I can't change what happened, Naomi. Not with Liam, and not what I've done either. But I promise you that I'm going to do everything I can to prove to you that you can rely on me. I won't hurt you again and I'm not giving up on us. You mean too much to me."

What he described sounded impossible. "I don't know, Kane. I need some time."

"I get that. You can take all the time you need, but I'm not going anywhere. It's getting late. Do you want me to call you a car?"

Relief that he wasn't going to stop me from going loosened even more of the tightness in my chest. "Yes, please."

Placing me gently down on the sofa, he packaged up the meal he'd ordered, a meal we hadn't even looked at, and walked me down to the lobby. As I settled into the back of the car, I reached into my pocket for the keycard to his flat and held it out to him.

Pain pinched his handsome features as he shook his head. "Keep it. Just in case you need it."

He closed the door without taking it.

As the car pulled away, I slumped back in the leather seat, wrung out by the day's emotions and yet, strangely, a little lighter at the same time.

Kane knew all of me now, including the broken pieces I carried, and he hadn't run.

But could I trust him? His behaviour was a pattern, one he'd relied on for a long time. How could I believe he wouldn't fall back into it the next time things got hard?

I couldn't answer that question on my own, but maybe there was someone who could help me figure it out, someone who knew that side of him better than I did.

Fishing my phone from my pocket, I chose a contact from my list.

"Hello?" the woman on the other end answered, her voice laced with suspicion and uncertainty.

"Hi, it's Naomi. Can you meet me for a drink?"

When we'd agreed on a meeting place, I gave the driver the new destination, and he dropped me off at an upscale pub in the City. I visited the toilet first, scrubbing my face clean of the evidence of my tears so that I was a bit more presentable by the time Kane's assistant, Natalie, walked in.

She eyed me warily as she sat down across from me. "I almost changed my mind about coming a dozen times between my flat and here. Usually, when Kane's girlfriends call me, it's because they want to know if he's cheating on them, but I suspect you already know about that."

"I do, and I've already spoken to him about it. We don't need to go over it again." I gestured to the wine bottle on the table and the extra glass. "Help yourself."

She exhaled, clearly relieved as she poured herself a glass. "What do you want from me, then?"

I got straight to the point. "I want your perspective. You've seen him with a lot of women, so you'll know better than anyone if I'm fooling myself here. He says he wants to commit to a real relationship but I'm not sure he's capable of that. Have you seen anything in the last six weeks that would suggest to you that this might be different for him?"

She took a sip of her wine as she considered the question before placing it back down with another deep sigh. "Can I tell you something without you thinking I'm a total bitch?"

Her bluntness made me laugh, the first thing that had in hours. "To be fair, I don't have the best impression of you already, considering the only other time we've met in person."

She grimaced in acknowledgement. "It's actually about that night in his kitchen. I knew right from the start that there was something different about you. He was way more interested than he's ever been in anyone, and that's part of why I went after him that night. I like our relationship, and I was worried you were going to change that. I thought I could change his mind. But just before you walked in, he reminded me that he was seeing you, and as soon as you left, he asked me to leave."

That matched with what he'd told me about that evening. "He still shouldn't have let it get that far."

"Probably not, but for Kane, that's still a pretty big step. He has *never* turned me down before, even when he was seeing other people."

The confirmation that he had cheated on previous girlfriends didn't help matters any, but I was more curious about what Natalie got out of the whole thing. "That arrangement really makes you happy?"

"I guess I liked knowing I could always fall back on him when I needed to feel wanted," she admitted. "That night, I'd just been dumped. The guys I go out with... I don't know. I never seem to hold their interest for very long."

I found that hard to believe. The woman across from me was beautiful and clearly smart and resourceful as well, considering how much Kane relied on her. "Maybe you just go out with the wrong type of guys."

"Maybe," she agreed, and I could have sworn I saw a flash of real loneliness in her eyes before she flashed me an unconvincing smile. "I don't suppose you know anyone?"

"Not anyone like Kane, but if you're open to something completely different, I could see what I can do."

"Well, trying something different seemed to work for Kane," she mused, which brought us rather neatly back to the main reason we were there.

I took another drink from my own glass, considering her earlier answer. "You said you knew from the start it was different with me. How did you know?"

Her smile that time felt more genuine. "Lots of little things. He checks his phone constantly during the day, even in meetings. He never used to do that. I know he gave you a key to his place which never happened before with anyone either. And meeting his parents? Forget about it. I've worked for him for six years and I've never met them. None of the women he's dated ever have. And when he got to the office this morning, I thought he might have been abducted by aliens in Thailand and replaced by a clone. I've never seen him looking so happy."

She tipped her glass in a nod to the circumstances that brought us there.

"Until he saw the post, of course."

*Of course.*

I sighed, looking out at the surrounding tables, everyone involved in their own conversations and their own little worlds. I wanted so badly to believe what she was saying, but I didn't know how much more heartache I could take.

"I believe that he cares about me, but I just don't know if I can trust him. Women throw themselves at him constantly and he told me he's not in the habit of denying himself. I don't know how I can be sure that he won't give in."

Natalie considered that for a long moment, swirling her wine around the bottom of her glass as she thought it over.

When her gaze finally lifted to meet mine again, it had taken on a conspiratorial edge. "Believe it or not, I do want him to be happy, and if that means being with you, so be it. If you trust me to help you, we could find a way to put him to the test."

**~Kane~**

I never realized how much pain Naomi had been carrying. After she left, I sat back down in the lounge, watching the sun set through the window, the room darkening around me as I thought back on all the times I'd been a jerk to her. Shame settled deep in my gut. There had been so many moments, so many careless words and selfish actions, and yet, despite all of that, despite everything I put her through, she still fell in love with me.

And then I hurt her even more.

Our conversation that evening shifted something in me. Hearing Naomi blame herself for Liam's death made me see how absurd it was to keep blaming myself for Abel's condition. We were both our own worst critics, punishing ourselves in ways no one else ever could. I'd never seen so clearly how destructive that kind of thinking was.

Maybe, if I could pull myself out of it, I could help her do the same.

Over the next few days, I gave Naomi the space she asked for and took whatever steps I could to fix the mess I'd made. I went back to the sexual health clinic and got re-tested. The results came back clear, and I sent them along to her, not expecting a response but hoping it would ease at least one of her worries.

I also tracked down the woman from the plane. When I introduced myself over the phone, she was understandably wary.

"None of what I said is untrue so you have no legal ground to stand on."

"I don't want to sue you," I promised. "I just want to apologize. I wasn't in a good place that day and I'm sorry that I treated you unfairly."

A long pause followed, as if she were trying to figure out what the catch might be. "You're not angry?"

"Only at myself. Is there any chance you might be pregnant?"

I held my breath until she replied. "I'm on the pill. I'll let you know if something went wrong, but it should be fine."

"Okay. This is my personal number, so call me if you find out otherwise."

On Friday, four days since I last saw Naomi, I had flowers sent to her office, simply to say I was thinking of her. My phone never left my side, just in case she decided to get in touch, but no messages came in and I forced myself not to message her.

She said she needed time to think, and I had to respect that.

The following week, Natalie had me on a tight schedule with business dinners almost every night. It felt like the waitresses flirted with me especially hard everywhere we went, but I had no interest in talking to any of them. I kept our interactions polite and nothing more.

On Thursday, I had a party to attend, an annual one that I had been hoping to take Naomi to. Since that wasn't an option, I asked Natalie the day before if she would be my plus-one instead.

"I have plans, but I can have a friend fill in."

"Please do." Going to those events alone was a nightmare.

The woman arrived at my office as I shut down for the day. Dark-haired and nearly as tall as me, she was absolutely gorgeous.

"This is Emma," Natalie introduced us before leaning close to me and whispering in my ear, "She's a lingerie model."

I could believe it.

Emma sat next to me at the party, her thigh brushing against mine at regular intervals, her hand 'accidentally' making contact with mine whenever she reached for her glass. In every glance and pout of her lips, she made it pretty clear what she wanted, and a couple of months ago, I would have been all over her. That night, however, I felt nothing. When I looked at her, I only saw that she wasn't Naomi.

Outside the party, I put her in a taxi on her own. "I've had a long day. Thank you for coming."

The door closed on her stunned face. She was probably about as used to rejection as I was to doing the rejecting.

Natalie gave me a curious look as she brought me my coffee the next morning. "You disappointed Emma last night. She'd heard so much about you and was looking forward to getting to know you better."

"She wasn't my type," I muttered.

Natalie laughed. "She's *everybody's* type. When did you become so discerning?"

I didn't bother answering. "What's on the schedule for today?"

Friday came and went without any word from Naomi. Though I still wanted to give her time, the ten long days without her wore on me, and I dug for any excuse to make contact. Lying in bed alone, I sent her a text.

> Hope you've had a good week. I brushed off dinner at my parents' last weekend, but I'll be going tomorrow. I assume you don't want to come, but the invitation is open. Just as colleagues, if you prefer.

To my relief, she responded, even if the response wasn't what I hoped for.

> The week has been okay. I'm at the pub with friends. I'll pass on tomorrow, but thank you for the invite.

I pushed down the lump in my throat as I replied.

> Okay. Have fun with your friends.

Mum met at the front door the next night, arms crossed and ready to lay into me about avoiding her for the two weeks. As soon as she saw me, though, her countenance shifted, and she pulled me into a tight hug instead.

"I don't want to talk about it," I warned her. Naomi's absence spoke volumes on its own.

Luckily, she didn't argue. "You don't have to, but I'm here if you need me."

After dinner, Abel and I went to his room to hang out, like we used to when we were younger. After a bit of our typical banter, he asked me the question I knew they were all thinking. "What happened with Naomi?"

I let my head fall into my hands. "I was an idiot."

"I figured that out," his robotic voice declared in its deadpan monotone. "Why?"

That was a fucking good question. 'How', I could answer, but 'why' was more complicated.

"I don't know." It might not be a good answer, but it was the truth. "Maybe I'm just not a very good person."

"Bullshit."

My head lifted, eyebrows raised at his uncharacteristically foul language.

"You're a good person with me."

He really had no idea. "There's a lot you don't know about me, Abel. I've treated a lot of people badly."

"There's a lot you don't know about me too," he replied.

I couldn't imagine that we were talking about the same sort of things. "Like what?"

"I have a girlfriend."

Those were about the last words I expected to hear from him, and I stared at him in bewilderment. "What? Since when?"

He shot me a grin, looking delighted with himself for having caught me so off guard. "For a few months. Her name is Amy."

He couldn't have stunned me more if he suddenly leapt out of his wheelchair and did a tap-dance. "Why didn't you tell me?"

"I didn't want you to be jealous."

I waited for his familiar laugh, the punchline to every joke he told, but it never came. He *wasn't* joking. He looked completely serious.

"I was going to invite her to dinner next time Naomi came," he explained. "But you had to screw it up."

"I'm fucking good at screwing things up," I agreed, shaking my head at the unexpected turn this conversation had taken. "I'm so happy for you. Where did you meet? What's she like?"

He told me about his visits to the local library where Amy worked as a librarian, how he'd asked her for help one day to find a book he wanted and how she'd learned to use his communication device so they could speak silently in the quiet rooms. His eyes lit with a joy I recognized every time he said her name.

I recognized it from the way I felt when I talked about Naomi.

In the car on the way home, I analyzed what he said about not telling me about Amy earlier because he thought I might be jealous. Truthfully, I was. He found someone he cared about, who cared about him in return, and he didn't overthink things or push her away. He hadn't fucked it up like I did.

For the first time in my entire life, I thought my twin brother might be the luckier of us two.

As the new week started, I dug through old emails until I found something my mum had sent me ages ago, something I'd barely glanced at when I received it. It came from a support group for people with siblings with additional needs, and it listed various resources available to deal with unresolved feelings of resentment or guilt.

At the time, I ignored it. I'd figured out a way to deal with my emotions, a way that seemed to be working since I had all the material success I could have ever wanted.

Now, I wondered if I could be doing better.

I reached out to a therapist listed in the email who was able to get me in for a last-minute cancellation on Tuesday afternoon. We started by talking about Abel, which I expected, but the focus quickly shifted to me, my relationships and the way that I tried to keep people from getting too close. We didn't even get to talking about Naomi, and already, it gave me a lot to think about.

That evening, I stayed in the office late to make up for the time I took off for the appointment, and Natalie stopped in before she left for the evening.

"Is everything okay, Kane?"

"Sure." I kept my eyes on my computer while I answered. I hadn't explicitly told her about Naomi breaking up with me, but no doubt, she'd put it together. She didn't miss much. "I'll see you tomorrow."

"I could stay for a while if you need some company," she offered.

When I glanced up, she wore the soft, seductive smile that usually led to the two of us getting naked on my desk.

For a brief moment, I yearned for those nights when things were simple and uncomplicated. But almost immediately afterwards, my mind flashed back to the time I had *Naomi* on my desk and the contentment I felt with her. *That* was what I wanted, nothing else.

"I'm okay. Have a good night."

Undeterred, she walked over and perched on the edge of my desk. Too close. "I can make you feel better than okay."

She leaned in, her mouth aiming for mine, but I gripped her shoulders tightly and stopped her movement before she made contact.

"It's not happening, Natalie. Not tonight, and not again. I don't think it's good for either of us."

Surprise registered in her eyes. "It's just sex. Nobody has to know."

"*I'll* know. And you deserve more than just sex. Stop wasting your time on men like me."

Her back stiffened, a sure sign I'd offended her even though I hadn't meant to. "Alright. I won't bring it up again."

"Don't quit," I begged as she strode back towards the door. "I don't know what I'd do without you."

She stopped, turning back to look at me over her shoulder, and to my relief, she smiled. "You'd be utterly screwed, and luckily for you, I don't want to see you suffer. See you tomorrow, Kane."

"Thank you. And good night."

She closed the door behind her and I checked my phone, just to make sure I hadn't missed anything from Naomi. The screen was blank, and with a sigh, I set it back down.

The work waiting on my desk used to be enough for me. Now, it wasn't even close.

**~Naomi~**

My phone buzzed, and my breath caught as I saw Natalie's name pop up.

Tried my best but he didn't take the bait.

The tension in my chest unraveled. Over the last two weeks, Natalie had been throwing women at Kane in ways subtle enough that he wouldn't suspect it was orchestrated. She sent him to business dinners where she knew the servers and had them flirt with him. She arranged for a friend who had been wanting to meet him to accompany him to an event.

And that night, she even tried to tempt him herself, falling back on their long-time friends-with-benefits relationship.

Each time, he turned them down. No hesitation. No engagement.

I exhaled slowly, my grip loosening on my phone. Technically, we were no longer together, so he didn't owe me anything. He could have cut his losses and moved on. He could have justified a fling by saying we were broken up.

He didn't do any of that.

I also checked in with Tom, the doorman at Kane's building, and he assured me no one had been to Kane's flat since the last time I was there.

It didn't guarantee he would never hurt me again, but it showed *effort*. Restraint. A willingness to change.

It gave me hope.

My phone buzzed once more with a follow-up from Natalie.

> Btw, he looks really sad. He's missing you.

I swallowed against the lump in my throat. I missed him too.

Strange as it might be, Natalie and I were actually becoming friends. We went for dinner and drinks together the same night she sent her friend to the party with Kane, and we agreed in advance that we wouldn't talk about Kane at all. We spent the whole time getting to know each other, and I found out she loved to read and had a soft spot for animals.

"Were you serious about wanting to meet someone outside your usual circle?" I asked her. "Because if you are, I might have an idea."

The next night, the same night Kane texted me to invite me to his parents' house, Natalie joined me at my regular pub night with my friends. My friend Jolie invited her co-worker Theo again, the same man she tried to set me up with several weeks earlier, and this time, I introduced him to Natalie.

He wasn't her usual type at all. He was quiet where she was bold, and he seemed a little awkward in the face of her confidence. But when

I nudged him to talk about his volunteer work at the animal shelter, they quickly bonded, their heads bent over his phone as he showed her pictures of rescue dogs. Then he mentioned the book he was writing, and when they discovered they shared a favorite author, there was no turning back.

On Sunday, she went to visit him at the shelter. By Monday morning, she had a date lined up with him later that week.

The next morning, another bouquet of flowers arrived at my office.

"It's beginning to look like a florist's in here," Pauline laughed. She'd seen the social media chatter about Kane the same as I had, and she knew things were up in the air between us, but I could tell she was still rooting for us to make it work.

Later that morning, I received a text from him, only the second time he'd reached out in the 16 days since we last saw each other.

I had a good talk with this therapist yesterday. If you're looking for someone to talk to about Liam, I can recommend her.

The therapist's name and contact details followed, leaving me staring at the screen in surprise.

My friends had urged me to try therapy after Liam's death, but the idea of talking about any of it felt too big and overwhelming. Now that I had told Kane, though, it didn't seem quite so impossible anymore.

Had Kane gone to talk to her about Abel? That seemed like a huge step for him. Rather than shutting down like he used to, he was pushing himself to open up.

When I looked up the therapist, I saw immediately that it was a private clinic, not covered by the NHS. Still, I decided to give them a call and find out what the price would be like. If someone as private as Kane felt comfortable talking to her, she had to be good.

I dialled, half-expecting them to have no openings or for the cost to be absurd. Instead, the receptionist responded warmly.

"I was told you might be calling, Ms. Law. In your case, the appointments would be fully covered, and we can work around your schedule to find a time that works for you."

My fingers tightened around the phone. Although she hadn't said it outright, there was only one possible explanation.

*Kane.*

I could see it as a way of trying to buy my forgiveness, but that didn't seem fair. More than anything, I think he just wanted to help make things better, in the only way he knew how.

I thought about him all the time, even when I tried not to. I missed his laugh, the twinkle in his eye when he was up to something and the feel of his breath against my skin. God help me, I even missed his self-satisfied smirk.

A dozen times, at least, I composed a text to him, ready to hit send before my head overruled my heart and I deleted it instead.

There was still one more thing I wanted to do before I made up my mind about giving him another chance.

So, on Thursday, I hopped on the train after work. After getting lost twice and retracing my steps, I finally knocked on the door of the right house.

Mrs. Davis greeted me with a warm smile, her eyes full of understanding as she opened the door. "It's good to see you, Naomi. Abel's expecting you. He's in his room."

We'd been in touch ever since my first visit, but earlier that week, he'd messaged me to invite me back for an in-person talk. Intrigued, I couldn't say no.

In his room, I sat down across from him. He'd already prepared some things to say and saved them to his device, so he was able to keep his eyes on me as the computerized voice spoke the words.

"I know my brother did something stupid. He didn't tell me what he did and I don't want to know. But he's really sorry about it."

I offered him a small smile. "I know he is, but I'm not sure that's enough."

"It's hard for him to trust people," Abel told me. "He doesn't like relying on anyone. I think sometimes he sabotages himself and pushes people away so that he doesn't have to care too much."

I'd noticed the exact same thing, and if anyone had any insight into Kane's background, it would be his brother. "Why is he like that?"

Abel hadn't prepared this answer, so it took him a while to tap it all out. I waited patiently, watching the man across from me who was so like his brother in some ways and so very different in others.

"It's because of me, I think. The way people treated me when we were younger. But it's not like that now. I have friends and I'm happy. He doesn't see it because he's not around, he's too busy working all the time. In his head, we're still kids and he needs to protect me."

That made complete sense to me. "He told me some of the things that happened when you were younger. He still seems pretty upset about them."

Abel nodded and tapped on the talker again. "I want him to be happy, like I am. He's happy with you. I know he's a pain in the ass, but can you give him one more chance?"

I stayed for dinner with the whole family before taking the train back to London. As the world rolled by outside the window, I thought over everything Abel said, about the conversations I'd had with Kane, all the time we spent together and the way he made me feel.

I thought about what he'd done since our fight, the effort he was making and how he was respecting my request for the space and time to make my decision.

I thought about what it meant to forgive someone, not just for their benefit, but for mine too.

And when I finished weighing the pros and cons, balancing the risks and rewards, I pulled out my phone and started typing.

# Chapter Twenty

**~Kane~**

I had to reread Naomi's short message a couple of times to make sure that I wasn't imagining it. For a full thirty seconds, I did nothing but stare at it.

> Can I come over for dinner tomorrow?

Maybe she sent it to me by accident? Could it have been meant for someone else? If I responded with an enthusiastic 'yes' and she replied that she'd sent it by mistake, I would be crushed.

Still, I had to respond, so I did my best to not come across as *too* eager.

> Of course. I'll order in. What would you like?

I watched the dots bounce as she replied, my whole life hanging in the balance.

> Surprise me. I'll be there just after six.

*Thank fuck.* She meant to send it to me after all.

It had been two and a half weeks since I'd seen her, the longest, most agonizing two and a half weeks of my life. Now, I still had to get through another twenty-two-ish hours before dinner on Friday, but at least I had something to look forward to again.

I found the business card from our time in Bangkok, the one that the man who cooked for us on the boat gave me from his brother's Thai restaurant in London. I ordered a variety of things, probably enough food to feed five or six people, to be honest, and laid it out on the dining room table before she arrived.

We'd never eaten in the dining room before. Normally, I only used it on special occasions when I hosted events, but I wanted that night to feel special. The stakes couldn't be higher.

Just as I had the last time she came over, I watched the security feed from the lobby, anxiety gnawing at my stomach until she finally appeared. Then, the nerves kicked in for a whole other reason. She came, but I still had to win her back.

I was standing in front of the lift when the door opened, unable to any longer than necessary to lay eyes on her in person. "Hi."

She gave me a small smile but didn't say anything as she stepped out of the lift. Fuck, she was beautiful. I'd always thought so, but after not seeing her for so long, the realization hit me even stronger than before.

"I'm glad you're here. Dinner's ready if you're hungry."

We walked through the kitchen, where she dropped off a small carrier bag she'd been holding, and into the dining room. Naomi inhaled deeply, taking in the rich, fragrant aromas.

"That smells amazing."

"Let's dig in, then."

We each took a seat, me at the head of the table and her on my right. The food gave us something to focus on as we passed dishes back and forth, exchanging easy compliments about how good everything looked, smelled, and tasted.

"How's work?" she asked, and I told her a few things before asking her the same question.

She shared an update on the research project I had funded, her passion for the work as evident as always, but still, she said nothing of a personal nature.

I was dying to ask her what prompted her to come over that night, what conclusions she'd come to during our time apart and what she was thinking about our future, but I forced myself to let her take the lead.

I'd been selfish enough in the past. This time, I would do things her way.

"The one thing I didn't get for tonight was crème brulée for dessert," I said when we couldn't eat another bite.

Naomi smiled. "That's actually a good thing because I brought dessert. Wait here."

She took our empty dishes to the kitchen with her, leaving me puzzling over her words. Why would she have brought food with her when I said I was getting dinner? It wasn't my birthday, and it wasn't hers either.

I hadn't figured it out by the time she returned with two plates and an entire chocolate cake.

A very *familiar* chocolate cake.

Dumbfounded, I watched as she cut two pieces, handing one to me before sinking her fork into hers, placing the large bite in her mouth, and moaning happily.

That moan had been haunting my dreams, but I was still so confused, I could barely register it.

"Is this my mum's cake?"

"Of course."

She stated it like it was obvious as she took another bite, eyes closing in bliss as her lips closed around the fork.

I didn't understand.

"Where did you get it?"

"She gave it to me last night when I had dinner with your family."

I understood all the words she said, but the sentence as a whole made no sense to me. "What?"

Naomi's attention remained focused on her cake. "Abel invited me over."

"He... what? How? Why?" I couldn't decide which question I wanted answered first.

At last, she looked over at me, a grin on her lips and mischief in her eyes. "If you don't eat your piece, I'm going to steal it from you."

I pushed the plate towards her without hesitation. "Take it. Just *explain*."

She laughed, shaking her head. "Because he's worried about you. He wants you to be happy."

I had the same impression after my conversation with him at the weekend, but I still didn't understand how Naomi fit in.

"What did you tell him?"

Her brown eyes met mine, just like on the night we met: hesitant, a little scared, but willing to take the leap anyway.

"I told him I want you to be happy too."

Hope stirred in my chest, my heart beginning to beat faster.

"You know what would make me happy."

She took another slow bite of cake, making me wait. Making me *suffer*.

"Do you understand that if you ever cheat on me again, I will—"

I didn't let her finish. I didn't *need* her to finish. The consequences didn't matter, because the mistake itself wouldn't happen again.

"I understand," I said firmly. "I don't want to be with anyone else. If you let me be yours, then I'm *only* yours."

I swallowed hard.

"I love you, Naomi."

The first time I said those words, just a few weeks ago, my world shattered the next day. This time, I hoped they would put it back together again.

"And I love you, Kane, though maybe not quite as much as I love your mum's chocolate cake."

She reached for my plate but I pulled it back, my heart soaring. I needed her eyes on me, needed to bask in this moment with her.

Naomi's eyes narrowed on me, a smile playing at her lips. "You're going to regret that."

Before I could guess her plan, she got to her feet, picked up the piece of cake from my plate in her hand, and smashed it into my face.

For a second, all I could feel was the sticky, sweet frosting smeared across my skin.

A second later, my lips curled into a grin as delicious new possibilities opened up in front of me. "So that's how you want to play this?"

*Game. On.*

**~Naomi~**

I squealed, trying to make a run for it, but Kane was faster.

With a wicked smirk, he wiped cake from his face, eyes dark with promise. Before I could escape, his arm snaked around my waist, pulling me onto his lap.

"Uh-uh," he murmured, trapping my wrists in one hand. His other hand sank into the remaining cake.

I squirmed, twisting against him. "Don't..."

I barely got the word out before he smeared it across my face and down my neck.

*Damn it.*

"Okay, but don't get any on my shirt," I huffed. "I didn't bring spare clothes."

Kane's eyebrows lifted, his blue eyes flickering with heat. "We better take it off then. Just to be safe."

A slow, delicious shiver ran down my spine. I'd already known where the night was heading, had made up my mind before I even walked through his door, but his behavior over dinner only cemented my choice. He'd been patient. Respectful. He'd let me lead.

Now, I was ready to let him take control.

He reached for the buttons of my shirt and I squealed again, jerking back. "Wait! Your hand."

He lifted it between us, finally noticing the icing smeared across his fingers.

"Well," he mused, cocking an eyebrow. "What should we do about that?"

I licked my lips in invitation and his grin widened as he brought his fingers to my mouth. One by one, I sucked them clean, swirling my tongue over each digit. He groaned, the sound low and desperate, sending molten heat straight through me.

His restraint lasted only another moment before he tugged off my shirt. His gaze landed on the bra I'd specifically chosen, the deep red one I'd worn in Rome, our first night together, and recognition sparked in his eyes.

I had a feeling he'd remember it.

Instead of immediately removing it, he swiped his fingers through more of the cake and dragged the icing across my chest.

I gasped, caught between amusement and anticipation. "What are you..."

Before I could finish, he bent his head and licked it off, tracing his tongue along my skin, nipping and tasting as he went.

A soft moan slipped past my lips.

Fuck, I'd missed him.

The bra came off and his mouth found my nipples, teasing and tormenting and sending waves of pleasure crashing through me.

When he started moving lower, I decided I wasn't about to let him have all the fun. I reached for his shirt, tugging it over his head before grabbing another handful of cake. Slowly, deliberately, I dragged the icing across his chest before leaning in to lick it off.

His muscles clenched beneath my tongue, his cock beginning to swell beneath me.

"Naomi," he groaned, gripping my hips to hold me still, but I had no intention of going easy on him. I ground down harder, rolling against him, until he let out a ragged curse, his control snapping.

Lifting me effortlessly, he set me on my feet and tore off the rest of our clothes. I turned back to the cake, scooping up another handful of icing, but before I could use it, his mouth found mine.

With a sly smile, I reached down and stroked the chocolate along the length of his shaft.

Kane groaned, his head dropping back.

"Please tell me you're planning to lick that off too," he rasped.

With a wink, I lowered myself to my knees and took him in my mouth. The sweetness of the chocolate mixed with his taste, his heat, his scent as I wrapped my lips around him.

"Fuck," he muttered, threading his fingers through my hair. His grip tightened, just enough to make my pulse race.

I sucked him until every trace of chocolate was gone, until he was thick and hard and on the edge, then I released him with a wicked pop and rose to my feet.

He didn't ask why. We were already on the same page.

Kane lifted me onto the table, spreading my legs wide around him. "So fucking beautiful," he whispered as he ran the head of his cock through my wetness before pushing into me as easily as he always did.

I gasped, arching beneath him. The feeling was impossible to describe. I'd felt so empty without him in the time we were apart, physically and emotionally, and now, at last, I felt complete again.

Although he tried to go slow, his control unraveled within minutes. Less than two minutes later, he let out a low, guttural curse. "Fuck. Sorry."

He looked so disgusted with himself, I had to laugh. "I'm not worried. I know you've got some other tricks up your sleeve."

He wasted no time in taking up the challenge, dropping to his knees between my legs. His tongue found my clit as his fingers took the place of his cock, and I grabbed onto the edge of the table as my legs began to tremble.

"God, Kane," I panted, writhing beneath his touch. "That feels so good. I love you…"

I meant to say more, but I hit my peak as his mouth clamped down on my clit and my power of speech evaporated into the air around me. Kane held me through it, drawing out my pleasure until I was boneless, breathless, and completely undone.

When I finally caught my breath, he pulled me onto his lap, wrapping me in his arms as I melted into him.

The last time I left this flat, I didn't know if I'd ever be back again, but I was so glad to be there. Glad he'd gone to the lengths he had to prove to me he could change, and glad that I didn't give in to my instinct to run from the pain.

Life hurt sometimes. It could be messy and hard and painful. It fucking sucked sometimes.

But other times, it could be unexpectedly wonderful.

"I don't think I'll ever look at your mum's chocolate cake quite the same way again," I whispered.

Kane's chest rumbled in laughter as he held me tight against him. "I'll have to ask her to make it every time we visit, just to watch you squirm," he teased.

I raised my head, ready to make a smart retort, but as his eyes met mine, the look in them took my breath away. Hope and happiness shone there, but strongest of all was love.

"I love you so much," he whispered, brushing the hair from my face. "Thank you for giving me another chance. I promise I won't fuck it up again."

"That's good enough for me," I told him, pulling his mouth towards mine again.

We were good enough for each other.

# *Epilogue*



*~One year later~*

**~Kane~**

The moment I stepped into the hotel bar in Rome, my eyes found her.

She sat at the counter, twirling a straw in her drink, lost in thought. Lost in the city where we began.

Everything else faded away.

I stepped behind her, leaning casually against the bar. "Are you waiting for someone?"

"Are you waiting for someone?"

Naomi turned, her eyes narrowed in suspicion and her lips twitching with amusement. "I was, but you're much better looking than he is. How about you take me upstairs before he gets here?"

I grinned back at her. "I would like nothing better, but I've got a dinner reservation that I would hate to waste. Maybe I can tempt you with food instead?"

She slid off her chair and took my arm. "Lead the way."

The streets of Rome felt different this time: warmer, lighter, and alive in a way they hadn't been the first time we walked them together. Naomi was in town for a work event with the Abel Foundation, and there was no way in hell I was missing the chance to relive a few memories. I'd flown in that afternoon and checked into the same penthouse suite I'd stayed in the year before.

She didn't know that part yet.

The only thing she knew was that I'd asked her to meet me in the bar, so when we arrived at the same restaurant from our first night together, her eyes lit up in recognition.

"You're a secret romantic, aren't you?" she teased.

I smirked at her. "Only when it comes to you."

They led us to the same private dining room, and as Naomi settled across from me, wine glass in hand, I took a moment to drink her in.

The last year hadn't all been smooth sailing. We'd argued and we'd faced challenges, but we'd faced them together.

I wouldn't trade a single second of it.

Naomi leaned in, one brow arched. "What are we doing here, Mr. Davis?"

I chuckled at the familiar question. She was toying with me, echoing the conversation we'd had a year ago, but she also knew me well enough to sense that I was nervous.

I set down my glass, inhaling deeply. "I have a problem I think you can help me with."

Her smile was warm, inviting, and breathtakingly beautiful. "What problem is that?"

"There's something I want to ask you, but last time I tried telling you how I felt, it went really badly." I paused, my voice dipping lower. "So, you have to promise to let me finish. Deal?"

Her teeth caught her lower lip, her eyes gleaming. She probably already knew where this was going. I hadn't exactly been subtle about the way I felt about her.

"My lips are sealed," she promised.

I exhaled, trying to push all the nerves away. Time to say the words I'd been practicing all week.

"Naomi, this year with you has been everything I could have hoped for. When we sat here together a year ago, I could never have imagined how much I would love you, or that you could love me half as much as you do. And I know that I will never want anything that doesn't include you as part of the deal."

She opened her mouth to speak, but when I raised my eyebrows, reminding her of her promise to let me finish, she obediently pressed her lips back together.

Her eyes continued to sparkle.

"I honestly can't imagine anything better than being with you, so I would like to suggest that we enter into a new kind of arrangement."

I reached into my pocket, pulling out the small velvet box I'd been carrying all afternoon. Naomi's eyes darted to it, then back to me, happy tears blurring her vision.

"I want you to be with me forever and I want to be there for you always. Naomi, will you marry me?"

For a moment, she didn't answer, and my heart began to pound. This couldn't be happening again, could it? Had I misjudged things? Was it too early?

Just before my thoughts began to spiral, I realized the problem and let out a sharp laugh of relief.

"I'm done now. You can speak."

She leapt from her seat and landed in my lap, her arms around me. "Of course I'll marry you. I love you, Kane."

Her lips crashed against mine, her body molding into me, and I wrapped my arms around her, needing to double-check that she was real and this wasn't a dream. Every time I thought she couldn't make me happier, she managed to prove me wrong.

I still had more surprises in store for the night, though.

Gently, I nudged her to my feet. "Come with me."

She glanced down at the empty table in dismay. "But we haven't eaten yet."

"I promise I'll feed you," I assured her with a laugh. "Just come."

We made our way into the restaurant's main dining room, a beautiful room draped with lights and flowers, filled with people who all began to applaud as we walked in.

Satisfaction swelled in my chest as Naomi looked around the room, her jaw dropping as she took in the faces of everyone who'd made the trip to celebrate with us. By the time she made it back to me, tears were starting to fall.

"You were pretty confident I'd say yes!"

Those sitting nearby laughed as I pressed a quick kiss to her lips. "I had a good feeling about it."

We circled the room, saying hello to my parents, Abel and Amy, Naomi's parents, and Liam's parents too. She'd reconnected with them as part of her therapy and we both enjoyed spending time with them. They were thrilled when I told them I was going to propose. Naomi's friends were there, including Natalie and Theo, and her co-workers from the charity where she used to work. Even our therapist made the trip.

The meal lingered long into the evening as we shared dinner and drinks, enjoying the good food and good company. A year earlier, the people who truly mattered to me could barely fill a dining table. Now, we had a whole room full, and I had a feeling it would only continue to grow. Naomi drew people to her wherever she went, just like she'd drawn me in.

Eventually, though, I wanted my fiancée to myself. We said goodnight to everyone and made our way back to the hotel, Naomi's hand in mind. The diamond on her ring pressed against my fingers, reminding me of our new relationship status and filling me with so much pride and happiness, I could barely contain it.

As we stepped into the lift together, Naomi pulled out the keycard for her hotel room, but I quickly snatched it from her hand and swiped mine instead.

"What are you..." she started to ask, but my mouth was on hers before she could finish. My hands slipped up her skirt as I pushed her against the mirror, my cock hardening against her. I knew she felt it as she pushed her hips against me, her hands running through my hair as she pulled me even closer.

When the lift door opened, I pulled her out into the suite's living room and savoured the way her eyes lit up when she realized where we were. We undressed each other as quickly as we could on our way to the bedroom, and once there, she pushed me down onto the bed, climbing on top of me.

I exhaled deeply as she sank down onto me, the feel of her warm body around my cock just as amazing as it had always been. She moved slowly at first, stroking me languidly as I rubbed her clit until she came. After a moment to recover, she started to go faster and my hands roamed across her beautiful body, a body I knew every inch of, but which never failed to fascinate me.

"You look so fucking perfect riding my cock," I whispered, the image in front of me blurring with the one from our first night together in that same hotel room, with that same fire.

"Fuck, Kane," she gasped, shuddering around me, and I followed right after her.

She collapsed against my chest, our bodies still tangled, and her lips brushed my ear.

"You know you're stuck with me now, right?"

I grinned into her hair, holding her closer.

"Good. Because I'll never, ever get tired of this."

# Keep in Touch

Thank you for reading Charity Case! If you enjoyed the book, please take a moment to leave a review.

For more about my other books and to keep up-to-date with new releases, find all the links here:
https://linktr.ee/melodytyden